Feral

Look for these titles by
Joely Skye

Now Available:

The Minders Series
Monster (Book 1)
Zombie (Book 2)
Minder (Book 3)

The Minder Series in Print
Beautiful Monster

Marked
Poison

Feral

Joely Skye

A Samhain Publishing, Ltd. publication.

Samhain Publishing, Ltd.
577 Mulberry Street, Suite 1520
Macon, GA 31201
www.samhainpublishing.com

Feral
Copyright © 2010 by Joely Skye
Print ISBN: 978-1-60504-557-3
Digital ISBN: 978-1-60504-520-7

Editing by Sasha Knight
Cover by Anne Cain

First Samhain Publishing, Ltd. electronic publication: May 2009
First Samhain Publishing, Ltd. print publication: March 2010

Dedication

To Samhain Publishing. Just one HUGE thank-you.

Chapter One

Ethan swerved, just missing the river's edge, and leaped uphill. If he pushed, he could reach the mountain, and if he reached the mountain, he could get to the cliff. It was better that he jump into forever than be captured, because these wolves wouldn't simply kill him, they would tear him apart, over and over again. He couldn't live through that hell a second time. Once—years ago—had almost destroyed him and had certainly destroyed what was human in him.

So he ran as cougar and ignored his body's rapidly draining reserves—it was the end of winter and he was racing towards oblivion.

The werewolves' sudden appearance had initially confounded him. He'd been alone for so long that when he came upon the pack, or more accurately they came upon him, he froze. Only for a moment, but that time of pure astonishment had been crucial in terms of the hunt—and that's what this was. They were attempting to bring him down. By his count, six wolves were chasing him, and they were close, too close.

Unlike hounds that bayed the few times they'd tried unsuccessfully to tree him, the wolves were silent, steady and very, very large. Why these shifters were after him, Ethan couldn't fathom. He'd been careful not to attract their interest. Though he knew, at least at an intellectual level, that not all wolf packs were sadistic, he'd been wolf-shy forever. His past had taught him to avoid them at all costs.

The winter had been long and harsh, and he wasn't as strong as he needed to be. For one thing, he'd lost too much weight and his skin hung loose around him. Nevertheless, his paws were large, larger than a wolf's, and he should have been able to outrun them on this snow. But he was one and they were many, enough they could switch off on the hunt, take turns being fresh.

They had planned this.

His muscles bunched, straining, propelling him forward despite his fatigue. The snow's crust sometimes broke beneath him, making him stumble before he pushed on. The key was not to panic, to remain determined. He reminded himself that this snow would break under his pursuers' paws too, and with greater frequency. And yet, the wolves were gaining.

Ten more minutes max. He could make it to the cliff. Despite his body's protest, he ran, and ran hard, barely slowing down. As long as he didn't collapse, he would get clear.

The wolf shot out of nowhere, dark against the white snow, racing towards Ethan at an angle. As if he knew of Ethan's plan and was determined to cut off his escape route. Ethan's confidence took a hit and it was hard not to falter.

He forced himself to aim straight for the predator. The large werewolf was male and as Ethan approached, the wolf eased up his pace and turned, apparently bracing himself for Ethan. Foolish thing, or was this one a sacrifice? For, one on one, a cougar, even a malnourished cougar, would best a wolf and kill it easily. Didn't matter. Ethan refused to go down that road. If he stopped to harm one wolf, the pack would be on him, attacking, and would forever claim their right to do it again and again.

At the last possible moment, Ethan leaped and he caught an expression of surprise on the wolf's face before he was past it, flying through the air.

As he landed, the snow's hard crust cut the pads of his front paws, but he welcomed the pain, let it spur him onwards as his hind legs pushed off the snow and moved him forward.

Unlike Ethan, the wolf was fresh. Ethan didn't think he could keep up this new, faster pace. Though he tried, *he tried*, marshaling the last of his energy. Yet he heard the wolf panting, the snow breaking as the wolf closed in.

He could turn, Ethan thought. He could turn and slice the wolf open, gut him with his claws. A pack of wolves he couldn't outfight, but this one he could kill.

No. Instead he ran harder, fighting to race ahead. The cliff. It was not that far.

Pain speared his right flank. It wasn't the jagged tear of teeth, but a sharp, clean puncture. No wolf was on him, so he ignored the sensation of having been shot and bunched his hind legs to push harder.

The effort failed and he stumbled, his right leg going numb and not responding to his body's commands. *Up, get up.* Ethan summoned all his will to push forward, and fell.

The wolf approached and Ethan, snarling, lunged to keep the predator at bay. The lunge was pathetic, with his hind legs giving out, and Ethan collapsed onto the snow. His body had betrayed him while a wolf stood watching, eyes brown, fur black.

It was like before. Years ago, the wolves had liked to watch him when he was down.

Ethan felt sick. It would happen again. They'd ripped him open a few times, waited for him to heal, and repeated their not-quite-lethal attacks. A terrible sort of play. A punishment. But for what this time? He hadn't consorted with one of theirs or attacked anyone. Revenge couldn't be a motive. Perhaps they simply wanted to toy with him.

They'd drugged him, he recognized, a dart in his right flank immobilizing him. So this episode was different. As was the dark wolf's somber appearance and his strange, unhappy whine. Last time, the wolves would have laughed at his helplessness by now.

They were wolves with different weapons and perhaps a changed agenda. One he couldn't guess at and one he feared. Ethan had never returned to his human form after the terror. He didn't know how long it had been since he'd become feral and didn't *want* to know. The point was, the point to cling to— he refused to turn human. His human was weak and would reach for solace, for companionship, for contact. Ethan simply could not afford it, or survive it.

He should close his eyes, shut out the dark wolf, but the anger in him wouldn't let go of that brown gaze, would not look away, even though he could no longer hold up his head.

The wolf whined again, as if in greeting. Lila used to whine, Ethan remembered rather hopelessly, though he'd spent so many years trying not to think about her. The wolf came closer, approaching Ethan's neck, and he braced himself for the attack.

The wolf nuzzled Ethan. Lightly.

What the fuck?

"Get back, Bram." The voice came out of nowhere, a warning, and the wolf obeyed by retreating a few steps.

Bram. Ethan remembered that name. His cat remembered all the names. Not a different pack then, though Bram had been a youngster last time. So the same pack had somehow tracked Ethan down. But *why?* He'd have felt sickened if the drug hadn't taken hold, allowing him to float in a painless, cloudless space full of only curiosity and anger—and even those emotions were becoming distant. Panic was completely at bay.

Bram stood between Ethan and the second wolf, and growled. Under other circumstances, Ethan would have felt like Bram was protecting him, which didn't make sense. Evidently, the drug was confusing him.

"Jesus, Bram, I could wring your neck." That gravelly voice sounded angry and alpha-ish. Somewhere deep inside himself, Ethan cringed. "What the hell were you thinking going one-on-one with a feral cat? He could have sliced you open. He's done it before."

Despite his best efforts, Ethan's eyelids drifted shut. He didn't entirely lose consciousness, but he wasn't aware of time passing. He kept his focus on himself, on his cat. He was only cat, not human. No shifting, not ever again. He had to keep a stranglehold on his ability to shift so he didn't give in to his weaker side.

"This was a *hunt*, Doug." A new, reproachful voice jerked Ethan back to the present. The words were spoken low, uncertain, and someone stood very near Ethan.

"What the hell else could it be after he ran from us?" the one named Doug answered. "It took me three shots to bring him down. This cat was fast, twisting and turning like a mad thing. I missed twice."

There was a long silence, and if Ethan had had the energy, he would have lifted his head to see the two shifter humans. But he could only listen.

"Bram, look at me," Doug demanded.

"Sorry." Sorry for what? Ethan didn't know. He only knew that brown-eyed Bram-the-dark-wolf was no longer a wolf. He must have shifted to human while Ethan had drifted along in

13

his drug-induced haze. God knew how long they'd been here.

But why turn from wolf to human? And why didn't they attack? What were they waiting for? For *him* to shift too? The worst thing was that they called to him, these shifters, standing nearby in their human forms. They called to Ethan the human, and he was scared he wouldn't be able to resist the pull.

"Get the fuck back." Doug spoke again, still annoyed. "You're not even wolf and he's still cougar."

Ethan would stay cougar. He was not going to change for them. As if from far away, he heard himself snarling.

"Bram," Doug warned. "If you can't act responsibly, I will not keep you on this job."

"He's down." Bram's voice filled with resentment. "And I know how to take care of myself."

"Right." The older man didn't believe Bram. Why not? Ethan muzzily tried to figure out what they were arguing about. He was losing track of the conversation. Another needle poked his flank and he barely felt the puncture.

Time passed, but Ethan grimly and determinedly remained cat.

Words came back into focus.

"Jesus, we've been here close to an hour. Shift already." The gloved hand of the alpha came down on Ethan's face, and despite his desire not to show weakness, he flinched. A thumb raised his eyelid and the blue eyes of his worst nightmares looked into his. "Okay, Bram, he needs encouragement and clearly he's harmless now, close to senseless. Get over here and touch him, coax him." The alpha spoke directly to Ethan for the first time. "Shift, buddy. It'll go easier on you if you do."

This asshole was no buddy of his, but all Ethan could let out was a soft, pathetic hiss. He began to tremble. His human so long suppressed was struggling to change, to shift, to be with these humans. To *talk*.

Couldn't go there, could not go there. Not with fucking *wolves*.

They knew of his struggle to stay cougar, but showed no mercy. A bare hand ran through his fur. Not a pat, but an awful caress that went down the length of his spine. They were playing with him, tempting him, and the human in him didn't know or didn't care. The human thought they were asking for his company, offering friendship. The human was an idiot who yearned for companionship.

His cat, on the other hand, was a solitary animal who needed no one and nothing, but food and sleep. His cat was much stronger. Usually. At this moment, his human craved contact and Ethan could not fight it down. Between the drugs and that shifter hand—fingers drifting through his fur, over his shoulders and back—he became terribly, fatally weak. Tremors rippled through him.

"Let it go, Ethan." A bare murmur, as if in comfort. Bram's voice was a lure and a betrayal. A false source of comfort.

Ethan refused to let it go. He fought hard to stay what he was, focusing on his cat, fighting down his human while those beguiling fingers softly stroked his exposed neck. Despite his best efforts, the blackness took him.

Chapter Two

Ethan lay on his back.

He never lay on his back. It was too narrow, the cougar's back, and much more comfortable to lie on his side. He attempted to roll over and his body resisted. Odd. His shoulders were too broad, his legs wrongly shaped, his tail...gone.

Panic. He pulled in air and scrabbled, trying to sit up. He couldn't see, couldn't move limbs properly. A noise came from his throat, and it sounded all wrong—human. God *no.*

Something pushed at him to rise. A hand. Hands. Someone behind him. Human-shaped. Arms surrounded him, clamped down on his wrists, wrapping his own arms around him like a human straightjacket. A chest pressed against his back.

Made no fucking sense. Prepare for attack. Cat... *Think!* Air pulled in again. *Breathe, Ethan.*

"Easy." A murmur.

Ethan bolted. No. Tried to bolt, but couldn't move, could only shake. He wasn't paralyzed, but confined. The clasp became a vise, and legs pressed down on his own while arms tightened around his. Someone enveloped him. How? Why?

He heard a keening noise and came to recognize that his own throat was making it.

"You're all right, but you need to calm down."

The voice spurred Ethan to fight harder, and he strained against the muscles and bones that held him. He was strong, even in human form, but not more powerful than this cage of arms, legs, back. He needed to shift. Cat. *Cat.* He needed to think to shift.

"Don't fight. No one is going to hurt you." The timbre of the voice gave his captor away, as did the strength that held him.

Wolf. Ethan was entrapped by a wolf. The thought tore at him and his heart banged harder, threatening. Everything threatened. His world started to turn gray and he battled to hold on. God knew what they'd do to him once he passed out.

"Easy." It was an effort for the stranger to hold him. The wolf actually nuzzled the side of Ethan's neck, a classic wolf-calming technique, but it worked on *wolves*, not him. Ethan would have tried to crack his captor's head, but he was shaking too hard and he was held too tight. Ethan had lost control. Weak, lost.

"Ethan." A soothing voice, deceptive, and yet some of Ethan's energy leached away. Human curiosity rose within him, tentative but building despite the terror. Fucking human. It coaxed Ethan to not want to fight. It created this terrible longing within him.

It made Ethan recognize that the wolf knew his name. And ask the question, *How?*

Cat. Ethan needed to shift so he could fight. His cat could outfight any wolf. His stupid human would want to make friends. Jesus.

Breathe for a moment, Ethan. Get yourself together and you can shift, wolf or no wolf.

"That's it."

His shuddering breaths went in and out. God, he couldn't find it in him to shift. Why not? Where was his cat? It was as if this human contact—no matter that the male was really a wolf—suppressed Ethan's cat. Instead his human wanted to ask questions.

The stranger eased his hold slightly. Not enough that Ethan could do anything, just to make him more comfortable.

He had never been held like this, and it felt unsafe. He shouldn't try to speak, but his human ignored that warning.

"I can't see," he managed though a long-disused throat. It hurt a little to talk.

"Open your eyes."

His eyelids flew open and light struck, blinding him with brightness. He cringed.

"Can you turn down the lamp, please?" The polite request wasn't directed at Ethan.

Talking to who? There was another person in the room. Of course, Ethan had heard the breathing but hadn't registered that second presence yet. Panic hit Ethan again, and the wolf increased pressure on arms and legs, an overwhelming embrace. He didn't want this, but with wolves it sure as hell was not about Ethan's wants.

"Ethan." More urgent this time. "You're safe here, but you need to *calm down*."

"Can't. Can't." Fool to admit it, but oh God, there were two wolves, and they were going to rip him open. One would hold him and the other, the blue-eyed one, would bleed him out. The helplessness of it all hurt. He'd spent years avoiding exactly this.

"No one's going to hurt you." Why did the wolf say that? Was it a new game? Ethan couldn't make sense of the situation, especially when his captor rubbed his face against Ethan's neck, making him shudder in confusion. "You're not thinking

18

clearly. You've been cat too long, okay? It takes some time to think as a human again. But it will come."

Never mind the human. Cat. But Ethan couldn't find his other self. His cougar was lost somewhere deep within, fighting to get out, but too far below the human surface to succeed. The internal fight sapped Ethan's will and the gray came again, a wave he couldn't stave off.

As Ethan fainted in his arms, Bram consciously relaxed all his muscles. His entire body had seized up while holding the cougar prisoner. Carefully Bram laid Ethan down on the bed and was tempted to push the sandy hair off Ethan's face. But no, it wasn't fair to unnecessarily touch the cougar without his say-so. Ethan was getting more than enough body contact from Bram as it was, and quite obviously the cougar didn't welcome it.

As Bram withdrew from the bed, he stared down at the shifter curled up on his side. Ethan looked like he was trying to protect himself and that thought gave Bram a pang of guilt.

Taking a moment to brace himself, Bram then raised his face to gaze defiantly at Doug who had watched the whole thing with great interest. At the look of satisfaction on his alpha's face, a surge of anger swept through Bram. Despite his better judgment, he blurted out the first words that came to mind. "That went fucking well."

Doug scowled. "Watch your tongue."

Fists clenched, Bram stalked around the foot of the bed. Ethan had radiated terror, and despite Doug's claims that the feral cougar required body contact and a safe human presence, Bram's embrace had done little to mitigate the overwhelming fear.

Doug's face turned impassive while his voice was full of

warning. "You won't speak to me that way again, especially in front of the cat, and I don't care if he appears unconscious."

Bram nodded almost immediately. After all, he did what his alpha told him to do. With the nod, his anger faded—it always did in the face of Doug's anger—and Bram was able give his alpha what he wanted, which was contrition.

"I'm sorry." Bram managed to mean it, even if what they were doing to Ethan did not seem right, no matter the extenuating circumstances.

"Okay. But Ethan isn't the only one who needs to calm down."

"I know. Sorry."

"It went quite well."

"*Quite well?*" Bram forgot all about being apologetic. The least Doug could do was acknowledge this was hell for Ethan. "I felt his heart beating out of his chest. I was worried he'd go into cardiac arrest."

The way Ethan's voice had broken on that last word, *can't*, had made Bram choke up.

Doug grabbed hold of Bram's nape and shook him. "Keep your voice down or you'll disturb his sleep. He needs the rest."

Bram bowed his head, accepting that hand on him.

"Normally I wouldn't put up with this kind of attitude, Bram, and you know it. However, I understand your nerves are a bit frayed." Doug's grip turned painful, squeezing Bram's neck to emphasize his point.

Doug was right, Doug was always right. Bram repeated the mantra. He had to put *all* his anger away and remember that he was doing a job. A job he wanted. He was lucky the alpha had chosen him to be involved in rehabilitating a feral cat.

Doug kept talking. "This guy has likely been a cougar for

eight years straight. After that length of time, it's frightening and confusing to become human again. Or so I've been told. I've researched this carefully, remember. I know exactly what I'm doing. Not that I need to justify anything to you."

"Yes," said Bram, enduring Doug's continued grip, trying not to resent the accompanying pain.

"Of course you can sense his terror. So can I. But it should lessen over the next few days as the cat gets used to being human. I told you this was going to take time and patience." The alpha's fingers pinched nerves and Bram hunched even more.

"Yes." Bram wanted Doug's hand *off*. Even if he craved contact with his alpha, he recoiled from pain of any sort.

"Do you have the patience, Bram?"

"I have patience," Bram returned immediately.

It was the response Doug demanded, and it was also true.

"I'm sorry, Doug." But only when Bram trembled under Doug's hold did the alpha release him. Bram resisted giving himself a full-body shake. The grip reminded Bram of late-adolescent punishments meted out, beginning with a neck-grab and becoming far worse.

However, this wasn't about Bram. It was about Ethan. If Doug had been interested, Bram would have told him that patience wasn't a problem *at all*. It was simply hard to feel, to smell, Ethan's terror.

"I thought he wouldn't fear me," Bram explained, still apologetic. "I'm sorry I wasn't better prepared."

"I warned you. You need to listen to everything I say. *Do* everything I say. It is critical you obey and if you can't control yourself and these outbursts, you're out of here."

"Yes. I'm sorry."

Mollified, Doug fixed him with a wry expression. "Of course Ethan is going to fear you. He's not a wolf, and you're not omega to this guy."

Bram flushed.

"In fact, you're a large wolf, a good-sized man. Ethan has no reason to be more trusting of you than anyone else." Doug paused. "Especially if he remembers you and associates you with Gabriel's reign."

"God I hope not." Bram had been sixteen back then, gangly but full-grown, and perhaps still recognizable.

"Assume he does." Doug wrapped a large hand around Bram's arm and pulled him farther away from Ethan. Bram didn't fight the alpha's now-gentle manhandling. Doug sat him down at the table and pointed at the plate. Obligingly, Bram shoveled in the food since he was still recovering from the chase and the shifting.

He paused and glanced at the bed. "Ethan needs to eat."

"He's too skinny," Doug agreed. "But it'll be less traumatic if he eats on his own rather than us deciding to immobilize him and stick in an IV. I don't want to make him crazy, so I consider that a last resort."

Bram nodded to acknowledge Doug's reasoning, and kept eating, but with an eye on his alpha who had more to say.

"The truth is, Bram, we have to careful. Ethan might have gone feral-vicious." At Bram's headshaking, Doug added, "It happens with cat shifters. My cousin apparently had to euthanize a number of them."

Bram shouldn't glare at Doug, he knew, but he never learned. Too many years as omega and he couldn't learn to control his anger and remain subservient. He couldn't learn control period. Sometimes he wondered how he survived. Still, he managed to keep his voice calm, respectful. "I remember what Ethan was like, Doug. He wanted to save Lila. He wasn't vicious."

"He wasn't vicious then, years ago." Doug lifted a warning eyebrow at Bram's challenge and Bram let his gaze slide away. "Look, obviously that's not what I want. I sure as hell didn't spend the last three weeks making our pack find this guy so we could kill him. What a waste of resources that would be."

Why exactly did we find him? Bram wanted to ask. It was a question that had not been answered to his satisfaction. But at the moment he didn't have the energy to voice it again. Not when Doug was already pissed off by his insubordination.

Doug slanted his gaze Ethan's way, triumph in that expression, as if the cougar was his prize. "Problem is, the last time Ethan was human, he had sociopathic werewolves playing kill-the-cat with him. It fucks a guy up." Doug turned back to Bram. "But I'm alpha now, not Gabriel, and *I* don't allow the pack to be crazy, murderous assholes."

Bram pulled in a breath of relief. Despite his misgivings about this venture, and on occasion about Doug, there was absolutely no doubt in his mind that the current alpha had made the pack a better place these last four years. Doug had probably saved his life by marking an invisible ring of protection around Bram that said "hands off". Whereas Gabriel had allowed omegas to be trashed. Repeatedly. At the memories, a furious shiver ran through him.

"I hated Gabriel," Bram said in a low voice.

"He's dead. You're not. In fact, you're here fixing an old wrong, which is how you should regard your dealings with the cat." Doug's blue eyes were cold and assessing, and no doubt found Bram wanting. "If you plan to do this properly, *you* are going to have to calm down, not just Ethan."

"I'm calm," Bram gritted out, but the old rage flowed

through him, brought to the surface by seeing Ethan vulnerable like this. Bram was ready to slam his fist in the wall and his vision threatened to turn red. Abruptly Doug grabbed Bram and bent him double, pushing his head between his knees. Bram tried not to resent this undignified hold, but it was hard. To make matters even more confusing, Bram needed physical contact more than he got it, typical werewolf that he was, so a part of him welcomed Doug's actions, no matter how domineering. Warm fingers pressed into Bram's skull.

"Breathe," Doug instructed, his voice dry. "And while you're at it, don't lie to me. You're not calm."

"Okay," he admitted to the floor, "I'm a little upset. I'm sorry. I thought..." But he couldn't say that he thought if he cared about Ethan and his fate, it would make a difference, that Ethan would feel Bram's concern, be soothed by it and wouldn't recoil from Bram's hold.

"I told you this would be a challenge." Doug gripped Bram's hair and pulled him up, allowing him to sit again. He gazed into Bram's face while Bram dutifully looked away. "I'm serious, I will pull you off this case if you can't keep your shit together. I'll do without you if I have to."

"I will keep it together, Doug." This job was too important to him, he *needed* it. He needed to contribute to the pack somehow. That and impressing Doug were both critical to Bram. Because if Doug lost total interest in him, well, Bram had no one else to turn to.

Besides, there was Ethan... Bram wanted to make some atonement, even if he'd only stood in the background while Gabriel had tormented the cat. Being there gave him some culpability.

Doug let go of Bram's hair. "Get some sleep before he comes to again. I'll watch him."

Bram picked up the large bottle of water and guzzled it.

Doug jerked his head towards an exhausted Ethan. "This guy is no cub, he's a full-grown cat. If he shifts on you and you're not prepared, you will resemble hamburger meat. At best."

"I know."

"You cannot let your guard down unless Ethan stabilizes."

"He will."

Doug eyed him, blue gaze unreadable. Was that doubt? Contempt? Annoyance? "He may not, Bram. Don't let hope ruin your judgment. Ethan ripped one wolf apart and after what he's been through, he'll do it again. He feels threatened here and that may not change, despite our best efforts."

"He's confused, but we'll reach him. He'll learn he's safe."

"He may stay confused. Not everyone can return from the feral state. However, for what it's worth"—Doug's expression hadn't changed, but there was a quality in his voice that suggested he knew how much this meant to Bram—"I wouldn't do this if I didn't believe there was a decent chance we can reach him. We just have to stabilize his human side. Ethan *cannot* shift and that means skin contact. After eight years, the human will crave it, but the cat in him won't like it. It will only want to destroy."

Bram didn't respond. Doug was the pack's alpha and only cat-shifter expert, and he didn't like any kind of argument at the best of times. But Doug hadn't seen Ethan in this compound long ago. A cougar trying to save an older she-wolf by sacrificing himself. Lila—Bram had decided never to forget her name—was dead, and Ethan's sacrifice had been heartbreaking, and in vain.

Chapter Three

Ethan woke weeping, human memories bearing down on him. Lila had lain beside him, her body shredded, and despite all his cat's efforts to forget that day, he could not.

He turned, and yet could not turn his mind away.

Hands on him, large and warm, pulled him up to cradle him.

That nuzzle and a stranger's comfort made Ethan sob even harder. He should have been embarrassed, but he was too weary for embarrassment. The arms did not clamp around him this time. Instead, hands soothed, stroking his face and his sides, making the weeping all the more painful. He found it hard to catch his breath.

"Ethan."

Lila had named him Ethan. He never knew why. She'd suggested the name to his mother, and his mother had liked it.

"Ethan." That voice sounded strained, even concerned. Why? Ethan should be suspicious, but the tears made him weak.

He turned his face towards the man, unable to resist the lure of human touch. Ethan had stayed cat for a reason. Cat didn't need others and didn't need to be held, but Ethan was stupid. He reached for his captor and wept. It didn't stop. His body couldn't contain the sorrow. The wolf murmured reassurances while Ethan's body shook with crying.

"Something is wrong." The urgent, low statement was not directed at him. "He's going to exhaust himself if he continues like this." There was a fierceness to the words, an anger. Ethan didn't understand. Why weren't his captors hurting him?

"Keep his back to you, Bram." The alpha issued a warning Ethan didn't comprehend, and a second set of hands descended on him, turning him away from the one who held him and, outnumbered, Ethan began to fight blindly.

A tight hold clamped down, immobilizing him, while his captor Bram growled, "Back off, Doug."

"What did you say to me?" Blessedly the second man moved away from Ethan.

"Sorry." Bram gasped, obviously in some kind of pain, his voice tense, his body tight as a wire even while his grip on Ethan remained gentle.

Ethan couldn't follow what was happening except that the second wolf was touching Bram and no longer touching him.

"But, Doug," Bram pleaded, "you're making it worse for him."

"Keep his back to you," Doug repeated, voice flat.

"I will."

The alpha stepped away. "I actually don't want him ripping out your throat."

Ethan was gasping for air, waiting for Doug to attack, waiting for them to slice him open. He'd forgotten he was waiting for that. How could he forget? Brace, brace. Why was he so *weak*? He couldn't think straight and he was going to pass out. Again.

As the world faded, someone buried his face in his hair—

his long hair. "Ethan." The voice sounded shaky, a little...desperate, a faint echo of his own terrible despair. "Shhh."

A claw, a wolf's claw, slashed across his stomach. His intestines spilled out. The human in him was exhausted but the cat fought on, shifting to save its life, to save Ethan's life, and when he came to, the werewolves were human and one held a knife.

"Where should we cut him this time?" Gabriel lifted the blade so the sun's rays reflected on it, and then he sliced downwards.

Ethan hit the floor and someone caught him immediately. A wolf, but his tormentor didn't lay him open like they had in the past. Instead, the wolf enfolded him.

Blearily, Ethan recalled this embrace. He'd endured it before, enough that it was becoming unnervingly familiar— human chest to his human back, human legs holding his legs down, arms wrapped tight. This embrace didn't slice him open. Or at least whichever wolf held him didn't. It was all about restraint.

"Ethan." Someone's face lay against his neck—it was a wolf's way to reassure him. The gesture shouldn't have calmed him, but it did. At least it made Ethan weary of fighting. Though he was a fool to relax, the hold tempted him, and he stopped struggling. After a moment, exhaustion reasserted itself, and despite everything, he laid his head back on the wolf's shoulders and simply breathed. He had never felt so bone-tired in his life.

The wolf could go for the jugular and Ethan wouldn't have the ability to stop him. Were they starving him, was that their plan? He began to pant in fear, but also with terrible hope, because whoever held him had yet to hurt him.

No teeth, just a nuzzle, and a sound of...satisfaction? Relief?

"Ethan?" Kind of tentative the way Ethan's name was said. "Can you speak?"

But Ethan lolled against his captor while his chest shuddered, breaths going in and out, grateful that today there were no knives, no claws.

They made him drink then. He hadn't even realized he was thirsty until another's hands guided him to the glass. Fluid at his lips, he started gulping and continued till nothing was left. His eyelids fell shut, the drinking having worn him out, so once again he laid his head against the wolf and fell asleep.

Again, Ethan woke, and he was hungry this time. Of course, the ever-present hands were on him, but they did not invoke alarm or make him recoil, despite the alienness of it all. His human welcomed the embrace and he rested against the manwolf, grateful his mind was not in a churning panic at this moment. Could one get used to this bizarre existence?

Very slowly Ethan opened his eyes and bright light didn't assail them. The room was dimly lit and unlike his previous wakings, Ethan felt capable of taking in what surrounded him. It seemed as if his vision, or whatever part of his brain processed his vision, was now working.

It was a small room, not well furnished, just the bed they sat upon, a chair and a table. Ethan looked around for the second wolf, the alpha who offered drinks and made dire warnings, but there was only the one captor.

Who was, unlike himself, dressed.

"Hey." That same soothing voice which was becoming unnervingly familiar, even if it was a false familiarity. They were playing on his weaknesses.

Despite the futility of it all, Ethan bucked against the hold that, as a matter of course, tightened. That face landed on his neck, right at the tendon, nuzzling, not-quite-kissing, and Ethan shivered and stopped struggling. Let out a long, shaky breath that revealed too much. But his captor had not used his tears or his exhaustion to torment him. Not yet.

Tempted to once again lean back against the wolf, Ethan instead used what little was left of his pride to sit more upright. He searched for his cat and found him, found the cat was no longer furious, no longer desperate to escape. Both halves of Ethan were nervous, but also puzzled.

"What"—Ethan had to clear his rough throat before continuing—"the hell is going on?" He'd wanted to sound matter-of-fact, but there was a thready aspect to his voice that embarrassed him, even if it was in part caused by disuse. He'd been human so long ago, and his cat wasn't much one for speech.

The hold relaxed a fraction and his captor waited, probably expecting Ethan to struggle again. But Ethan worked to stay still.

"I'm Bram." Not exactly an answer.

Ah, yes. One of *them*, but Bram had lurked in the background years ago, a skinny, frightened, banged-up teenager. He hadn't touched Ethan, for whatever that was worth. Probably not much. Ethan needed to keep up his guard without getting uselessly panicked.

"Bram," he repeated.

"Yes."

Ethan hoped for more explanation, but none came. "Uh, why are you holding me like this?"

"I'm sorry."

At the words, for he couldn't fathom what this stranger was sorry for, Ethan tried not to show his fear, because wolves could smell everything, and they let you know it. Bram's face came back to his neck, moved forward towards his throat, and Ethan found himself sinking into Bram's hold. He wanted to turn, to return the embrace. His foolish, foolish human was as weak as he'd always known him to be. No wonder the cat had kept such a stranglehold on his existence. It was the only way to survive.

"Ethan." Even Bram's voice relaxed him. "I'm holding you so you don't hurt me."

His entire body reacted in surprise at this strange admission. Strange *lie*, he corrected himself. This one was a liar. Still, name-calling wouldn't get him far, whereas questions might. It made sense to talk to Bram and see if the wolf would tell him more. Christ, Ethan hadn't done conversation for a long time, but it wasn't too difficult to ask, "Why would I hurt you?"

Bram rested his chin on Ethan's shoulder. "Wolves and cats do not always get on."

It made no sense; it wasn't even true. Lila, his de facto foster mother, had proven it. "Why not cage me then?"

"I'm a shifter too. I know cages make us crazy."

The door opened, and to his embarrassment, Ethan jolted, pulling in a harsh breath. Bram the wolf gave him a reassuring squeeze and Ethan tried to calm down though two against one when he was a human, and a malnourished human at that, weren't good odds.

"It's okay," Bram assured him. "It's only Doug. He's been here before. We think you need to eat."

"I need to piss. My bladder is ready to burst." Ethan looked down at the dark arms holding his so tightly.

There was a long silence as the two wolves considered this

information. They stared at each other until Doug nodded.

"Let him go." At once Bram complied, slowly and obediently relaxing his arms and dropping them from Ethan as he backed off the bed.

Seemingly shocked that he'd been released, Ethan didn't move right away. A tremor ran through his naked too-skinny back that was all spine and shoulder blades. He hunched and tensed, as if ready to spring. Then, slightly feline in his movements, he twisted around, crawled across the bed and stalked to the bathroom. There was no door, but Bram and Doug turned away.

Next thing they knew the shower was on.

"Go watch him," ordered Doug and Bram did.

Washing himself thoroughly, Ethan ignored him through the transparent shower-stall door. About five minutes into his shower, he poked his head out. "I want scissors." He yanked on his long, tangled hair.

Bram glanced at Doug who responded dryly, "Tell him his food is getting cold."

When Bram opened his mouth to relay the message, Ethan said, "I heard. I have excellent hearing, as you may know." He jerked his hair again. It was down to his waist. "I want to get rid of this fucking hair. It's going to give me a headache."

Again, Bram looked to Doug who sighed. "I suppose it's a good sign that the cat wants to look civilized." He left the room, presumably in search of what Ethan had requested.

"I think he's gone for them. The scissors that is," Bram informed Ethan.

"Good." Ethan paused, his hazel eyes glowing with dislike. "Enjoying the show?"

At the mocking tone, Bram stiffened and tried not to reveal his embarrassment. Yes, shifters were casual about nudity, but they didn't usually stand staring as someone showered. Though perhaps Ethan was referring to the bigger picture. "I'm just here to make sure you're okay."

"Ah. So, that's what this whole thing is about, this hunt, this abduction, whatever the fuck it is you're doing in bed with me. You wanted to check in, make sure I was *okay.*" Ethan glared. "You'll be asking me to thank you next."

There was no sense in answering. If Ethan didn't know that other shifter humans called to *his* human, that physical contact reinforced his human shape, well, he was going to learn. Doug had stumbled upon that all-important fact when he'd researched cat shifters and reclaiming their humanity. If Ethan didn't think he needed to be human ever, there wasn't much Bram could say right now to convince him otherwise. Perhaps Ethan hadn't even considered himself feral.

Into the awkward silence, Doug returned. He slapped scissors and a razor into Bram's hand, but looked at Ethan and jabbed a finger. "You so much as nick yourself, or Bram here, you will not get these back and I will shave you myself."

Ethan's response was simply to curl his lip in distaste before holding out his palm in silence. Bram handed him the scissors, handles first, and dragged the wastebasket over to the shower. Ethan got to work, though it wasn't easy to cut the matted hair. Big clumps were discarded into the plastic bag, both from his head and his beard, until a manageable amount was left.

Next, Ethan stepped out of the shower and began to shave. Bram hastily retrieved shaving gel from Doug and passed it over before Ethan cut up his face. He wondered what a clean-shaven Ethan would even look like.

The cat did a thorough if awkward and slow job, obviously unused to the razor, and he ignored Bram the whole time. Ethan ignored his stomach too, which was now growling with hunger. The cat was not quite skeletal, but his hipbones jutted out and ribs could be counted. The bony spine made Ethan appear vulnerable, but Bram knew, from holding him, that Ethan had hidden wells of strength left.

After a while, Bram suspected that Ethan was trying to make some statement by the amount of time he was spending in the bathroom. Well, Doug had said the cats would want to show control and as long as they showed it by thorough personal grooming, and not by attacking anyone, it seemed relatively harmless.

Ethan finally stepped away from the mirror, the sharp planes of his face evident, his newly short sandy hair already displaying its curl. Bram handed him a towel. When Ethan finished drying himself, he wrapped the towel around his waist.

"Want some clothes?" Bram asked.

"You mean I get some?" Ethan's hand clasped the towel, knuckles white, and his voice, striving for snide, quavered slightly. He probably heard it himself, because his face heated up and his shoulders stiffened.

Trying to react casually, Bram walked over to the table to pick up sweats and a T-shirt, and gave them to Ethan who deigned to take them. He was shaking, probably from hunger and exhaustion, though perhaps also from trying to maintain his pride in what had to be a difficult position—being held against his will.

"You had clothes before. You actually ripped off the last pair of sweats," Bram explained and Ethan shot him a glare of disbelief as he pulled on the clothes.

"Your food's cold." Doug didn't hide his impatience as he

34

pointed to the table.

"We cats don't care about food temperature." Still Ethan walked over and gingerly sat on the chair, as if the action was a strange one. A long time had likely passed since he'd last sat on a chair.

"That so," drawled Doug as Ethan ate a mouthful, and Bram wished Doug would shut up and let the cat eat in peace. "How many cats have you known besides yourself?"

Ethan drew his mouth in a tight line.

"None?"

Ethan ignored Doug and instead ate at great speed. Even fast for a shifter, he was almost inhaling the food.

Leave him be, Doug. However, Bram couldn't say that to his alpha.

"I've spoken with one other cat shifter," Doug informed Ethan, who shot him a wary, startled look. "Callie prefers her food hot, though like most of us shifters she isn't picky."

As Ethan finished what was on his tray, he looked up at Bram, then Doug. "Callie. A female," Ethan said in obvious disbelief. His contempt would have been more effective if his expression didn't resemble one who was cornered and if there wasn't a tremor running through his body. Ethan needed more sleep, and less fear. Bram could smell the fear even if Ethan fought to keep the emotion off his face.

"I was surprised too." Doug nodded as if he and Ethan were in agreement. "Females are rare enough among wolves."

Something in Ethan seemed to collapse at that. Bram wondered if Ethan was remembering the she-wolf, Lila, who had been his companion those eight years ago. Doug didn't pursue the conversation. Perhaps he finally realized he'd said enough. Instead he picked up the empty tray. Before he left the room, he threw a water bottle at Bram. "Get him to drink."

When Bram approached Ethan, the cat ducked away and dragged himself over to the bed. He pulled himself up into a ball and lay with his back to Bram. So he simply placed the bottle on the table and sat on the chair. Now that Ethan seemed more aware of his surroundings, it felt invasive, this watching. But there was no question, the cat required surveillance. To be rehabilitated, Ethan needed to remain human. Making this breakthrough, conversation, was a critical first step, but they had a long ways to go.

After a while Ethan's breathing changed and Bram let out a silent breath of relief. The cat shifter was back asleep.

Chapter Four

Ethan woke with a start, eyes opened, fists clenched. *Fists.* He groaned. He didn't miss the paws that much. After all, human hands were capable of more interesting actions. But Ethan missed his claws. They had protected him on more than one occasion.

He'd woken from a nightmare, another human trait—having nightmares that scared the shit out of you. His cat wasn't much given to vivid dreams. He was sick of the nightmares, and what was he doing in these clothes? He began to rip them off.

Someone stayed his hand and he jerked away, gasping.

"Ethan." The voice wasn't Bram's. *Fuck.* It belonged to the other one, the alpha with the eerily familiar blue gaze. Trying to stave off the panic, Ethan backed away, careful not to look the wolf in the eye. Alphas took direct gazes as a challenge, and next thing you knew, they were attacking.

Christ, how to get out of here? His head was together enough to realize he *had* to escape these wolves. He just needed to keep the confusion at bay. He gritted his teeth.

"Ethan."

He wanted to cover his ears. Stupid, but he hated the note of authority in the alpha's voice. Not that he responded to it like another wolf might, but the goddamned alpha would expect

Ethan to respond.

Ignoring the outside world, he looked inward, searching for his cat. He needed to shift, absolutely needed to get out of this human skin and escape. His human knew nothing of escape. If he could only find his focus...inside...there. *Yes.* He felt his cat rise within him. The very beginnings—

Hands descended on him and Ethan lunged away. Didn't make it far before he was lifted into the air and slammed face first into the mattress. The alpha yanked Ethan's arms behind him, clasped wrists together and pinned them high up on Ethan's back. High enough that his arms were being wrenched out of their sockets, even while his legs were spread apart. Weight crushed down as the alpha kneeled on Ethan's thighs and pressed on his wrists.

Between his panic and bearing the full weight of the wolf, Ethan couldn't breathe. His chest hurt.

"Turn your head to the side." The alpha's voice sounded neutral, almost bored, and Ethan did as he was told. He wasn't contrary enough not to obey and suffocate by breathing in the soft bed. Why was he so stupid when he woke up in this room? Half the time he couldn't really think. After he turned his face, he began gulping breaths.

"You're going to calm down." Flat tone. A statement. A *command.*

Yeah, right. A fucking wolf on his back and he was going to calm down. "Or *what?*"

"I'll sit on you until you do."

Ethan snorted, as if it were funny, though it wasn't. He should have been revolted by this unwanted hold, but at least the armlock felt impersonal. His legs hurt. Doug—yes this was Doug, Ethan remembered—was a lead weight, and Doug's large hand, the one not gripping his wrists, was resting on the small of Ethan's back, under the cotton T-shirt. It wasn't a caress, there was no affection. Doug was simply placing his palm against his skin so that Ethan could no longer find his cat, couldn't even think of shifting. His cat was gone and Ethan could only lie here and breathe, because his human wanted to keep this form. Even when he was being punished.

"What are you doing with me?" he asked, unable to keep the plaintive tone from his voice.

"You were trying to shift."

Ethan didn't deny it.

Doug continued, "I'd prefer that we simply make conversation. Truth be told, I'm not particularly interested in wrestling you down. But you didn't answer to your name."

"You're an alpha. I don't talk to alphas."

"Is that so?" Doug didn't take offense at Ethan's statement. "What are you going to do if I release you?"

"Nothing. Sit up." He also wouldn't mind getting some circulation back in his arms and legs, but pride forbade him from saying so. Doug had to know exactly what he was doing. Ethan needed that circulation to shift. "I won't even attack you, Doug. I'm sure you're relieved to hear *that*. You might have to throw me back down on the bed again."

"You're confused when you wake up. That's normal."

Ethan snorted. "Normal, huh? I'm not sure I know what that is."

"Promise me you're going to stay human. Then I'll release you."

"And if I don't promise anything?"

"We'll sit here for a while." Doug patted Ethan's back with the palm of his hand. Impersonal, yes, but Ethan still shuddered.

"I have no choice."

"That's right."

After a few more minutes of silence, Ethan's skin was crawling. He hadn't minded Bram restraining him, hadn't reacted like this, but he couldn't stand Doug on him any longer. "I'll stay human. I promise."

The words stuck in his craw but he couldn't wish them unsaid.

Slowly Doug eased off Ethan's legs and released Ethan's arms. He scrabbled away to the headboard. Trembling in reaction, he thought he might throw up. Doug was no Gabriel, but Ethan's gut told him this asshole was dangerous.

He rubbed his bruised, numb wrists. "Where's Bram?"

Doug cocked his head. "Why?"

Ethan glanced away. He didn't like looking into those eyes anyway. "No reason."

"Bram is sleeping. You've exhausted him. He's watched you closely for two days straight."

"How generous of him."

Doug grinned. "I like your spirit, cat."

Patronizing dangerous asshole. Ethan bit back an insult. He didn't feel like being sat on again. "Um, why am I here?"

"You've been cat too long."

Ethan blinked, that wasn't the answer he'd expected. "According to who? You? Is there a past-due date I don't know about?"

Doug laughed as if Ethan had made a great joke. "Not exactly. But being feral is a problem."

"A problem? For you? It's none of your business what I do. I'm hardly a member of your *pack*."

The alpha regarded him silently, his expression suggesting that Ethan had it all wrong.

"I have to piss. If that's okay with you."

Doug pointed towards the bathroom with a be-my-guest gesture, and Ethan retreated, taking his time, trying to get his head together.

When Ethan came back, a freshly hot prepackaged meal was passed to him on a tray. He was suddenly ravenous and could barely think beyond eating as he shoved food in his mouth. His human mother—he winced at his memory of her and pushed her away—would have been appalled at his table manners. When Ethan finished, Doug handed him one of those ubiquitous bottles of water.

Ethan grabbed it and before he opened it, demanded again, "Why am I here?"

"We have to kill the cat shifters who are feral too long."

Ethan couldn't quite suppress his flinch.

At Ethan's reaction, satisfaction lit Doug's expression before he continued his explanation. "So I thought we'd capture you before you became all cougar all the time. You know how vicious a cougar can be."

"I know how vicious wolves can be."

"That too," Doug acknowledged. "I can be quite vicious, but not without provocation. Don't provoke me, and we'll get along fine."

Ethan drank water and worked at tamping down the fear. *I know assholes when I see them, Doug.* But Ethan kept his mouth shut. He was ready for Doug to leave the room. This had been more than enough interaction. After being alone for years, having an alpha in his bedroom, in his fucking bed, was overwhelming him.

However Doug was warming to the conversation, settling in for the long haul, though at least, thank God, he sat in a chair, not on the bed. "Thing is, I don't like the idea of killing shifters. So I've researched you guys, and I've developed a new strategy. You're my test case." He smiled. "People will be very interested in you."

Ethan gave up trying to hide his fear and swallowed. "Being a test case doesn't sound too promising. But I guess you know that."

"I think you're promising," Doug said quietly.

This situation was making Ethan queasy. He wanted to ask for Bram again, which was not only stupid but unwise. Bram was no friend of his, even if his human body thought otherwise. Ethan pulled that body into himself. He'd been feral. He bloody well knew it, and they held it against him, held it up as something to experiment with.

"So you see," Doug continued, "I am searching out feral cats before they are unreachable. And taming them."

"Unreachable," Ethan said in scathing tones, bravado overrunning his fear. "What happens when they're unreachable but they don't want to be hunted down, captured and forced to stay in one small room?"

"Unreachable means they've become vicious killers of humans, of human children."

Ethan shook his head, adamant. "I would never attack a human."

"No?"

"No. I was a cat, but not unaware. I was not an unthinking beast. You know *nothing* about me."

"I know my cousin Gabriel tortured you. I know you killed a werewolf."

Ethan lifted his chin and met Doug's gaze dead on. "Gabriel is a vicious killer, not me. Euthanize *him*. I was protecting...someone." He would not say Lila's name to this wolf.

Doug rose and walked over to Ethan, eyebrows lifted, expression interested. Ethan needed to figure out how to be less interesting to this alpha. First step would be to *shut up*, but he couldn't manage to keep his mouth shut for any period of time. He had this horrible desire to talk now that he could. Even when, especially when, this asshole said such ludicrous things.

"I'll agree that Gabriel was a vicious killer," Doug acknowledged. "But since he's dead, no one can euthanize him. *I* am now in charge of the Winter pack. And you were in my territory. I decided to bring you in."

"I am here so you can judge me? If I'm deemed a child murderer, you'll kill me?" A slightly hysterical note had entered his voice, and he didn't have the strength to suppress it.

"I won't kill you now that I can talk to you." Doug paused. "If you stay human and cooperate, there will be no problem."

"No problem," Ethan repeated. "You are unbelievable."

Doug stared him down and Ethan shrank a little.

"Let me go, please." Ethan shouldn't ask, and shouldn't ask with a pleading note, not after everything he'd been told, not given the way Doug regarded him as a *test case*. But the room was getting smaller and smaller, and his lack of control unbalanced him.

"No."

"*Now*."

"You're almost starving to death, Ethan. Let us fatten you up."

Ethan was being fattened up for some kind of sacrifice, but

it meant he had some time. *Careful, be careful. Don't lose it completely.* "I want to be left alone, that's all."

"Sleep," commanded Doug and he dragged the chair closer. He sat there and waited for Ethan to obey his latest command. Doug was toying with Ethan, and Ethan had to keep his shit together.

"I can't sleep. Not with you here."

"Try." Those bland, smug, hateful tones almost sent Ethan over the edge. He pulled in three long breaths, no longer looking at the alpha as he slid down to lie on his back and stare at the ceiling. He listened to Doug breathing beside him for the longest time.

Ethan was tired of sleeping, tired of waking, and *still* damnably exhausted. He sat up and looked down to see that he was naked again, and braced himself for someone to put their hands on him, since that seemed to be their MO.

"Hi."

Ethan jerked his head up to find Bram standing in the room, but no Doug. He could barely contain his relief.

"You took off your clothes in your sleep." Bram pointed to the small pile on the floor.

Ethan glanced at the clump of oversized clothes before looking at himself again. His body was in crappy shape. A long time ago, he'd been young and toned. Since then he'd lost his humanity and now? Scrawny limbs, knobby knees, he could see his ribs. He raised his face to scrutinize this dark man who carefully kept his gaze trained on Ethan's face and off the rest of his body. What role was Bram playing in the werewolf game of Tame the Cat?

"It's just me here." Bram offered a half smile and to Ethan's consternation, he wanted to respond to that smile. Mighty desperate for friends, his human, and Bram was the only possible choice. Doug had crossed himself off the list with, among other things, grinding Ethan's face into the bed.

"Hungry?"

"Always. Ready to feed your test case?"

Bram frowned, but didn't respond, simply handed the tray to Ethan who sat cross-legged on the bed and inhaled the contents. As usual, eating made Ethan groggy. He didn't know why he had to be so wiped out all the time. He'd never get out of this room at this rate. He'd fall asleep in the middle of an escape and they'd find him snoring two meters from the building.

"Are you drugging me?" Not that he'd necessarily get the truth, but at least Bram projected earnestness.

Bram slowly shook his head. "Nope."

"Someone else is drugging me?"

The slightest hesitation before: "I really don't think so."

"Then why am I so tired?"

"We think it's because you haven't been human for years, so it's exhausting for you. Everything feels new with the different senses, different body, so there's an adjustment period."

Adjustment period sounded so innocuous that Ethan had the urge to laugh in Bram's face despite his serious expression.

"Also, you're malnourished."

"I'm scrawny," Ethan agreed. "You must get tired of holding me."

Bram went quiet, apparently searching for an appropriate

response if the look on his face was anything to go by. Interesting that he cared so much about what he said. He finally settled on, "No. I don't get tired of it."

Good. Maybe Ethan could somehow use that. Even if a traitorous part of Ethan welcomed Bram's touch.

"Doug said that I had exhausted you." Ethan got off the bed and went to the bathroom, then glanced up as he returned to see the wolf standing awkwardly, unsure about the new direction this conversation had taken.

That was good too, Ethan reflected. Bram didn't appear particularly sophisticated or confident. Perhaps the alpha brought in dumb wolves to guard feral-cats-turned-test-cases. Ethan stared into those liquid brown eyes and Bram's gaze sheered away. Obviously not an alpha. Thank God.

"I just needed to sleep," Bram said eventually.

"Like me then." Bram looked startled by that statement, so Ethan added, "Or wait. That won't do. You wouldn't want to be thought to be like me. *Feral.* In need of being forcibly contained. Apparently I might randomly attack all kinds of innocent creatures."

Bram's big brown eyes turned puppy-dog sad. "Ethan—"

"Aren't you supposed to restrain, sorry, hold me? Keep the cat human and all that."

Bram's gaze turned more intense and despite everything else, Ethan was his stupid, sorry self and reacted to that gaze. He'd known it would be like this if he ever returned to the human world. His human needed intimacy, it seemed, and Bram was the logical choice. The *only* choice since Doug revolted him, which was straightforward thinking in its way, but absolutely insane. Dangerous.

"Never mind," he muttered, turning away to grab a pair of sweats and pull them on. They held all the cards and they could use his need for human touch against him. He hadn't realized, hadn't wanted to realize, how lonely he'd become as cat. He sat on the edge of the bed, back to Bram.

"Ethan." Bram's palm came down on Ethan's bare shoulder and he couldn't hide his response, a welcoming shudder. But he also didn't want what had become the embrace de rigueur— Bram's chest against Ethan's back. As Bram settled behind him, Ethan spun quickly and clasped his arms around Bram's shoulders, sank his face into Bram's neck, searching for his carotid.

Bram went rigid. His hands gripped Ethan's upper arms as if to push him away, and Ethan held on more tightly. Before Bram tried to throw him off, Ethan kissed his neck and let out something like a purr. He should have been embarrassed by his body's response—they were playing him beautifully—yet it simply felt right to hold someone.

Perhaps Bram expected an attack on his neck, but Ethan, despite Bram's hard, stiff clasp on his arms, sank into him more, pressing his chest full against Bram's, sitting deeper into his lap.

Ethan let out a groan of relief at this two-way embrace. It was a release of sorts to be held like a fellow human being and not like a captive. He traced Bram's collarbone with his lips, intoxicated by Bram's scent, by the taste of his skin. It no longer mattered that Bram was a wolf. An awful compulsion gripped Ethan's body and all he felt was need. His dick grew hard against Bram's stomach. And he wasn't the only one. Bram's cock was hardening, rising up to rest between Ethan's ass cheeks, and Jesus that felt good.

Bram's hands slid up to Ethan's shoulders, to his neck, and anchored in his hair. Gently he pulled Ethan's head back. He felt woozy in Bram's grip, those strong palms cradling his skull.

"Listen, Ethan." Bram sounded urgent.

Ethan pushed up on his knees, brought both hands to hold on to Bram's biceps, stared at the wolf, at those dark eyes, pupils wide with desire and confusion. Thank God Ethan wasn't the only one confused.

"What are we doing, Bram?"

Bram didn't answer though there was a kind of despair in his expression that Ethan found encouraging. If Ethan had been the only one affected by these bizarre last few days in this bed, he would have lost all hope.

"Ease your hold on me, Bram," Ethan said softly, applying slight pressure to Bram's arms.

"Sorry. Am I hurting you?" Bram moved his hands down to Ethan's shoulders.

He wasn't, but Ethan used the opportunity to duck in and bring his mouth to Bram's. He took it, delved inside before Bram, openmouthed, could stop him. Ethan swept his tongue across Bram's, lapped at his mouth, tasting the wolf and wanting more, so much more. He wanted to fuck. Here. Now. He thrust against Bram's belly.

Bram jolted backwards. "*No.*"

At the wolf's shock and retreat, Ethan could only blink. He'd seen desire. Bram had responded sexually, even if that kiss was all Ethan giving and Bram receiving.

"No?" Ethan repeated as Bram warily slid off the bed.

What were they doing to him, making him human like this? Making him desire Bram? The entire sequence of encounters was orchestrated, Ethan was sure of it. Was it to keep him on some kind of hook?

Ethan licked his lips and watched Bram observe his

mouth. The wolf's chest heaved once, and Ethan took some satisfaction in seeing that Bram was not unaffected. Bram might be part of the plan on how to treat a test case, but he was not sure of his role here. Nevertheless, the words that followed were flat, resisting. A rejection.

"This is not why I'm here."

Something in Ethan deflated. What the hell was he thinking? He was a prisoner and he wanted to fuck his captor. How asinine was that? Bram was shocked Ethan had kissed him. Every time he thought he was getting his head on straight, he'd do something completely, completely wrong.

Ethan retreated to the headboard and strived to keep his composure. He pulled his knees up to hide his body's reaction and tried to ignore his painful hard-on. "What's the problem? Don't like men? Don't like cats? Don't like ferals?"

"No."

"No, what?" When no answer was forthcoming, Ethan added, "Sorry, I lost my head. I have to remember what I am."

The earnestness on Bram's face meant—what?

"Better go spit me out. Brush your teeth," Ethan suggested.

Bram glanced away, something like desperation crossing his features before he sucked in a deep breath. Dragging a hand across his face, he looked back at Ethan. "I don't want to take advantage of you."

"Like hell." Ethan snorted. But Bram looked miserable, and it occurred to Ethan that he'd better figure out how to be smart *now*, because otherwise he was not going to survive this ordeal. There was opportunity here and he needed to be quick enough to take it. His next words were calculating more than anything else. "You wouldn't touch me with a ten-foot pole except it's your job. It's what your alpha has demanded you do. I hadn't quite realized that till now."

"No. That's not true." The words were softly spoken, with some distress.

Ethan let his head fall back and placed an arm over his face. He could play this convincingly because there was a strange fury in him for being spurned. After all, Bram was *supposed* to touch Ethan, to keep him human, to keep him sane. But Ethan was not supposed to touch Bram. *Certainly* not supposed to kiss him. Despite that Ethan was quite certain Bram had liked it, or at least reacted to it.

"Ethan."

"Get the fuck away. You must have drawn the short straw to be given this job." He had to be careful not to lay the petulance on too thick. That would be unattractive, and Ethan absolutely had to remain attractive to Bram.

"I wanted this job." Carefully Bram placed a hand on Ethan's ankle, and Ethan didn't jerk away. His skin surrounding that joint soaked in the human touch. He even enjoyed it, goddammit.

"Yeah? Well, you know what it's like after you've shifted to human after a long spell as cat or wolf. You know I'm primed for sex. My making a move can hardly have surprised you." In the distant past, Ethan had always made a point of waking human alone so he hadn't had to deal with insane sexual drives. But these wolves weren't giving him that choice and they knew it.

"I'm sorry." Bram sounded sincere. Ethan moved his arm away from his face and regarded the werewolf. "The truth is, I admire you."

"*Admire* me?" Ethan couldn't help it, he laughed. What could Bram admire him for? Weeping? Sleeping? Eating? Kissing him?

"Yes." There was a stubborn, rather endearing tilt to Bram's chin, like he intended to stick to his point.

"So...what's the problem?"

When Bram couldn't seem to find words, Ethan came up with his own. "Do you somehow see this as a conflict of interest, is that what's going on?"

"Yes. A conflict of interest." Bram seized the term eagerly. "If it makes you feel any better. I-I don't..." Bram became overwhelmed by whatever he was trying to say and Ethan got curious. He cocked his head.

"You don't what?" he asked softly.

"I don't kiss, get kissed. That's just not me." A wave of heat washed over Bram. Ethan could see it and didn't know what to make of it or the odd declaration, but he slotted away that observation and that revelation for future use. "I wouldn't say this to anyone else but...you're so offended. I didn't want to offend you, Ethan. I'm sorry."

"You may be sorry. However, I don't believe you, about the kissing." Ethan watched Bram's face burn, but he made himself continue. "Werewolves are really into sex, touch, affection. More than cats. That much I remember." From Lila and her descriptions of her pack, and from Lila herself acting all motherly towards Ethan. But he wasn't going to speak her name.

Bram looked away. "Not all werewolves." His mouth twisted. "Some are *special.*"

He wouldn't meet Ethan's gaze, sat very still, yet didn't release Ethan's ankle, as if that hold was important.

Not all werewolves, eh? Well, if Bram was for real, if he was showing Ethan his true emotions, there might be room to maneuver because Bram could be played. And while it had been many years, at one time Ethan had been very good at playing men. It was time to relearn old skills.

Chapter Five

Bram clenched his fist by his side, as if that single gesture could convey to Doug what he had to say.

"Did Ethan get under your skin?" Doug asked.

"We have a problem." *He kissed me.* But Bram didn't want to actually say that. It felt disloyal, which was silly. Doug wouldn't use it against Ethan. Doug wouldn't give a shit.

The alpha glanced at the sleeping Ethan on the screen. "Actually, I think the cat is doing great, much better than expected. Trey's had to kill all his ferals. This one has been human for three days and coherent for one day."

Bram frowned. From time to time, Doug mentioned Trey, apparent cat expert and cat killer. Bram didn't much like the sound of this werewolf cousin of Doug's.

"You look troubled, Bram."

Bram kept his voice quiet, tentative. Doug liked tentative and was more receptive to what Bram said when he appeared uncertain. "It seems wrong to hold Ethan captive and keep him in one room. Now that he's lucid it might do more harm than good."

"*Seems* being the key word here." Doug lifted his chin towards the outside window. "Do you think he wants to know he's surrounded by werewolves out there? That he's being held at the Winter pack's headquarters?"

Bram scrubbed his face. "No. At least, not yet."

"'No' is the correct answer. It's better Ethan stays cocooned away from the real world. Yes, he's got escape on his mind. You can tell by the way he looks at the door, and what could be more natural? His cat will want to be free." Doug grinned, that triumph in his expression again. "But not his human. His human craves our company. He wants to talk to us. He responds and even initiates conversations. It's very good, Bram."

It sure as hell didn't feel *good*.

At Bram's dubious look, Doug added, "He's been alone for many, many years, and it hasn't been healthy for him."

"Yeah, but he's a cougar. They need to be alone. They're not pack animals like us."

"They need time alone, yes. But they're shifters, not animals. They have their human side."

"I know that," Bram snapped.

Doug leveled him a warning look.

Bram raised his palms in apology. "I'm sorry. That's not what I meant. I didn't mean to say Ethan was an animal." He could have accused Doug of twisting his words and putting him on the defensive, but Bram didn't want to get sidetracked.

"My point," Doug said with great patience, "is that Ethan is part human and constant solitude is bad for him. It fucks him up."

"Okay," Bram agreed, just like Doug wanted him to. Bram felt tired. He wasn't used to arguing and disagreeing this much with his alpha, and he found it stressful. Easier to bow and scrape and apologize, though that was hell on what was left of his ego.

"Is there something you want to tell me, Bram?"

Bram stared at the floor, preparing himself for his next words, and they were hard to force out even if Doug likely knew. Given his fascination for the cat, he had probably watched the screen. Bram cleared his throat. "Ethan came on to me."

Doug eyed him steadily, no surprise in his expression. "How did you react?"

"I set him apart from me." Bram could feel heat flooding his face but he met Doug's gaze briefly.

"Good." Doug paused and a ghost of a smile appeared. "It's actually a good sign that he wants you. It shows that his human side is alive and well and working. We want that."

Bram shook his head. "It's not good, it's wrong." It wasn't fair to Ethan, being captive, being drawn to his jailer. Bram felt that in his gut. Even if that kiss, that eager tongue on his, still had him hard.

"Of course it's not wrong," Doug said calmly, bringing Bram's thoughts back to the important issue—Ethan. "He's trying to bond with you."

"*Bond?*" Bram hadn't thought cats formed bonds. Ethan was just reaching for whoever was there. And Bram was surely there. He'd been watching the cougar for three days.

"Yes. Cougars form bonds. That one female cat shifter—"

"She's real? I thought you were making her up for Ethan's sake."

"Don't interrupt me."

"Sorry. Sorry, Doug." Christ, Bram didn't know how much longer he could apologize to Doug without getting sick. It was exhausting, this constant apology. It should have been natural, since Bram was omega, and yet it never was.

"She's real, yes," Doug said finally. "I didn't lie to the cat.

Anyway, she's apparently bonded to a human. So Ethan is bonding to you, which makes sense. You've spent the most time with him and should continue to do so."

"It doesn't seem right, to lock him up. To force him to bond with me because he sees no one else." A relationship was being forced on Ethan, and even if a part of Bram craved a relationship, he didn't want it like this. Sordid. Under Doug's control. On screen.

Doug rolled his eyes. "Stop whining, Bram. It's irritating. The fact is Ethan's entire life has been unfair." Doug held out three fingers and started ticking them off. "Our pack gutted him more than a few times." Second finger. "He's been feral, though quite obviously not irreversibly so, thanks to us." Third finger. "His friend Lila was killed before his eyes."

Doug paused, as if his dimwitted omega would take a while to soak up this information, before he continued. "Being attracted to you is hardly Ethan's worst nightmare. At least you're concerned for his welfare." The alpha's expression actually softened. "You're not so bad, Bram. Don't loathe yourself, and don't bring your self-loathing into it."

"I'm not," Bram said quickly, trying to forestall a conversation about himself. Those lectures never ended well. "This isn't about me."

Doug's smile turned patronizing, indulgent, and Bram had this very unomego desire to slug him.

Don't react. Don't get off track. Turn the subject back to what's important—Ethan. "The point is he's too vulnerable to bond with anyone. It makes things...wrong, twisted. He's a prisoner, malnourished, fearful most of the time—" *Shit.* Doug looked pissed.

"Are you suggesting that what I'm doing is wrong?" Doug asked quietly in clipped tones.

"No." *Maybe*, but Bram couldn't say that. Too dangerous.

"You need to trust me on this. I expect your trust, Bram, after all I've done for you." Doug paused, giving Bram a chance to respond. He didn't take it. Doug sighed. "I'm the bad cop in this situation. That will make him turn to you even more, and that's better for his mental health. He *needs* to connect to someone. Do you not see that?"

Bram found he could no longer nod, no longer agree, so he just stood there, but Doug didn't notice. "Also I'm the alpha. Cats are unlikely to be drawn to alphas. They don't like authority. But omegas...that's a different story. You're perfect."

At the word "perfect", Bram snorted.

"Don't lose sight of what we're trying to accomplish here," Doug lectured on. "This is nothing, a slight awkwardness. You'll get past it."

It doesn't feel like nothing.

Placing a hand on Bram's shoulder, Doug squeezed, but instead of letting go, he held on, his grip firm. "Is the problem that you need an outlet after that kiss? I can give you that."

Bram went still, wondering if Doug meant what Bram thought he meant. His heart rate picked up. The oblique offer filled Bram with an awful anticipation and he shivered in reaction.

"Kneel," ordered Doug. "You need this."

Bram breathed quickly, confused thoughts tumbling through his brain. Before today Doug had always kept their transactions away from the office.

"I don't mind if you take yourself in hand this time. I know you're under stress." Doug's other palm came to rest on Bram's shoulder, and he applied pressure, forcing Bram down to his knees.

"Unzip yourself, Bram. You know you want to. I can smell your arousal."

Looking down, he obeyed, finding his dick while Doug undid his own zipper. The alpha made his signature move, fisting Bram's hair and lifting Bram's face towards his groin. Sometimes this was the best part of the sex, that hand on Bram's head. Not affection exactly, but purpose, and tension in that grip showed that Doug was not unaffected, that it wasn't only Bram who wanted sex.

Bram parted his lips and Doug's penis slid past. The cock hardened, thickened as it seated itself at the back of his mouth. Something in Bram unwound, knowing that he could make his alpha hard, that Doug allowed him this. It was the only time he could truly please his alpha and despite everything about his life, Bram was wolf enough to want to please his alpha.

Bram stroked himself while Doug withdrew and entered again. As always Bram's gag reflex went to work, but they both ignored it because Doug was a large man. The stimulation, the act of being fucked, electrified Bram like nothing else did.

He stroked himself harder. If he didn't come before Doug did, he might not be allowed to. A rising lust rose within Bram, his balls tightened, and Doug pulled harder on his hair, bruising the scalp.

They continued, finding their rhythm, Doug rough on Bram, while Bram was rough on himself, fighting to reach climax sooner rather than later. It became a contest, the tension unbearable, not knowing who would reach the end first. His body seized.

He arched, coming in his hand. Doug entered his mouth again, keeping Bram upright, that hand holding tight to Bram's hair as the pace picked up. He counted silently: once, twice, five more times before Doug spurted, spunk filling Bram's throat.

Doug remained pressed against the back of Bram's mouth while Bram's entire body slackened. The salty, sour semen slid down his throat and he took it, every last drop. He licked Doug, circling the head carefully so Doug came away clean. The alpha slowly released Bram's hair, the signal for Bram to sit back on his haunches. He managed it, if a little shakily.

Doug stepped away and tucked himself back into his jeans. The alpha wasn't gay, wasn't attracted to Bram, but he liked being given head and he knew Bram needed some sexual contact. No one else would have Bram. This was their compromise.

Bram zipped himself up and found some wet paper towels to clean the floor. The euphoria of anticipation and sex was fading, and with it came the knowledge that there were better ways to have sex. He knew it, longed for it. But there were also worse ways, especially for an omega, and he knew firsthand about those too. Still, his face was beet red with heat and a strange kind of squeezing hurt.

Doug didn't like to see him like this, in the aftermath. "Go back into Ethan's room."

Bram shook his head. Though Ethan didn't have the keen nose of a wolf, he would smell Doug on him. Bram didn't want Ethan or anyone else to know. This fucking was only between Doug and himself.

"Don't shake your head at me. Do it."

Raising his gaze, Bram said, "I'd like to shower first, please."

But Doug wasn't looking at him. "Later. I need to go out. I have others in my pack besides you. Get inside and babysit the cat or I'll march you in there."

The trouble was, sex with Doug took the fight right out of Bram. He closed his eyes briefly and turned towards that locked door. Really, what the hell did it matter? Ethan was sleeping anyway.

Bram grabbed a water bottle. If nothing else he'd drink to try to get rid of the taste of Doug.

Ethan woke slowly. It was a nice change from jerking awake, but as awareness built so did dread. He was in this fucking room with two jailers, an asshole and someone Ethan hoped to manipulate. Rather awful really, but his fears of being forever locked up trumped everything. He had to get out.

Only Bram was present and given Doug's oppressive bedside manner, Ethan felt relief. He pushed himself up to sitting and took a long look at his visitor.

The wolf wasn't watching Ethan, which was a bit of a change. He stared, unseeing, into the space in front of him. Ethan opened his mouth slightly and pulled in a breath. The air carried the scent of sex and Doug. Overlaid by mint, yes, but definitely there.

The realization was like a sucker punch to the gut and Ethan's intake of breath was audible.

Somehow, Ethan hadn't seen it coming, that Bram and Doug were lovers. Bram was much less likely to betray a lover, especially an alpha lover. These wolves were loyal and power meant a lot to them. Doug was sure as hell powerful.

Bram turned to face Ethan, his gaze narrowing, brow furrowing. No doubt because Ethan looked ill. He shut his eyes, rolled onto his side and curled up, putting his back to Bram. A sick feeling of despair enveloped him. He'd been better off with hatching an escape strategy, even if its chances of success had been small. He hated this feeling of wishing he were dead, and he wanted to shake it off, but living in a one-room prison was painful.

After a few minutes he heard movement and sensed Bram rise and walk around the bed to the side Ethan faced. There was the soft creak of knees as the wolf crouched down to eye level.

"Ethan?" Bram said softly, worry in his voice.

Ethan raised his eyelids and stared without answering. Bram's dark hair was usually mussed, but Ethan imagined it was more mussed than usual. Lips weren't too obviously kissed though. Probably it had been a quickie. There was a kind of heat on Bram's face, what Ethan had thought of—many long years ago—as an afterglow. However, on close inspection, the expression in Bram's eyes seemed a little bruised, out of sync with the rest of Ethan's observations. He feared he was imagining that expression, looking for ways out that weren't there. Looking for Bram to be a weak link.

"Are you all right?" Bram asked.

"No." Ethan gave a humorless laugh and propped his head on one hand to observe the wolf more carefully. "Are *you*?"

Bram's eyes widened. "Sure."

"Sex good?"

The wolf went very still, face heating more, but that was no afterglow, that was embarrassment. Even shame.

Ethan found himself frowning, and hope rising. Something was out of whack. It was up to him to discover what exactly.

He pitched his voice to sound wry, sympathetic. "Or not so good?"

Bram stayed still except for the slight flaring of his nostrils, yet the wolf's unhappiness affected Ethan and he offered a half smile to ease Bram's discomfort. "Which happens to the best of us."

Bram's eyes swerved to the right and he cleared his throat.

"Are you thirsty?"

Ethan sat up and crossed his legs. "Bram," he coaxed, trying to get the wolf to focus on him. It felt cozy in this room when it was only him and Bram, and it was time for Ethan to take advantage of the weird atmosphere. God knows it had been used against him these past few days.

But Bram shook his head, once, definite, then rose and retrieved a bottle.

"Okay, I'd like a drink." Ethan held out his hand and made sure his fingers brushed Bram's. The wolf's arm jerked slightly and Ethan looked at Bram, whose gaze had jerked too.

Shit. This wasn't exactly fun. Unless he was a very good actor, Bram was a bit of a mess. Someone Ethan would have avoided in another life when he liked things light and easy. He swallowed a good two-thirds of the bottle of water, then wiped his mouth while trying to figure out what to do with this sad-looking wolf. Sympathy was fine, sympathy was good, but Ethan still had to be smart about it.

He eyed Bram and spoke neutrally. "No wonder you didn't want to kiss me. Not when your alpha is your mate."

Bram gave himself a whole-body shake, reminiscent of a real wolf's movement of shaking off water. He gritted his teeth. "I'm an omega."

"So what, omegas and alphas don't mate? Sorry, I don't understand pack dynamics all that much."

"Would you like something to eat?"

"Not mates, then."

Bram gazed at him, long and hard, not answering. But there was fire in that gaze, which told Ethan two things. Bram and Doug weren't mates—a mated wolf would never deny the bond—and Bram was an angry omega, sometimes beaten but not completely down. Ethan had to find a way to use that anger to help him.

An angry omega had issues with his alpha, whether or not they were fucking.

Maybe Ethan stood a chance after all.

Chapter Six

The next day Bram appeared on cue as Ethan was waking. Not from a particularly restful sleep, but there'd been no nightmares either. Small mercies and all that.

Bram looked weary, like all the enthusiasm for Project Ethan had been sucked out of him. Maybe good, maybe not.

"Good morning." Ethan rubbed his eyes. "It is morning, right?"

"Sure."

"Sure, it's morning? Or sure, Ethan, it doesn't matter since you live in a windowless room?"

Bram studied the table upon which he'd laid breakfast. "It's morning. Late morning. Did you have a good sleep?"

Bram's diffidence was kind of endearing, or would have been if the wolf hadn't been holding Ethan captive. At least Bram didn't smell of Doug anymore. All washed off and there'd been no rematch. Ethan figured if they were having sex too often, there was the danger of a strong bond, angry omega or not. Occasional fuck buddies would better work in Ethan's favor.

He finally lifted a shoulder in response to Bram's rote question. The wolf usually asked about his sleeping, probably after watching him for hours. "All I do is sleep. With practice,

I'm becoming very good at it. Gets a bit dull as my only hobby though."

Bram gestured at the food and drink brought in for Ethan, all prepackaged, high-energy shit. His mother, Ethan thought, the memories weren't all that clear, would have called it junk food. At any rate he gobbled them down and wondered if he was already putting on a bit of weight. It sure as hell wouldn't hurt. He needed more strength.

"I'm also getting good at eating and drinking," Ethan said, picking up the conversation again and giving a nod towards the empty tray. "I'm wondering what my next party trick is supposed to be. Not sex, I can assume. You and Doug have each other." But Ethan allowed a little innuendo to enter his tone, a little invitation.

To his surprise, Bram met his gaze, a warning in his eyes. "Don't talk about Doug."

"No? The topic is off limits?"

Bram slowly swerved his eyes up and to the left, added a slight tip of his head before looking back at Ethan. "It is for me."

Ethan waited a beat, letting Bram pick up the empty tray, before he briefly looked into the top right corner of the room.

He didn't know much if anything about these things, but there might have been a camera embedded in the wall—black, circular, with something lens-like in the middle.

The air whooshed out of him. They were fucking filming him? Jesus. He stood up, feeling shaky, feeling like he couldn't get a good handle on his situation. Then he plonked back down on the bed.

"Tired from eating so much?" Bram suggested. His tone was flat and bland, carrying the faintest distaste.

Ethan turned away from the camera and spoke to the bed. "Yeah."

"I'll be back."

"Fantastic."

And Bram left.

Of course, if Ethan's brain was in any kind of working order, he would have realized he was being watched. How else did they know to come in while he was waking up? Every single fucking time. He let the resentment wash through him and went on to the next question.

Why would Bram reveal that fact to him? It had been surreptitious, as if Bram could get into trouble for pointing it out. So why bother? Perhaps to prevent further seduction attempts.

Ethan clenched his jaw. His privacy was already shot. He would not allow a camera to get in his way, distasteful as it was, because his situation had gone well beyond distaste.

"He ate," Bram told Doug, throwing the empty tray in the bin for dirty dishes. He'd be washing them later.

"I gathered that." Doug gazed intently at the screen, which showed Ethan lying on his back staring at the ceiling, unmoving. "What happened? I thought he wanted to talk to you, but he kind of gave up and went back to bed."

Bram shrugged. "Maybe he got pissed off that I didn't want to talk about you."

Doug leveled a stare at Bram, who was careful not to squirm. "Then talk about me. Conversation is vital. We're going to have to show he's functional."

"Functional," Bram repeated slowly, not liking the sound of it.

"Yes. We're trying to bring him back to civilization, remember?"

And God knows we're civilized. But Bram shut up, because he didn't want to argue with Doug and lose. Instead he asked, "When?"

"When what?"

"When do we have to show he's functional?" Bram wanted to know the bigger picture, but Doug was not generous about information.

Doug shrugged. "A few days, maybe less. My contact is being a little vague. Depends when he can get away."

"Then what'll happen?" Doug was watching him thoughtfully, so Bram strived to sound casual, even if the alpha would scent his anxiety. "I don't want him to come to any harm."

Doug clapped a hand on Bram's shoulder. "Don't worry, they'll take care of him."

"Who?"

Doug actually laughed. "Did you think we were going to keep him forever? This is extremely draining. We're just the first step."

"But who will take care of him?" Bram was alarmed by the phrase. "I thought Trey was a cat killer."

"Jesus, Bram, don't get hysterical on me." Losing his pretense at patience, Doug glowered. "What is the matter with you? Of course it's not Trey. He's gone to ground. No one even knows where he is these days."

Bram blinked. Why Doug thought Bram should know this fact about Trey, he couldn't fathom, given that Doug played his cards close to his chest and rarely told him anything. In fact the amount of information thus far in the conversation seemed excessive. Perhaps a side benefit of yesterday's sex with Doug. The alpha tended to feel guilty afterwards and offer Bram compensation. Usually not information, but Bram would sure take this.

"Gone to ground?" Bram ventured. "What does that mean?"

"He disappeared." The alpha's lips thinned, as if thinking he'd said enough. "That's all you need to know."

"It would be helpful if I understood the endgame, Doug, so I knew what I'm preparing Ethan for. Don't you think?" Bram added, because Doug liked questions that implied he was being asked for guidance.

"We're handing him over to people who know how to look after Ethan's kind. They have no interest in killing him, believe me. A cat is very valuable in their eyes. They are incredibly keen to understand a cougar shifter."

This was news to Bram. To date, Doug had talked like just he and Bram were going to be involved in rehabilitating a feral cougar. Bram swallowed. "Government?"

"Not exactly." At Bram's doubtful expression, Doug said, "What? You think it's a good idea to keep him *here*, among the wolves who tormented him before he went feral? Or, you think we should have left him alone, to stay feral and go insane so he had to be euthanized by someone like Trey? I understand you find some of this unpalatable, Bram, but there are worse fates. Your stupid reproachful glances piss me off."

"Sorry." Doug wanted to be appeased, so Bram added, "I didn't understand but what you say makes sense. I'm sorry I have so many questions, but I didn't know more people were going to be involved. I'm just concerned about him, because I've spent the last few days with him."

Doug nodded. "Do you need me to spend the afternoon with Ethan? Is he getting to you?"

"I'm okay."

"Well, get back in then. I don't think he's falling asleep and he shouldn't be alone. I sure as hell don't want him turning cat now."

Hiding his relief, because Bram did *not* want Doug with Ethan, Bram obeyed his alpha. He opened the first door, closed it and took a deep breath while facing the second door. If he were claustrophobic he'd have problems in this closet, but instead it was a fifteen-second reprieve while he locked that first door, unlocked the second and stepped into Ethan's room.

At Bram's entry, Ethan sat up on the bed, looking fairly fragile, truth be told. He was wiry, despite his malnourishment, and almost reached Bram's height. Half the time his face gave nothing away. Other times, there were lightning-quick expressions of anger, fear and desperation.

Bram hated being partially responsible for that. His heart turned over and he didn't know what to do with these emotions that were intensifying with alarming speed. He *knew* he longed for companionship, he *knew* Ethan's attempts to draw Bram closer were based on expediency, not any real kind of friendship. And yet to Bram *something* felt dangerously real.

But there was more at stake than Bram's emotions. He feared for Ethan's well-being, given that Doug's contacts were going to view Ethan as valuable. Which made the cat sound like an asset, not a person.

"Come here." Ethan sat on the bed, cross-legged, and leaned forward, intent on Bram.

"I am here." Bram firmly closed the door behind him. Not locked from this side, but Ethan couldn't escape through the second door because its keyless lock required a number be punched in.

Appearing faintly amused, Ethan said, "What? Not budging

from that door? It's almost as if you don't want to be here."

"I want to be here."

"Could have fooled me. You look like you're ready to bolt." At this moment, Ethan's face gave nothing away, and Bram didn't see it as a good sign.

"I can't leave, actually."

"*Can't?*" A bright anger sat in Ethan's eyes. "I dunno, Bram. I am forced to stay in this room, because you people won't let me out. But I'd hazard you have a bit more freedom and you don't *have* to do anything."

Bram walked over to the bed and crouched down on his haunches so that Ethan was above him. A submissive gesture that came naturally, though whether Ethan would recognize it as such, Bram didn't know. It didn't matter.

He rested his elbows on his knees. Hands dangled between his legs and he looked at them, not Ethan. Okay, Ethan wasn't wolf and he certainly wasn't alpha wolf, but Bram still chose to speak without eye contact. "What do you want?"

No answer. After quite a while, Bram lifted his face to gaze at this tawny, ethereal creature. Probably not always ethereal, but the malnourishment gave a certain effect.

As did the glowing eyes. Bram's heart clenched.

Slowly leaning forward, Ethan brushed a knuckle across Bram's cheek. He spoke softly. "What are you doing down there, Bram?"

Unable to come up with any kind of answer—Bram wasn't used to his face being touched—he just smiled.

A small answering smile—it appeared genuine—crossed Ethan's features. "Are you one of those people who think too hard?"

"No." *I try not to think.*

Ethan pressed his thumb lightly against Bram's forehead, making upward strokes. "Don't frown so."

Bram once again moved his eyes in the direction of the camera, trying to warn Ethan. Doug would be watching them, and he couldn't stand that. Bad enough... Well, bad enough.

Doug slammed into the room and while Ethan jerked in reaction, his gaze didn't leave Bram's face. Bram felt like Ethan was silently asking for his help and Bram realized in that moment that he wanted to give it. *Had* to give it.

Figuring out how to help Ethan, though, would be his challenge. One Bram wasn't sure he'd be able to meet.

"Come here." Doug was talking to Bram and to Ethan's dismay the dark werewolf actually cringed before he rose and walked over to his alpha. Ethan stared at where Bram had been. The wolf had wanted those touches. His eyes had dilated and there'd been a kind of yearning in his expression.

But he was scared, of his alpha perhaps. Was Doug the jealous kind?

Doug dragged Bram out and suddenly Ethan was alone again. Well, Ethan and the camera. This time he observed it for a few minutes. It didn't look easy to break, and breaking it might lead to a worse kind of surveillance. Better to know about its existence and not let on to Doug he knew.

Ten minutes later the door opened again and it was, as Ethan had feared, the alpha. Ready to lay down the law though Ethan wasn't entirely sure which rule Doug thought Ethan had broken.

Warily, Ethan spread his hands without looking Doug in the eye. "No shifting. I promise. I've decided to be good."

"Is that what you've decided?"

"Yes." Ethan smiled.

"You want to fuck."

Ethan's smile felt strained, but he refused to let it drop. Ass. Hole.

"That's normal. Wolves and cats are similar that way. We like to fuck when we return to human form. And you. You're a shifter who's been human for the first time in eight years."

Eight years. Gawd. Ethan's smile evaporated and his body sagged. He hadn't thought he'd been out that long. It took a moment to sink in, that length of time. He was twenty-nine, and the loss of human years made him feel a little sick. He'd lost his twenties. He'd lost his youth.

Doug appeared amused by Ethan's reaction to that piece of news. "Oh, we hadn't mentioned the eight years before?"

"No," Ethan said shortly.

"If you want to fuck, I'll bring in a wolf who likes fucking men."

Ethan shook his head while he clamped down on his fear, refusing to let Doug smell his emotions. It sounded like a threat and Doug knew it.

"No?" said Doug softly. "Then back off from Bram. You approach him again and I'll send in someone else to take care of you."

"Fuck you."

Doug's lip curled. "It would only ever be the other way 'round. But I'm not inclined."

"I don't actually want to be raped."

A short shake of his head. "I don't do rape, don't allow it in my pack. So don't worry."

"Oh," said Ethan with a careless wave of his hand, "I'm not worried. What the hell would I have to be worried about here?"

"Clever, Ethan."

Not really. He was seething and it entertained this werewolf.

Doug stepped closer, looming over Ethan. "I meant what I said about Bram."

"I'm sure you did."

Doug waited, so Ethan added, because he wanted the alpha *out* of this room, "I understand."

"I'm glad to hear it."

Doug left, and Ethan lay down and put an arm across his face.

"Turn it on again." Doug shut the door behind him and Bram tapped the keyboard. Ethan came back on screen, lying on the bed with his face covered by his arm, as if protecting himself.

Doug had expected Bram to obey and not watch him give Ethan the ultimatum, so Bram pretended he had not kept the surveillance on. Consequently, a question was in order. "What did you say to him, Doug?"

"I told him to leave you alone. He agreed to do as I asked." Doug paused and frowned. "Why are you looking miserable? I took care of the problem."

"Thanks."

Doug paused, assessing Bram who wished he could dissimulate better than this. "You were pretty upset yesterday with the idea of Ethan kissing you. Ran against your ethics or something. Don't tell me you've changed your mind today."

Bram shook his head emphatically. "I haven't changed my mind."

"Good. I thought about it last night and decided you were

right. It's a bad idea to get physical with the cat. I want him to keep his head on straight."

Head on straight. *Right.* But Bram just nodded.

"What's he doing?"

"Lying down," Bram said tonelessly and they both watched Ethan on the bed, chest rising and falling as if he was in distress.

Doug quirked his mouth into a smile. "Bit of a drama queen."

Bram shrugged.

Clapping him on the back, Doug announced, "I'm out for a few hours. You can watch him from here if you'd prefer. If you find it too intense to be inside his room."

"I might just do that."

Doug strode out.

Bram waited a full half hour before he turned the camera off—Ethan hadn't budged the entire time—and went into history. There he found video of himself watching Ethan from yesterday, forty-seven minutes worth, and spliced it out. Then he set it to play again and again. Yes, if Doug came back early and paid attention, he could figure out it was a false loop. Fortunately, Doug trusted Bram to do as he was instructed.

Bram ignored the pang of disobeying his alpha and walked back into Ethan's room.

Chapter Seven

Ethan didn't react to Bram's entry, even when he approached the bed. Bram stared down, wishing he knew what to do.

Let him go free.

It was the obvious answer and Bram didn't trust it. If Bram opened the doors and let Ethan walk out of the building, he wouldn't get far. There was a razor-wire fence that surrounded the pack's headquarters. Yes, a legacy from Gabriel's paranoid rule, but the thing was, Doug had never seen fit to tear it down. *One day it might protect us from the government* had been his last explanation.

Bram retreated and sank down into the corner, directly below the camera and out of its eye. Sure the camera was switched off, but under the circumstances, it didn't hurt to be overcareful.

"What are you doing?" Ethan spoke to his arm still covering his face.

Bram tossed several answers around in his mind and couldn't find anything he liked. He settled on, "I don't know."

Lifting his upper body so he rested on his elbows, Ethan looked across at Bram, then glanced up at the camera. He briefly closed his eyes before he rolled off the bed and came over to Bram on all fours.

Stalked over, Bram thought, and there was grace in it.

Day-old stubble adorned Ethan's jaw and his badly cut hair stuck up haphazardly. The bones of his face were too sharp, even if he had put on a bit of weight since staying here. Bram thought he was so beautiful and could never tell him.

"Are we out of sight?" Ethan asked softly.

Bram nodded. He had hunkered down in the corner with his knees up, his legs blocking Ethan, who had stopped just out of reach.

"My cat wants out, out of this room, out of this body." Ethan's gaze burned, which made Bram feel hot. "But I think that might be a death sentence here."

"No one is going to kill you."

Ethan's mouth twisted. "That's what Gabriel once told me."

"Doug is no Gabriel."

"And yet, I am still his sacrifice, no?"

Bram wanted to shake his head, but he remembered that there were people out there who Doug said would *take care* of Ethan. Was that a sacrifice? "I don't think so."

"I suppose I should take some comfort from the fact that *you* don't appear to want me to be a sacrifice."

"I don't," Bram whispered.

"What do you want, Bram?"

The air seemed to thicken, a tension, and Bram didn't know where to look. Ethan's gaze refused to let go and while usually it was a good thing to look away from someone and cede way, that wasn't the case here and now. Ethan was no werewolf. Instead he was a captive cougar asking for something Bram was in no position to give. Freedom.

Pulling himself up into a crouch, inches from Bram, Ethan reached out a hand and placed it on Bram's knee.

He tried to stifle his reactive shudder but didn't succeed.

Ethan waited until Bram got used to the heat of his hand on his knee.

"Bram?" asked Ethan in a low voice.

Bram gave up pretending he was unaffected. "It's hard to breathe."

Cocking his head, Ethan regarded Bram as if trying to interpret a foreign language. "You held me, not that long ago. You held me repeatedly."

"That's different."

"Okay." In one movement, Ethan turned and slid sideways in between Bram's knees, a surprising invasion that Bram couldn't resist. Then Ethan turned so they had their familiar embrace, his back resting against Bram's chest.

He should push Ethan away. It was the right thing to do, but slowly and carefully Bram wrapped his arms around this thin stranger who jerked in the hold even while moving deeper into Bram's lap. They were awkward and difficult with each other, but Bram did not want to let go. Neither did Ethan, for Bram could smell his desire.

"Your cat is...?" Bram didn't know how to ask if Ethan's cougar was desperate to get out.

"Okay. For now, anyway." Ethan turned his head to lay his cheek against Bram's chest.

"You're okay, you mean."

"I'm not okay, you must know that. But...this is better. Can you tell me why I like to hear your heart beat?" It was an oddly wistful question and Bram felt completely out of his depth. Was he supposed to even answer? Well, he couldn't. Ethan gave a shuddery sigh that echoed something inside Bram. "I don't really think you're okay either, Bram."

Bram held Ethan tighter, and breathed in Ethan's scent. There was something a little wild and foreign, something cat, or maybe just Ethan. It turned Bram on.

Ethan had to know, had to feel his erection pressing against the small of his back. Bram nuzzled Ethan's neck in apology, and Ethan repeated, "Okay."

"Okay what?"

He didn't answer, simply leaned back, head against Bram's shoulder to rest there. Bram shouldn't, but he raised one hand and stroked that long neck. Ethan groaned, turned his face into Bram's neck and licked the skin.

Bram jittered in reaction and Ethan said, "Shhh. Settle down." Before Bram could declare that was impossible, Ethan slid his tongue along the dip above Bram's collarbone, and Bram jumped again.

"You have me at a disadvantage." Ethan spoke against Bram's throat. "So many disadvantages. You can smell my arousal, but my sense of smell is not quite so acute. On the other hand, I can hear your heart beating too fast, your breath going in and out quickly."

Bram clamped down hard on Ethan so he couldn't move.

"Why are we like this together?" There was a kind of wonder in Ethan's voice.

Bram cleared his throat. "I'll let you go."

"I don't want to be let go. But I need you to help me. You know that."

"Doug," began Bram, but didn't know what to say beyond that. Doug was in charge, not him.

"Doug is going to kill me."

"*No.*" Bram didn't believe it, and wouldn't allow it.

"Like Gabriel."

"Doug despised Gabriel. They're not at all alike."

"I think you're wrong."

"You haven't been hurt," Bram pointed out.

"Not physically, but this containment is hurting me. I need out, Bram."

"Even if I let you out of here, you wouldn't escape. We're at the pack headquarters."

Ethan's entire body stiffened. "Oh God. Not here again."

"It's not like last time," Bram insisted.

"No. Because last time someone helped me get away."

Despite himself, Bram stroked Ethan's face. A kind of silent promise because Bram couldn't say anything. While he hoped his loop of tape was still running, there was always the awful possibility that Doug had returned and was listening.

"Oh," said Ethan, voice toneless. "I really thought you might help me. I thought I could be more persuasive than this. Out of practice. Out of practice with a lot of things."

"Patience," Bram mouthed, subvocally, and Ethan jerked his head around, trying to make eye contact.

"The camera has sound?"

Bram let his eyelids fall in assent.

Ethan fought to turn full around to face Bram, fear in his expression, in his scent. "Doug has made it clear he will punish me." His voice rose. "Doug—"

Bram cut him off with a kiss. Not very elegant, not like how Ethan had kissed him earlier, it seemed almost a fight, a clash of mouths, and Bram angled his body away to prevent Ethan from leaning into him.

But Ethan had to shut up.

Breaking the kiss, Bram met Ethan's gaze and mouthed,

"I'll take care of it."

"By fucking him."

"Enough." Bram glared. He should get out of here, but Ethan looked a little crazy with fear. Suddenly the cat turned away, sliding his sweats down as he settled back against Bram again.

Bram watched as Ethan brought his right hand down to his own hard cock to jerk himself off, and Bram's dick turned to steel.

"Hold me while I get this out of my system," murmured Ethan and Bram slung an arm across Ethan's ribs and held fast. "I need this. God knows I need something."

Ethan's dick was weeping pre-come and he began to pump himself.

Bram couldn't speak, he just breathed Ethan in and nuzzled the cat's neck and didn't let him go. He'd never held on to someone while they jerked off. In fact, doing so had never occurred to him though his skin suddenly felt electric, like that moment before he and Doug started having sex. However, this embrace was lasting longer, and Bram's chest hurt with a strange weight—desire, longing, loss.

"Oh God," Bram let out as Ethan picked up the pace. He was breathing harshly in Ethan's ear. More blood pooled south and he wondered if he could come simply like this. His tension and Ethan's rose in unison.

The cat's throat vibrated, a kind of catlike pleading sound. Almost a purr, but there was a striving there too. A need. Bram leaned over to lick and nuzzle Ethan's vibrating throat. In reaction, Ethan moaned long and low, then his back arched. He came in his hand, milky ejaculate pumped out to spill over Ethan's fist as he gasped. Bram felt like he was breathing with Ethan, uneven, short breaths of wonder.

Ethan slumped in Bram's embrace. The worst of his tension had eased and Bram liked holding this more relaxed Ethan. There was a kind of trust in this moment despite Bram's own tension. His balls ached, his dick hurt with pleasure-pain and his brain couldn't process the next step—because Ethan was turning around to reach for him.

Everything in Bram shut down and he balked. "Back off."

Ethan froze.

"Doug can*not* smell you on me. It's too dangerous. Back away and clean up."

Ethan looked as dazed as Bram felt. "The camera—?"

Bram made a slicing motion. "I think I can take care of it. Just...go shower. I have to leave."

"But you..."

Bram shook his head emphatically.

The expression on Ethan's face was almost bereft, which made it worse.

Bram had to leave, before things got even more out of hand. "I'll be back. I promise."

Ethan's eyes were large and almost golden. "Bram," he whispered.

"I am going to help you." With that declaration, Bram fled.

Ethan retreated to the washroom to have a long shower and tried to process what had happened. He wasn't quite sure.

That went fucking—ha—well.

So much for sophisticated seduction. He'd jerked off in Bram's arms, Bram had flinched when he'd reached for him, and mostly Ethan had pleaded with Bram to help him.

Gawd. He was screwed. To top it all off, Doug would

probably come back in and pay Ethan a visit. The idea of which made Ethan's skin crawl. Not only because of how Doug treated him, but because of Bram's reaction to Doug. The alpha didn't only treat cats like shit.

Ethan tried to step back from the confusion and think about what it meant. Thing was, wolves should yearn for touch as much as a cat who'd been feral for years. And despite the rather horrific past few days, Ethan could be sure of one thing—Bram liked touching him.

But not vice versa. The wolf's jumpiness was frankly disquieting and made him seem even younger than he really was. Ethan guessed Bram was in his mid-twenties, a few years younger than himself. Of course it was hard to know whether or not he should count his feral years. Perhaps he was really twenty-one.

He sure as hell didn't feel twenty-one. He felt old and weary and overcome. Desolate too. His body had yearned for some kind of connection with the wolf and, in one sense, had connected. His mind flipped back to the moment when his release shot up his spine and his come spilled over his hand. He had been caught there, in Bram's hold, ejaculating—his first time in years and in his captor's imprisoning embrace. His body had gone stiff and then eased away in a kind of boneless wonder, melting into the damned wolf.

He'd wanted to face Bram, reach for him and return the favor, which had resulted in Bram bolting out of the room— after saying he would help.

Maybe he would. Maybe those words meant something.

But it was more likely that Bram would go to Doug, his alpha and his lover, and Ethan would never see the dark wolf— or freedom—again.

Chapter Eight

Taking several deep breaths, Bram tried to keep it together. Ethan had rattled him, yes, but the thing really shaking him to the core was the decision he'd just made. The decision to move against Doug, his alpha. His pack.

Bram would be considered rogue. He'd have to leave.

Don't think now. God knows he'd have plenty of time to think about it later.

It took Bram two attempts to punch in the right numbers and exit the second door that held Ethan captive. With his shaking hands, Bram shut the door behind him, glanced around the outer room and let out a breath of relief at seeing no one else there. He'd feared Doug would have already returned and discovered the unending loop playing.

Bram pushed away from the door. He had no time for alternate scenarios and what-ifs, even if his mind was racing. Fact was, if Doug came upon him, he'd smell anxiety and ask Bram what the fuck was going on. Quickly Bram keyed into the camera feed, shut down the fake loop and disposed of it, then put the camera back to real time. Yes, close observation of the video would reveal the cut. For Ethan would have jumped from lying on the bed to disappearing into the shower, and there was a missing half hour.

But Ethan—and Bram—would be long gone by the time

this tape was analyzed. At least if Bram had anything to do with it. Better still would be if Bram managed to erase all the footage.

But first things first. He needed to think clearly about the best course of action. Most nights Doug went off to bed and left Bram to watch over Ethan. So night would be the best time to escape. Running out of here now, cutting the chain-link fence in broad daylight—not smart. Despite his desire to do everything immediately, now that he'd made up his mind about his future, and Ethan's, Bram had to wait at least a few hours, and he had to pick the right time to act.

That meant some planning, some patience, and keeping a cool head. The last requirement was a bit scary. Bram was noted for his anger, his lack of control, his erratic behavior. It was why he'd been ordered to stay away from humans when he was teenager, and why he continued to stay away from humans. The wolf in him couldn't be trusted not to shift.

Focus, Bram, focus on Ethan. It was not exactly the time for self-absorption.

Bram did have a strength of will, he knew he did, and he was going to use it over the next couple of days. After that, well, it wouldn't matter so much.

So he sat on that chair and calmed down and watched Ethan through the video feed. Eighty-three minutes later, Doug walked in and threw off his jacket. Bram looked up, bleary-eyed, as if he'd been watching that feed the entire day. He stretched.

Doug frowned at him. "You can get up and move around, you know. I doubt the cat is going to shift in a millisecond."

Bram forced a halfhearted smile. "Just being careful. Not much happened."

"What's wrong?" Doug pulled in a breath and Bram tried to remain calm and not give off fear signals. "You seem out of sorts. Unsettled."

"I'm tired." Bram swallowed. "I thought it best not to go into his room, given his reaction to me earlier today, but I think it's hard for him to be alone. He just lies on the bed."

Doug shook his head. "God knows how you survive, Bram. You're such a softy." There was even affection there, which made Bram inwardly wince. "Take a break. I'll watch Ethan for a while."

It was what Bram needed, what he wanted in order for his plan to work, but his heart also sank because Doug looked a little too smug, as if he had his own plan in mind.

"What?" asked Bram nervously. "Is something going on?"

Normally such questioning might have annoyed Doug, but Bram's anxiety was obvious and the alpha put on his reassuring face. "Good news. I heard from my contact. Got a definite arrival time. So don't worry, we're going to get this cat to a better place soon. I know you don't like him locked in this room. It's getting to you. I can smell your distress."

Good that Doug had settled upon a reason for Bram's distress but bad about the contact. "When is the arrival time?"

"Tomorrow."

Bram blinked. His window of opportunity had shrunk. He had to do everything tonight and he had to do it right. "You said days from now."

"Yes, I did. Now I say tomorrow. What of it?"

"Nothing, sorry. But. What will they do with him? Once they have him."

"Enough with the questions." Doug jerked his head towards the door. "Go. You're tired and out of sorts. Sleep. I want you to be alert tonight while you watch him, make sure nothing goes wrong."

Bram clamped down on his desire to know more when he couldn't afford to make his alpha suspicious with further questions, because Bram needed to be the one who watched Ethan tonight. If Doug had an inkling of his true thoughts, helping Ethan escape would become very, very difficult.

Slipping out the front door, Bram dragged in a lungful of cold air, exhaled and watched the air condense from that breath. The freezing weather braced him as he walked across the compound to his trailer. He shucked his jacket and dutifully ate as much as he could. Tonight was going to be eventful and he needed energy stores. Finally he lay down on his bed, ostensibly to rest, but his restiveness made that a challenge.

He had to be optimistic about his chances of succeeding. Going in with a sense of dread was one thing, and unavoidable, given that he was betraying his pack. But going in sure he was going to fail was asking to fail. For Ethan's sake, he refused to do that.

Well, he could count himself lucky that he didn't have to go searching for wire cutters. He'd bought a pair a couple of years ago and hid them under his bed. Though he'd never taken them out, they'd been an odd source of comfort on certain nights. When things got really bad they were his keys to escape, a means of cutting through the fence if life as the omega, the outcast, became unbearable. It hadn't happened of course. Instead, taking the crumbs of Doug's social favors had gotten Bram through his worst times.

That was over. He'd never wanted to be feral but alternatives were limited to nonexistent. If he had the self-control to live among humans, he could have chosen to mix with them and keep his human side, but his shifting was too unpredictable. Even now he could feel his wolf seeking to take over. It was always that way during stress, and Bram could imagine how well he'd do shifting in the middle of a city, horrifying humans, perhaps even hurting them.

He let out a long, painful breath. He was going to miss Ethan, which said a lot about Bram's situation, he knew. Worse, while Doug could be oblivious to many things about Bram, he doubted the alpha was going to overlook the fact that Bram had set the cat free. He might even try to hunt him down. Doug held grudges.

And yet, there was a certain freedom now that he'd decided to do what was right and handing Ethan over to Doug's contact couldn't have felt more *wrong*.

Three hours and no sleep later, Bram walked back to the holding cabin. He passed a few people who ignored him. His sense of doom had lessened as the time to act approached though he felt fatalistic about what was to come. He wasn't able to carry the wire cutters quite yet. He had to wait till dark, and he'd duck out and get them to cut that escape hole for Ethan, and himself.

Then he could appease his wolf and shift. Despite the fact the moon was only a thin crescent, Bram would welcome turning wolf. His human self felt bone-weary. He needed a reprieve. Life as wolf on the run would be simple, straightforward, and Bram would have no one to answer to. Perhaps that would be enough to compensate for the loneliness that lay ahead of him.

Ethan roamed. If one can roam a small room in which you are captive.

Don't think. The thinking was making him crazy. He hadn't actually been alone while awake for any period of time. That would have been fine if he were either not captive or if he were cat, but the combination of being human and completely at the mercy of these assholes was making him nuts.

His cat was rising within. They wanted him to stay human. Even his human, after so long as cat, wanted to stay human. But his cat was frightened, his cat wanted to be able to defend himself against Doug, and his cat wasn't listening to the human logic that said that if Ethan turned cougar again, he would be attacked, drugged, maybe killed.

The latter he could handle. But captivity and drugs... Ethan was going to lose it. More than he was losing it now.

So he paced, glancing from time to time at that corner of the room where the camera's eye watched him. There might be other, less obvious cameras.

He dropped onto the bed and let his head fall into his hands. All this effort to capture him and hold him in this room, it didn't make sense. He couldn't fathom why they gave a fuck about his existence. Back when Gabriel had captured him, yeah, it had made sense. It had been a horror show, but it had made sense.

Eight years ago Ethan had consorted with a female werewolf—simply not allowed by "wolf law", whatever the fuck that was and never mind that Lila had been a friend of his mother's and, afterwards, a mother figure. In trying to protect Lila, Ethan had killed a werewolf—and was consequently punished for this act of murder. When Ethan had fought that punishment every step of the way, Gabriel had seen fit to use torture.

An awful kind of logic in all that, but still logic. Now? Not so much.

Not so much a way to escape either. Last time he'd been able to play dead for good reason. Now they fed him and hugged him.

Gawd.

If he had access to a phone—ha!—he'd dial that number Lila had given him long ago. She'd made him memorize it, saying the phone number belonged to a go-to guy if he ever got in trouble and couldn't reach her. He'd never gotten a chance to use it, and neither had Lila.

Ethan still remembered those numbers. Some kind of ode to Lila, he supposed. If he had access to a phone, he'd be willing to see if this guy, yes another werewolf, would help a cat shifter. Obviously he was feeling desperate.

He threw himself back on the bed. What was the point of even thinking about it? Some stupid grasping at straws. Because, this many years later? Phone numbers changed. Besides a werewolf was going to think Doug's treatment of Ethan was hunky-dory and exactly what a feral cat needed.

His skin began to tremble. It had been quite a while since he'd shifted from human to cat. He wasn't quite comfortable with the transition anymore, though he used to be. If he were stronger, he'd fight it. Or maybe if he cared more he'd fight the cat off. But Bram was gone, scared away by God knows what. Ethan's plea for help? Well, he supposed it was scary when you're already at the bottom of the heap and someone even lower asks you to lend a hand. It wasn't too difficult to recognize that Bram needed almost as much help as Ethan. Maybe more. At least Ethan recognized when he was being treated badly.

Bram seemed to have no such understanding of himself, seemed to think Doug was supposed to be an asshole.

Ethan pulled himself into a ball and turned on his side, putting his back to the camera. His heart began its long, sliding beat that presaged its own conversion to cougar. His bones began to melt into something else. His skin, no longer quite skin, prickled with heat, and his mind faded to gray. *Enjoy the show, guys*, was his last thought.

"Hi, Doug." Bram felt wary, but that was hardly a new emotion of his. Doug shouldn't find it remarkable or out of line.

His alpha looked across at him, bored. He'd been leaning back on the chair, arms behind his head, and he brought himself forward. He gave Bram a lopsided grin, one Bram had always found endearing. "Funny, how something can be so boring and exciting at the same time."

"Yeah."

Doug eyed him, perhaps taking in Bram's disapproval. "Not only is it best for Ethan, to go to people who can handle feral cats, it will help our pack, Bram."

He swallowed, not wanting to hear this, not wanting to hear that Ethan's existence and Ethan's handover was a benefit to his pack.

"These people know about us wolves, they know about our headquarters, and they could cause us real trouble. However, if they regard us in a friendly light, if they see us as helpful, things will go better for us. That's important. While knowledge of our existence"—Doug waved a finger between himself and Bram—"is not yet widespread in society, it probably will be one day. And even if we are never accepted as real, people in a position of power, in government, in military, in paramilitary, do know and will know. I don't want the Winter pack to be seen as a liability or a source of danger. Something to be shut down or, worse, terminated. Better they see us as a responsible gateway to shapeshifters. We take care of our own and we take care of ferals. See?"

The earnestness on Doug's face almost undid Bram. He

wanted to confess all. He wanted to talk about the wire cutters under his bed.

Except Ethan was in there and Doug was ready to sacrifice him for the health of the pack. Bram could not be a part of that.

"Have you understood anything I've said, Bram?"

"I understand," Bram said in a low voice.

"I have to wonder sometimes, the way you stare at me, so blank faced. I end up wondering if anything is going on inside that head of yours."

Bram forced himself to say more. "I understand what you're trying to do and why you're trying to do it."

Apparently satisfied, Doug nodded and turned back to the computer screen. His eyes widened and his entire body stiffened in alarm. "Jesus Christ."

"What?" Bram moved closer to get a look, worried about what he'd find Ethan doing. And Ethan wasn't there, at least not the man. A cougar lay across the bed. "Oh God." Bram's chest went tight with panic. His plan hadn't included Ethan shifting.

"That was one fast shift," observed Doug, voice a bit jerky with excitement and nervousness. "I looked, say, ten minutes ago. Trey didn't mention that cats could shift this quickly."

Bram ran a hand up and down his face, wondering how far down tonight's chances of success had plummeted. He breathed in only to sense Doug's rising anger and braced himself, even welcomed Doug's focus on him. Anything to keep Doug away from Ethan.

"Goddammit." Doug rounded on Bram. "Did you not go in that room *at all* today? You know he needs human contact. I made that clear from the beginning."

Bram couldn't decide if it was wiser to admit he'd been in

Ethan's room or not, but when he caught sight of Ethan rising from the bed and prowling the room, as beautiful as he remembered from the day of the hunt, Bram's mouth dropped open. A tawny-colored cougar, black around the mouth and eyes, moved with feline grace. His loose skin swayed a little as he circled the room.

Then he jumped back on the bed and snarled directly at the camera.

"How the *hell* does he know about the camera?" Doug demanded.

"Well." Bram searched for the right thing to say. "He's been locked in the room for a number of days with not much to do, and he's not unobservant."

Doug jabbed a finger at Bram. "You fucked up."

Bram didn't bother to point out that Doug had suggested earlier today that he watch Ethan from outside the room. Under the circumstances, it was better to take the fall. "I'm sorry."

"'Sorry'," Doug mimicked. "That's fucking helpful. Thanks, Bram, for being sorry. Exactly what I need." Doug got right in Bram's face, forcing him to retreat. "What I need are fucking solutions."

Bram nodded and looked away.

"If I shoot him, he'll be forced to shift in order to heal, and quite frankly, it would serve him right. I *told* that bugger he had to stay human."

Bram did not want Ethan shot, but he had to tread easy here. Doug was close to enraged. "Drugging him worked well last time he was cougar, didn't it? He turned human then, remember? If you drug him, there's less danger if he fights the shifting, tries to stay cat and bleeds out."

Doug pooh-poohed that idea. "Why would he fight the

shifting if he's wounded?"

Bram met Doug's gaze. "He's going a little crazy in that room, Doug. You must know that. It makes him unpredictable. He might prefer to die rather than stay captive."

Doug seemed almost taken aback. "I hardly think he's suicidal." He waved at the screen. "This guy wants to live."

"He's complex. After all, we didn't predict he would shift."

"What I didn't predict is that you would screw things up." Doug shook his head sharply. "Nevertheless, we'll go the tranq route, as you've suggested. I want to keep him safe given we're handing him over tomorrow. They might not want a dead cougar." But suspicion sat there in Doug's eyes, as if Bram was less trustworthy after this development. "Ethan is going to attack, be it gun or tranq. A bullet would bring him down immediately. A tranq is slower."

"I'll do it."

Doug laughed, no humor in it. "I may be pissed off at your negligence, Bram, but I don't want you shredded either."

"I know." Bram did know, which made this moment harder. He had to dig deep to stay the course, to do what was right. He pulled in a breath and Doug probably thought he was summoning courage. Which he was, but not for the reasons Doug thought. "I don't think Ethan will want to kill me."

"You're fooling yourself."

"Maybe. But I don't think so. You said yourself that he was trying to bond with me. That means something, even to a cat." Bram paused. "Give me the tranq. I'll do it."

Doug glanced at the screen. Ethan had jumped off the bed again and, with his claws, pulled off the blanket and sheet. He attacked the mattress, shredding cotton and foam that had made up the futon. "Well, you're right about one thing. He's going crazy in there. I thought he'd last another day."

The alpha went to the mini-fridge, turned the combination lock and opened it to retrieve the tranq.

Bram felt like everything was moving in slow motion.

Doug glanced up at him from the crouch, worried. "You're freaking out."

"A little," Bram admitted. "But I can do this."

His alpha straightened, tranq in hand, and accepted Bram's statement. "You'll be too close range to use a tranq gun. You're going to have to jab him with a needle. Still think you can do it?"

Bram nodded.

Doug ripped open the plastic, held the syringe. "Sure?"

Again, Bram nodded.

"You seem too nervous."

"I'm nervous, but I'm also sure."

Doug handed Bram the syringe and he held it uncertainly. "I press down here, right?" He rested his thumb on the end of the plunger.

Annoyance and frustration entered Doug's eyes. "Yes. I'd hoped that was obvious."

Bram dropped his gaze, properly submissive as he regarded Doug's thigh, which was about where Doug had hit Ethan when he was running from the pack. The upper leg was what he wanted.

He swung his arm forward. The needle sliced through the material of Doug's jeans and pierced flesh. Bram pushed the plunger fully down.

Then he jumped back out of reach as Doug took a swing at him, empty syringe still stuck in his thigh. Doug ripped it out, disbelief and rage in his face. He stared at Bram, gaping. "You little shit."

He went after Bram, face white, a fury in him that Bram hadn't seen in years. Doug wanted to kill him, and Bram sidestepped his second attempted punch.

"What the hell are you thinking, you asswipe?" Doug swayed, just slightly, but enough to realize he might be in trouble. The alpha jerked away from Bram, heading for the door. Heading, Bram realized, for help. He'd hoped Doug would collapse before it came to this, but he had no choice. He tackled his alpha, landing on his back, and Doug couldn't take the weight. He toppled, grunting as he hit the floor. Bram wasn't that much smaller than Doug and had no trouble keeping him down. Doug kept struggling even while his rage became diluted by confusion and drugs.

Abruptly the alpha stopped moving. "Bram. Get off me." A command and even now it was hard to resist when Doug used that tone on him.

"I'm sorry." He shook his head, though Doug couldn't see him.

"Off, Bram, *immediately*. I'll be willing to talk about this if you get off me. Something squirrelly is going on in that head of yoursh. But I'm will. I'm willing to...make allowanshes."

"I really am sorry, Doug." He'd never meant it more in his life.

"Bram." But the urgency was sluggish. "Bram. C'mon."

"So sorry."

In a last-ditch effort, Doug bunched his arms under him and tried to rise, despite Bram's weight, but all he managed to do was raise his head.

"Think. No. Bram."

"Go to sleep, Doug. It's the only thing you can do now." How odd it felt to say something like that to his alpha.

For perhaps the first time in his life, Doug obeyed Bram.

Chapter Nine

Staring down at Doug, Bram watched the alpha's face go slack and felt the body beneath him become loose as the alpha slipped into unconsciousness. No longer wanting to touch him, Bram couldn't get off Doug fast enough. Despite this recoil, he forced himself to grab hold of the alpha and drag him into the backroom. Doug wouldn't be hard to find there, once people figured out something was wrong, but until then, he wouldn't be obvious to someone popping their head in.

Trying not to shudder, Bram shook himself out and walked away. He shut the door behind him without looking back. Doug was down. First challenge met.

He picked up the empty syringe and returned it to the fridge. Spinning the combination lock, a kind of grim humor took hold. Doug had thought he was the only one who knew the numbers, but Bram had watched more times than he could count and had memorized the numbers just in case. Although the "just in case" scenario had always been vague and ill thought out, and had nothing to do with a cat shifter.

Bram pulled the lock off the fridge handle and opened the door to place the used syringe back beside the others. Better that whoever found Doug hadn't a clue why the alpha was unconscious. The more time they spent trying to figure out what happened, the more lead time Ethan would be given.

Bram relocked the fridge and pushed out of his squat.

Next he disabled the video, changed the master password to something unguessable and started the process of wiping the computer clean. No one would be able to access the computer in the short term, and when they could it would be empty. No sense keeping footage of Ethan as cougar or man. The fewer people who could recognize Ethan in the future, the better. Bram closed his eyes, mentally shying away from the enormity of what he was doing. Instead he focused on the next necessary step.

He marched over to face the door, wanting to get Ethan out immediately, before his plan came crashing down.

But no. First he had to retrieve the wire cutters. Wolves would smell a cat shifter loose in their compound. It didn't take much to rouse them. So once Bram opened these doors, Ethan had to race for freedom. Speed was critical, and Ethan could not hang around while Bram ran to his trailer to pick up a tool.

Spinning on his heel, Bram banged out the door and sprinted to his trailer. He didn't need a jacket now and soon he wouldn't need one at all. He passed a couple of wolves who ignored him, par for the course, and tonight he was grateful. He wasn't shaking yet. If he could stay this focused, think everything through, quickly, he might succeed.

He slammed into his trailer and fell to the floor to grab the wire cutters from under his bed. Up he rose and slipped out the back door in order to stay in shadow. Racing straight for the nearest portion of the fence, he felt the subzero temperatures. The freezing air energized him, made everything feel clean and crisp. One snip at a time, he cut a hole in the linked chain, big enough for Ethan to get through.

Ethan. Bram finished the job, stood and nodded to himself. He was prepared to face the cat. Carrying the wire cutters with him—his smell on them would implicate him—he jogged to the holding cabin and threw the tool under the stairs. They might find them later but, by then, it wouldn't matter.

Just before he reentered the building, fear pressed upon him, like a physical weight in his chest. Someone could have stumbled onto Doug's unconscious body and Bram wasn't sure what to do if another wolf was in the holding cabin—except take them out. Yet incapacitating one werewolf, his leader, had been more than enough violence for Bram tonight.

Doug would never, ever forgive him. Bram shoved that thought away. No time. He swung open the door to face an empty room, no evidence that one of the pack had come by. The computer was still erasing itself. He felt giddy-sick with relief.

He shook, just a little, and had to grit his teeth, force himself to move to that door that shut Ethan in. Bram pushed the handle and pulled it towards him. He left it wide open, unlike ever before.

The cat might attack. Bram accepted that and hoped he'd be able to tell Ethan where to go to escape the compound. Bram didn't care otherwise. He was feeling rather pessimistic tonight, at least about his own future, though Ethan's successful escape remained very important to him. Bram couldn't bear the thought of going through all this and failing Ethan, who deserved to be freed.

Bram unlocked the second door, pushed it slowly inward with one hand while he raised his other arm to protect his throat. His gaze fell upon the cougar.

Ethan, who would have heard him approaching, crouched nearby, ready to leap. Their eyes met for one long moment, assessing each other as if they were complete strangers. However, the hazel cat eyes were still Ethan. Bram felt like he was looking into a mirror of sorts, into the eyes of someone who knew exactly who he was and what he felt. It was a sensation he'd not before felt or was likely to feel again.

"I..." His voice cracked but he pushed the words out his thick throat. "Ethan." The word shook with intensity and Bram worked to get a grip on himself. "I've made a hole. Fence. In the fence, for you." Christ, he had to make sense. He literally shook himself, trying to keep his head together, and Ethan crouched there unmoving, except for shoulders bunching and eyes blinking very slowly.

Bram cleared his throat and this time the words came out with some coherency. "Doug's unconscious. I drugged him. I've cut a hole in the fence for you to get through. You can get out. You need to get out. *Now.* They're coming to get you tomorrow, and I don't know how long Doug will be down."

Maybe it was Bram's imagination but understanding lit Ethan's eyes. Bram continued, "Once we leave the room and this building, we have to move fast. The wolves—the pack is outside here, we're in the Winter pack's compound—they'll *smell* you." Ethan rose from his crouch. "We have very little time. Do you understand?"

The cougar walked right up to Bram who couldn't move, who felt like he was stretched tight like a rubber band before it snapped. Ethan rubbed his large head against Bram's hip, and purred. It sounded like an affirmation and Bram remained stock-still, unsure what to do. Ethan rubbed his head against Bram a second time, almost butting him as if he was asking for a response, and Bram couldn't resist replying. He let out a long shaky breath and sank to his knees to wrap his arms around Ethan for a brief, hard moment, pressing his face into that amazing fur. He absorbed the vibration of Ethan's chest, determined to remember the feel of that purr.

"We have no time, Ethan." Bram pushed up, wiped his face.

"Follow me. Once you're out, don't look back, because they're going to hunt you again if they can. They're wolves, and they want you for something. I don't know what that is, but there are powerful people who would like to keep you captive."

Ethan chirped. Bram regarded him and the cougar actually moved his head in an uncatlike and awkward nod. Bram nodded back. It was time.

He took off and the next few moments passed in a blur. Later Bram had a hard time remembering the exact sequence of events, but he must have led Ethan directly to the escape hole. At its threshold, Ethan hesitated, and it felt like they had more to say to each other. But really, there was nothing to say, even if they could have communicated.

"Please go," Bram whispered fiercely, angry that he was wiping his face again. "Don't look back."

Ethan tilted his beautiful head, blinked once and moved through the ragged hole to disappear into the black. His tawny coat turned to shadow and melted like snow into night.

Bram was left standing there, hands hanging loose, mind emptying out. He was supposed to run too. It's why he wasn't wearing a jacket. He would shift soon, but not quite yet. First he wanted to cause some confusion before Doug woke up though Bram needed to be gone by the time Doug was again coherent. If Doug got his hands on Bram, he feared he would admit to everything he had done tonight.

Bram wandered, pacing between the hole in the fence and the holding cabin. At some point, minutes not hours later, a wolf caught the cat's scent. So began the hue and cry. A few wolves surrounded him, more than once, demanding to know what had transpired, and Bram managed to convey his utter bafflement. Given his very real confusion, it wasn't a stretch. Bram still couldn't wrap his mind around what he had done.

There was talk of Doug and finding him and the cougar escaping.

The second-in-command grabbed Bram's shoulders, fingers pressing into flesh, and forced his gaze on Bram's. "You stink of cat. Why?"

Bram blinked. He'd embraced Ethan and it showed. "I don't know."

"Did he attack you?"

"No. No, he didn't."

"Then what happened?" The wolf glared at Bram like he was a blank wall that needed to be torn down, before he pushed the omega away in disgust. Bram stumbled back, alone again. Ignored. He slipped away when a shout went up that Doug had been found—definitely Bram's signal to leave.

It was over, his sojourn here at Winter pack. He had a small window of time before Doug woke, perhaps only an hour.

In human form, Bram ducked through the hole and ran a short distance. If nothing else, his shaky hold on his control allowed him to ease into the shift quickly. He embraced the pain, the oblivion that came with the brutal rearrangement of bone and tissue.

It was hard to know how long it took to turn wolf, but the post-shift disorientation passed swiftly. He clambered to his feet, shook himself out, and smelled the cold, the cat, the end of winter. He saw the shapes and shadows more clearly than his human had.

It was time to run, and he did. He even followed Ethan's trail for a short while. It was so tempting to continue along that path and try to catch up with Ethan and run with him. But that scenario was more dangerous for the cat so Bram veered off. If he was right, Doug's sense of vengeance would demand that Bram be chased down and punishment meted out. The hunt would be for the omega wolf and revenge, not for the cat.

Ethan ran. At first it was mindless, simply fleeing the stifling prison that lay behind him, putting distance between himself and the Winter pack, crossing through forests and over farmland. But over the course of the night, he realized that he was instinctively headed in a specific direction—southeast towards the city that had once been his home. A city he hadn't seen in years.

It wasn't till the second day that he began to recognize his surroundings, and at that point, he thought he might be free. He'd expected another hunt, truth be told. He'd even feared some weird betrayal by Bram, who was one fucked-up werewolf if he'd ever met one.

Perhaps that omega wolf's tears had been sincere, though Ethan suspected he hadn't fully understood the cause of Bram's distress, and likely never would. It was hard for him to process let alone understand this past week. Being locked in that room didn't allow for much in the way of context or understanding, and he sure as hell wasn't responsible for Bram.

Nevertheless, their parting was going to haunt Ethan if he couldn't do something about it. Bram had sacrificed a part of himself if he'd gone against his alpha, Ethan knew that much.

But the time to worry about Bram, let alone do something about it, was not now. First Ethan needed to be on safer ground. He couldn't return to his old feral home, where they'd smoked him out. He wasn't even sure he wanted to return. After being forcibly taken and after living human for a number of days, Ethan was attracted to the city, to humanity, both his and others'. It was a place he had long avoided as cougar, and it had its own sources of danger, no doubt about it. However, there was a certain safety in the city. One could get lost in it; the wolves would not find it easy to track him there.

It felt like the longest flight of his life, and it only lasted two full days. He ran, pushed himself until he was exhausted, and then kept going until he slid into the suburbs that had at one time, in another life, been familiar when he was oh-so-young and optimistic about life.

It was late evening, with enough shadows that his cougar could stay hidden as he navigated something that felt simultaneously familiar and alien.

The snow was melting here, spring on its way, more evident in the city with its multitude of buildings, streets and people. He let his mind flit to Doug and what could have possibly motivated him to imprison a werecat. Ethan didn't understand it though he wanted to. When his thoughts turned to Bram, he shied away from thinking deeply about the dark wolf.

Do you understand?

Bram's words, and Ethan had only comprehended that he had to flee immediately or throw away everything Bram had accomplished. So Ethan ran and didn't look back.

Years before he'd fled and not looked back. But years ago, Lila had been dead. Bram was not.

So Ethan had a phone call to make. Yes, phone numbers changed or went out of service, and Lila's so-called friendly contact might be nothing of the sort. But Ethan owed Bram this one attempt at getting help.

He eased along the alleys, staying to shadows, going deeper into the city. For Ethan needed to dial a number he'd been given long ago by Lila when she thought someone could help her survive.

Ethan needed to phone a wolf named Trey.

Chapter Ten

Ethan jingled the stolen coins in his pocket and hoped there were enough. The twenty-four-hour laundromat he'd remembered was still in operation, though dingier than last decade. Fortunately, it continued to harbor abandoned or mislaid clothing, as well as a coin machine—which now stood broken and empty, its contents having been transferred to his new and overlarge jacket.

He would pay the company back, somehow. It might take some time, admittedly. He'd never liked to steal, even though he could quite easily. He was fast, he was observant, and he could disappear in a way others couldn't. But he'd always maintained principles to keep him steady and on track.

Don't use your gift for the wrong reason. Something his mother had drilled into him by the time he was nine. Good thing she'd succeeded by then, because she'd died shortly afterwards, and Ethan had been left to raise himself, with some help from Lila.

Ethan sighed, too tired to push memories of his mother away, although it had been so long ago and he could no longer remember her face clearly. That hurt almost more than her death now.

He picked up a handful of quarters and fed them into the pay phone's slot one at a time, his fingers slowly going numb with cold. It was early morning, still before sunrise, and he hadn't eaten enough given his activity over the past two and a half days. His human body didn't stay warm in winter when he wasn't properly fed.

Hopefully he'd have leftover money to buy some breakfast and something hot to drink.

He counted ten quarters and kept going. It had been difficult to find a working pay phone. They were few and far between compared to eight years ago. The one in the laundromat was gone for some reason.

Forty quarters in, he decided to stop feeding the machine. His grasp of today's currency and costs was nonexistent, but ten dollars should connect him to someone. If there was someone to connect to.

Slowly and carefully he punched in the numbers, worried he'd get it wrong, though God knows ten numbers wouldn't be a challenge to anyone else. The receiver beeped through the number and the phone rang. Ethan expected an automated voice to cut in and tell him the number was out of service, or to get a wrong number.

Instead, the phone kept ringing. Five times, and Ethan began to lose hope as he slumped against the phone box. No one was home and he'd have to stay in the city and try again, though they might not ever be home. He might not ever reach this mysterious Trey.

The seventh ring cut off and a voice—male—said, "Hello. Trey Walters speaking."

Ethan swallowed. It had been a long time since he'd spoken to anyone on the phone and never had it been as important as now. He could barely get the first word out. "Hi."

"Who is this?"

Ethan hesitated, but he'd already decided telling Trey his

105

name wouldn't do him harm. Trey couldn't reach through the phone wires and grab hold of him. Even if he had super-duper tracking devices, the likelihood that Trey stood right around the corner waiting to catch Ethan was remote. And giving over his name might help Bram's cause. Maybe. "I'm Ethan Marcelle."

He heard a slight intake of breath as Trey paused. "Hello, Ethan." He sounded surprised. "You've been gone for a very long time."

He gripped the phone more tightly. "Do you know me?"

"You're Lila's friend. She mentioned you to me." The voice went lower and sadder. "Years ago obviously."

Ethan's sluggish heart picked up speed. He had never spoken of Lila to anyone since her death. It was hard to talk of her. He'd had no practice.

"Yes, I was her friend." The words came out hoarse.

"I was sorry to hear of her passing."

"*Passing?*" Ethan echoed. Trey made it sound like Lila had succumbed to some unfortunate disease.

"After she got hit by a car, or so I was told." There was a flat wariness in Trey's voice that invited Ethan to dispute this account.

Ethan leaned his forehead against the cold window of the phone booth. "Whoever told you that lied. She was killed. *They* killed her. Her own pack. I was there." He had no idea whether Trey, a wolf who was acquainted with the Winter pack, would believe a cat.

"Is that so?"

Ethan's heart sank. This wolf was not different from the others. He might not belong to the Winter pack, but he'd buy into any of their false histories.

"She was supposed to call me if she felt threatened." Trey

was speaking carefully. "You must know that packs don't like to kill their females. They're considered precious and rare."

"Not if they consort with cougars." Ethan didn't hide his bitterness. They'd accused Lila, his mother figure, of many things, including taking the risk of breeding some kind of hybrid.

"Where are you calling from, Ethan?"

"A pay phone." Pause. "I thought the number wouldn't work, this many years later."

"I've been careful to keep this number available and safe. Not too many people know of it though."

There was an awkward silence. Ethan wasn't sure how to broach the subject of Bram.

"So I take it you're not phoning to report Lila's murder."

"I'm happy to report it. It's been my first opportunity."

"First opportunity in eight years?"

Ethan gritted his teeth, but he felt that the more truth he shared with this wolf, the more likely Trey would help Bram. "I stayed cougar after Lila died."

Trey whistled and Ethan expected some kind of lecture. Wolves didn't approve of their own kind going feral, let alone a cougar. "I'm surprised you came back, Ethan, if that's the case."

"It is the case," Ethan responded sharply. "Lila's dead, you couldn't help her. But I'm worried about another member of the Winter pack. Since Lila told me you would protect her, I thought you might protect or be able to help someone else. Even if he's a male. Even if he's an omega."

"Oh, especially an omega," drawled Trey and for the first time Ethan heard anger in the voice over the phone. "What's going on?"

He pulled in a breath and tried to tell his story with an even tone. "They captured me. This Doug guy wanted me, what the hell for, I still don't know. But Bram defied Doug—"

"The alpha."

"Yes, and helped me escape. I'm scared they'll kill him for that defiance. This was at their compound." Ethan closed his eyes. "Can you do something for Bram?"

"How long ago did you escape, Ethan?"

He winced. It was too late, he'd known that already, but he'd had to try. "More than two days ago." He could hear the defeat in his own words.

"Doug likes to serve his revenge cold, Ethan, so I may be able to help Bram."

"You think?"

"That wasn't a promise. I'm in no position to make any."

"No, I know."

"Where can I reach you, Ethan?"

"You can't. I've been feral. I have no place. I barely managed to find a pay phone. I don't know how long I can last in the city." The sun was beginning to rise and while he'd enjoyed slipping into the nighttime city and prowling dark corners, he didn't know how he was going to handle daylight and crowds. He was no longer comfortable in his human skin. Eight years as a cat did that to a shifter.

"All right. Phone me tomorrow at four p.m. EST. Can you do that?"

"Yes."

"I'll update you then. If you miss the time, I'll be gone."

"Where are you?"

"Don't ask."

"But can you get there quickly?"

"Yes." Trey paused. "Phone me, Ethan. I'd like to talk to you again."

"I can do that." He could stay here for another day. He'd make himself last that long. "I will."

"Good." Trey clicked off the phone without saying goodbye and Ethan was left to stare at the receiver before he slowly hung it up.

Four quarters came back to him, and he picked them up and returned them to his pocket.

He stood inside the glass box and looked through the windows. Snow continued to melt, the sky was lightening from black to gray, and a man walked by on the sidewalk. Ethan had blocked the outside noises while talking to Trey but it all came back to him. The noise would only increase as everyone in the city woke up.

He'd been used to this at one point, though whether that could happen again, after his time in the wilderness, he didn't know. Nevertheless, he needed to feed himself in this city, and tomorrow he needed to hear what Trey found out about Bram, so he was here for the next thirty hours.

Trey had seemed sincere. Ethan wasn't even going to consider the possibility that Trey was not on Bram's side.

He used the money for one meal, but had to save the rest of the quarters for the second phone call. He didn't know what to do with himself and by late afternoon, he found himself headed to a suburb, a townhouse, where long ago he'd been welcome, even loved a little. Robert would be forty, and Ethan wondered how the years had treated him. He hoped Robert was healthy, happy.

It was a three-hour walk but he had time to kill. Dark was falling by the time he reached Robert's street and his mouth dried up as he thought about rapping on that front door.

He delayed that action, scouting out the environs, trying to determine who was home. Trying to see, for goodness' sakes, if Robert even lived here.

It didn't take all that long for Ethan to determine that Robert did indeed still make his home here. But he was not alone, and tonight Ethan couldn't face meeting a stranger. Ethan managed to be glad that Robert had someone who loved him, for Robert had been loveable, but the loneliness threatened to gut him and Ethan had to slip away.

His teeth chattered and it wasn't from the cold. In so many ways he'd been wise to stay cougar—even if the past years had had everything to do with instinct and nothing to do with wisdom. Awaking this longing for human contact was debilitating and hurtful. If wolves came upon him now, it would be all over.

But they didn't, and to be realistic, a city attack was unlikely. Wolves, especially wolf packs, avoided city life, what with their dependence upon the moon and their need to run together. Cougars, being more solitary creatures, adapted more easily to the streets and buildings and traffic and people. Not for the first time, Ethan wondered if Doug had been lying or telling the truth about the other cat shifter he claimed to have met.

That night Ethan ate by loitering at the back of a couple of restaurants—he had done this often in the old days—and retrieving their throwaways from the garbage.

Not the most glamorous way to get a meal to be sure, but

he didn't have to worry about getting sick. One thing his too-skinny body remained was immune to disease. Shifting did that to a guy. Once Ethan felt stuffed to the brim, and he'd badly needed to fill himself with calories before he burned out, he went prowling again—the human kind of prowling—and no longer felt cold. He'd last the night okay.

He didn't intend to shift back to his cat form, at least for a day or two. But the loneliness pressed down on him like a terrible burden, eight years rushing to the surface of his human skin.

All the same, he felt incapable of actually approaching a human in this city. Yes, he'd eaten in a diner, ordered food and paid money. But even during those simple transactions, he'd acted oddly. Paying in quarters had raised the cashier's eyebrows. His vagabond-like clothing had people regarding him with suspicion.

Don't worry, I'm just a cat shifter.

Ha. Truth was, he didn't have the resources to initiate any kind of human transaction. He refused to go to a shelter for the night. Too many bodies in too small a space.

That night he found a vent and slept on top of it. When he woke, he scavenged for food and remembered what he didn't like about the city. But he got through the day. At four p.m., nerves taut, he made his second phone call to Trey.

There was no preamble on Trey's part. "Bram's gone. No one can find him."

This time Ethan didn't try to control his voice, and it sounded high and unsteady with the guilt of Bram's sacrifice. The omega had rocked the status quo and he was going to pay for Ethan's freedom. "Do you think they killed Bram? Do you think they're lying to you when they say they can't find him?"

"No." The flat negative was reassuring to Ethan's ears. Trey appeared to have no doubt about it. "There's a trail. Bram left here alive. In fact, I'm going to follow it out as far as I can. At least get an idea where he's headed. But with the melting snow and Bram's head start, I don't have much hope of actually finding him, and neither should you."

So. It sounded like Bram had escaped. That was good, wasn't it? "I wish I could know he was safe."

"If it makes you feel any better, I beat the crap out of Doug."

Ethan smiled at the image, but didn't speak.

"In fact, I'm the new alpha here now."

"Huh?" Christ, Ethan hated alphas, even over the phone.

Trey snorted at Ethan's reaction. "It's big news, actually, but you're a cat. Pack dynamics aren't your forté. I didn't like how Doug's been running the show. I disapprove of kidnapping and abuse. So I challenged him and won. I'm taking over. I needed a new job anyway since I got fired a while ago."

"What will you do if Bram comes back?"

"He'll be safe. I've made that clear. It's one of the reasons I'm doing this, Ethan. Bram's likely to try to return eventually. The pack will call to him. Unlike cats, wolves generally don't do well on their own."

"I hope you're telling me the truth."

"No need to hope. I am. Look, you phoned me. I dropped everything to do what you asked me to do."

Ethan didn't say anything. He didn't know what to say. He'd done what he could for Bram, who was maybe safer, maybe not. But Ethan couldn't really know Trey's agenda. Couldn't really know that what Trey said was true.

"Ethan?"

He stayed silent, trying to think this through clearly. Trey was associated with the Winter pack and Ethan had to careful around him. Maybe whatever Doug had wanted Ethan for, Trey now would.

Trey's voice went lower, became more confiding. "Call me in a week or so. I can tell you what I find of Bram. Or, call me anytime. I'll talk to you. I can even introduce you to another cat shifter."

The offer made Ethan suspicious.

"Ethan?"

Very quietly Ethan hung up. The temptation to meet one of his own kind was strong. He had to resist. Trey might be as big an asshole as Doug or even Gabriel. Alphas were treacherous creatures. He'd had firsthand experience with that. Twice.

He stood in the pay-phone box, feeling stunned, looking blindly out the dirty window, aware people were passing by but not really seeing them.

His entire reason for entering the city had been to phone Trey, who might have been able to save Bram. Maybe Bram would have been better off if Ethan had never picked up the phone, but he couldn't undo it. It was over. Done. Ethan had no other resources to turn to.

He could shift tonight, leave the city and return to his life as a cat.

The human in him balked. It was too soon. He *needed* to stay in this skin. He needed to keep hold of his humanity. It had been years as cat, yes, but this past week as human would not let him go. Not yet. It was not something he could relinquish.

He'd lost all social skills. At twenty-nine years of age, he didn't know how to function, couldn't even fucking read, and could barely punch in the right numbers for a phone call. Ethan scrubbed his face.

Robert had always been kind. Boyfriend or no, Ethan didn't think Robert would turn him away from his doorstep. It would just be for a few days, just to talk to someone who might care a little.

Bram had cared, sure. But Bram and Ethan's relationship, such as it was, had been forced upon them both. Besides, Bram was gone.

Ethan pushed out of the phone box and strode down the street. It would take him three hours of walking and he'd be hungry by the time he arrived, but he could reach Robert's house.

Chapter Eleven

Ethan lifted his hand, made a fist and rapped at the back door. It was near midnight, he'd dithered that long. Somehow he'd rather be turned away from the back door than the front. Besides, he didn't like the glare of the streetlights much. He hadn't recalled that they burned this brightly.

Robert was home. So was a second man, but that didn't concern Ethan. It took a few minutes for someone to answer the door. A sleepy-looking, thirty-something guy with bed head peered out, then switched on the light.

Ethan winced at the sudden brightness and had to squint to see that the boyfriend was a little alarmed, probably by Ethan's shabby appearance.

"I need to talk to Robert," Ethan said quickly before the door got slammed in his face or the police got called. Or both. He wasn't sure how bad he looked.

The nervous boyfriend shut the door. *Shit.*

"Jeremy?" Robert's sleepy voice sounded puzzled. "What's going on?"

"Robert?" Ethan called, trying to keep his voice calm while hoping it carried through the door. There were mutterings and murmurings, mostly Jeremy's. "It's Ethan. Robert?"

Negotiation continued but ended with Robert snapping,

"Let me see."

Robert flung the door open. He was forty, hair receding now, eyes a little older, but still Robert, and Ethan's chest squeezed with gratitude at the sight of a familiar face. It was extraordinary to see a familiar face. He'd been fond of Robert.

"It's me, Ethan."

Robert's expression didn't change and Ethan feared his ex didn't actually recognize him.

He stepped closer, Robert backed up and Jeremy barked out, "Stay where you are," as if Ethan was a threat to them.

Ethan shuddered, at the noise perhaps, or at being commanded. He'd wanted to see Robert, an old friend. He looked down at himself. Perhaps he appeared to be homeless, which wasn't that far off the mark. He raised his gaze to meet Robert's, hoping to be remembered. Had he changed so much he was unrecognizable?

"Robert?" During one long-ago conversation when Robert had wanted to delve into some of Ethan's secrets and Ethan had kept him at bay, Robert had declared that he would never turn Ethan away. But his throat thickened and he couldn't refer to that perhaps-forgotten statement that had once meant so much to him.

"Jesus, Ethan, why are you only wearing socks in winter? Don't you even have boots?" There was distress in Robert's voice, but Ethan shivered because Robert had said his name.

"I really need your help."

"Don't—" began Jeremy.

Robert flung up a hand to silence him and turned his hard gaze on Ethan. "It's been..."

"Years," Ethan finished. He didn't intend to stay long, especially with unwelcoming boyfriend here. He needed a few days at most, just to get oriented. "But—"

"God, come in. You must be freezing. Those clothes don't look very warm." Jeremy added a muttered "or very clean" and Robert frowned, then motioned Ethan forward.

His old lover didn't reach for him and Ethan was glad. He didn't want to be touched. Robert backed up to allow Ethan into the house and closed the door.

Robert eyed him, not without compassion, but not without suspicion either. "Are you in trouble?"

"No." Or none that Robert would understand. In the past he'd feared Ethan was involved with drugs in some way or the other.

"Are you hurt?"

Ethan shook his head.

Robert gave a wintry smile, an echo of his old grin, but welcoming all the same, even if his words were not. "I often wanted to see you again, but not quite like this."

Ethan blinked at him, unsure what to say. *Sorry?*

"Would you like a shower?" Robert implied he needed it and started walking towards the stairs.

"Yes, thank you."

Jeremy snorted, and Robert turned on him, clearly put out. "Jeremy, do you mind?"

"I mind," he returned, disgruntled. "I mind bringing strangers into *our* home."

"I know Ethan."

"A long time ago. People change."

Do they ever, Jeremy, but I couldn't begin to explain. "I won't stay long," Ethan promised them both. "I won't cause trouble."

Robert paused, doubtful, but raised a hand and swept it

towards the stairs. "You remember where the shower is. Get in. I'll bring you a towel and a set of clean clothes."

Ethan looked down at his wet stocking feet. They were like ice and he welcomed the idea of hot water thawing them. "Thank you."

Robert's face softened. "Get in the shower before you turn blue."

An hour and a half later, Ethan was warm, clean and fed. Robert had remembered his outsized appetite and had also noted he was too thin. The glowering Jeremy never left Robert's side, despite his obvious exhaustion and complaints about having to work the next day. Perhaps he expected Ethan to jump his old lover.

Ethan was too tired to do anything of the sort. Nor did he have the desire. Whatever they'd shared belonged to another era and to two very different people.

"Do you need anything else?" Robert asked.

"No. Thanks." In borrowed clothing, Ethan stood on the threshold of the guestroom.

Looking ready to stumble back to bed, Robert simply nodded.

"Good night." Ethan shut the door and went to lie down. The bed was comfortable and for the first time in many days he felt relatively safe. He fell asleep immediately, the strain of the past week catching up on him.

For more than twenty-four hours he slept, with only a couple of bathroom breaks. At one point, Robert came in to check on him and Ethan roused himself enough to assure Robert he was okay, he just hadn't slept for days, and Robert let him go back to sleep.

It was close to nine o'clock in the morning of the second day that Ethan felt half-alive and ventured to get up for real.

He listened to the house and only heard one person moving around. It sounded, if his memory could be trusted, like Robert's movements.

Swiftly Ethan pulled on the clothes—they smelled of Robert—which fit close enough. How nice to be wearing something that was clean and didn't come out of a laundromat. Buoyed by sleep and clothing and a house that was semi-familiar, Ethan exited the guestroom and jogged down the stairs.

He saw Robert in the kitchen, pouring coffee, and smiled. No smile was returned. In fact, as Ethan approached, Robert became grimmer. His gaze moved to the left, but Ethan was dumb or unaware or simply not yet awake. His brain was definitely slow to pick up the right cues.

It wasn't till he entered the kitchen that he realized Robert was not alone. Ethan pivoted to see a large man standing very still, arms crossed. As Ethan looked into his blue eyes that were alarmingly like those of Gabriel's and Doug's, Ethan breathed in through his mouth and smelled wolf.

He jerked his gaze back to Robert, hurt by his ex's betrayal.

"Don't look at me like that," snapped Robert. "You told me you weren't in trouble."

"He's not in trouble." That was Trey's voice. Somehow he had managed to reach through the phone lines after all. His voice, though, was flat, calm, neutral. Not really like Doug's or Gabriel's voices. The wolf spread his arms. "I've no weapons. I've come alone. It's pretty hard for me to take you in, Ethan."

Meaning it was hard for a wolf to bring in a cat by himself. At least in theory. Though Trey was a larger, bigger man than Ethan.

119

Ethan blinked. "But how did you find me?"

"I phoned him," said Robert.

Again Ethan pivoted, a sense of betrayal returning. "*Why?* Why would you do that? And how—?"

Robert gave a helpless shrug, as if Ethan should already know the answers to his questions. "Ethan, you disappeared on me. I didn't know what to think."

"Ethan." Trey waited for Ethan to focus back on him. "Eight years ago, I convinced Robert that you were in trouble and if you ever came to him, I could help you."

He looked back and forth between Robert and Trey. He didn't feel like trusting either of them. Worse was his sense that Robert shouldn't have trusted Ethan, who had brought a wolf to his door. Ethan had no idea of the quality of this wolf's character.

"Ethan," urged Robert. "You show up on my doorstep in the middle of the night looking half-starved and indigent. You didn't even have boots." This clearly bothered Robert. "You need help and you never wanted mine. So I called Trey."

He frowned, wondering what story Trey could possibly have told Robert.

"I'm going to work," Robert continued. "If you disappear off the face of the earth again, do me the courtesy of leaving me a note this time." An expression, something that resembled an old painful hurt, entered his eyes. "I worried about you, you know."

Ethan looked away. Saying sorry seemed inadequate. Saying "I know", even worse. "It's hard to explain, Robert."

"It always was," Robert said wryly.

"I *wanted* to." It came out more fervently than Ethan expected.

"You always did." Robert sighed, collected his things and

left for work.

"I'll leave you a note," Ethan called.

Robert just nodded, then was gone.

Ethan turned to Trey, who gazed back expectantly, and Ethan found himself wanting to trust him. His reasons for doing so were weak. It was seductive to have a human-shifter, who was not, at least yet, his jailer, in a room with him. Unlike Robert, Trey was someone who could understand him. Unlike Robert, Trey knew Ethan was a cougar. He had also professed to care about Bram's fate. Ethan clenched his jaw.

"I haven't slept for three days, since you phoned me, but I'm glad you've caught up on some of your sleep." Trey pushed away from the wall.

"It's touching that you're so concerned about my health."

"I'm concerned about all shifters' health. That's my job."

Ethan expected a deadpan expression, but Trey looked back at him and Ethan read sincerity on his face. "Right."

"It is right. Bram's gone. I followed his trail till yesterday, then lost it. However, I think with some help, I might be able find him again. The area where he disappeared has limited terrain before it goes urban or at least suburban."

"Oh, so you're going to get his loving pack to hunt Bram." Ethan felt his anger rising.

"Nope. I have a number of other contacts, singleton wolves, who'll help me. Despite my new job, I don't particularly like dealing with pack dynamics." Trey paused. "You might help me too."

It was getting too weird and Ethan didn't understand the half of it. He backed up, waving his hands in the air. "Why the hell would Robert phone you? He's not stupid. He doesn't trust that easily."

"I convinced him I wanted to help you. He was extremely distressed by your disappearance years ago."

"You *convinced* him. How? Did werewolves develop powers of mind control while I was gone?"

The corner of Trey's mouth kicked up into a smile. "No. Not us. I was FBI at the time, I had good credentials. I can be quite persuasive when necessary and I explained that you'd come up through the foster system."

"I didn't. I looked after myself."

Trey shrugged. "With all your mysteries, it wasn't difficult to get Robert to believe you were in trouble. And it wasn't difficult to get him to believe I wanted to help you. Because I did."

"Right." Ethan flushed then, because he sounded like he was nineteen years old, not twenty-nine.

"You're rattled. You have a right to be. You've been human for just over a week after being cougar for years. You've been accosted by the Winter pack twice and you watched them murder Lila."

He was also starving, but didn't want to admit that weakness. As casually as possible he picked up a muffin that Robert had left sitting on the counter. He took a bite and chewed. "What do you want from me?"

"The same thing you want from me. Help with finding Bram. He shouldn't be feral. He won't fare as well as you have."

Ethan couldn't help it. He laughed. When he was done, he added, "There's actually nothing *wrong* with feral, if wolves leave you the hell alone."

"You're a bit of an exception, and you're a cougar." Trey shook his head, his expression thoughtful. "You're also damn lucky Bram got you out before someone could ID you. So you owe him."

"ID me?"

"There are very sophisticated tracking devices and from what I understand, Doug was about to pass you over to a group of people who would have stuck a transponder in you, in which case you wouldn't be wandering around the city by yourself right now. These people can be hard to escape once they have their claws in you. The paramilitary wants to understand shifters and you do not want to be their means of doing so."

Ethan swallowed, finding the muffin a bit dry. "You found me."

"Sure. By other means."

Ethan didn't even know if he could believe this guy. It could all be bullshit, but instead of expounding, Trey returned to his earlier point.

"We have to find Bram. From all accounts, he is a highly social wolf. On his own, he won't do well at all."

"I don't want to hunt him," Ethan protested. "I know what it's like to be hunted."

Trey's gaze became a bit hooded, a bit impatient, probably with Ethan's assumptions. "You know what, Ethan? So do I. We're not *hunting*. We're trying to find the boy."

Chapter Twelve

Find the boy.

Well, thought Ethan, since Trey was probably in his forties, maybe Bram seemed like a boy. More than once, Ethan had been tempted to say something like, *I thought you told me he was twenty-four.*

But that was pedantic and beside the point. Especially since Trey and his crew came out every full moon and did a sweep of an area. It had been three months since Ethan and Bram had fled the Winter pack's compound.

During the first month, Ethan had been unable to relax, on constant lookout for betrayal and lies from Trey. He'd even made a point of setting up an emergency cache in a cave a half day's run away—a retreat in case he had to flee at short notice.

Nothing bad happened. In fact, Trey handed Ethan ID and rented him out a place to live.

Exhausted by his constant wariness, Ethan gave in during the second month and decided to trust Trey and the wolves he'd been introduced to. Even if he still thought getting stabbed in the back was a distinct possibility.

Trey got Ethan a job.

By the third month Ethan started thinking of them as friends. If the wolves hadn't worked so hard in searching for

Bram, Ethan might have thought he'd been tricked, for reasons beyond comprehension, into this rather strange life where his new best buddies were a pseudo-pack of loosely related wolves who came to visit once a month.

Pseudo because there were only four of them and they didn't live by pack dynamics, but rather like a family. They didn't even all live in the same city, given that Trey was still in charge of the Winter pack and the others had homes in different states or provinces.

Despite the friendship they offered him, Ethan didn't run with the wolves. He was welcome to, but it made him uncomfortable, reminded him of the times wolves had run *after* him. Instead, he did his own kind of searching—none too effective. But to date, Trey and the gang hadn't found Bram either.

Just in case, Ethan stayed within hearing range of them, because if they ever did scent Bram, they'd throw up a howl and he was to come immediately. Trey figured Ethan was the only one Bram would know, having never met Trey and having no reason to trust any of them. Rogue wolves had reason to give another group of wolves large berth. It was easy to get killed in these situations. But presumably Bram would be reassured by Ethan's presence.

In truth, Ethan wasn't entirely sure Bram would trust him, but he was willing to give it his best shot.

He still felt guilty that Bram had gone rogue after he'd freed Ethan, *because* he'd freed Ethan. It was one of the few things he shared with Trey—guilt. The werewolf felt he should have intervened in the Winter pack before. In fact, Trey thought he was responsible for the welfare of any and all shifters who'd ever existed, which was an interesting way to live, Ethan supposed, though hard to fathom. Ethan was used to living on his own, only responsible for himself.

Perhaps he'd been isolated too long.

Even now he was alone, but at least there were others in the vicinity. It was approaching dawn, and almost time for them to give up for the night like so many nights before, when the unexpected but hoped-for signal came—a long, low howl rose into the waning moonlight. Ethan went still, listening. When he had been chased, there'd been howls once he was cornered, usually a chorus of them. It had been their way of letting the pack know they had cornered their prey.

But Bram wasn't prey. Still the resemblance was unsettling, and it was with a mixture of anticipation and dread that Ethan moved towards the howling wolf. He started out at a loping run and picked up speed until he was racing forward. Trees passed him by in a blur.

At the howl Bram froze and reconsidered his next move. He'd come across the intruders' scents the night before, but had managed, he thought, to elude them. Instead they had backtracked when he'd expected them to keep going east. He'd assumed they were passing through, and he hadn't recognized any of their scents so they certainly weren't some of his pack searching for him.

However, that howl was a signal that something or someone had been found, and that someone was probably him, because it was from awfully close by.

There were potentially four wolves tracking him, but why? Strangers weren't interested in rogue wolves unless they got in their face. Usually. Could Doug have hired someone to bring him in? The idea struck Bram as odd, given how Doug had tended to avoid non-pack wolves when possible. They were harder for him to control.

It was his own damn fault for coming back this way. It wasn't that he intended to return to his pack. That would be foolish. But he'd disliked the heat that was settling in farther south where spring had already passed. So he'd headed back to the Midwest, even toying with going up into Canada. He felt a need for wide-open spaces, and they were easier to come by in the north. He probably should have headed north right from the get-go, but there hadn't been a lot of thought involved in those first couple of months.

Those months as wolf had scared him enough that he'd forced himself to be human for a week and tried to think things through while he'd scavenged for food around some locked-up, years-abandoned shed. At that point he'd realized that he couldn't face going entirely feral, that he wanted to try to find some balance on his own. Lone werewolves were rare, but they did exist.

The howl came again. Just one, calling to the others. Bram had planned to run, but if they were set on finding him, it was four against one, either in terms of tracking or a fight. He would face them.

It wasn't a natural choice for an omega, but Bram wasn't feeling natural or omega. Rather he felt reckless. Part of it, he knew, was a wolf's desire not to be alone. Could he submit to being part of a pack again? He didn't have high hopes they'd treat him well. People who hunted others usually didn't. Still he would find out what the hell they wanted and try not to die in the process.

With that Bram trotted towards the howl. Maybe they would kill him, maybe they would maim him, maybe they would chase him off property they considered theirs.

Time to find out.

There was a breeze in the air this early morning, coming

towards him from one of the wolves, blowing down the hill, and Bram used it to pick up any scents that might alert him to danger.

It was only when he came quite close that he realized this wolf was female. Rare, though she-wolves were not unique. Still, she seemed like less of a threat and something in Bram loosened. While he did not want to be the creeping omega that had to ask for everything, he really wasn't interested in busting everyone's balls to show he was at the top of the heap.

She whined in greeting as he came into the field where she sat, ears forward, face alert, and he saw a beautiful dark wolf. She rose and trotted towards him, tail wagging, like he was her long-lost brother or something. Her golden eyes were striking.

He wanted to protect her, which was not a surprising reaction. Even if she wasn't part of his pack, she was female and valuable.

Valuable. It confused Bram. Where were the others? It wasn't always safe for a she-wolf to be on her own. In the past, males like Gabriel had gotten a bit nutty about she-wolves and had liked to control them or kill them when they became too defiant.

Was she actually going to come right up to him?

A bark sounded from an upwind direction and then, out of nowhere, a white wolf streaked across the field. Her protector maybe, but Bram had no intention of hurting her and signaled that. He stopped, keeping his posture friendly, and whined in greeting.

There were more wolves, but these two—the white wolf had reached the she-wolf and danced around her once, to her evident irritation—were not threatening.

Bram whined again, wary, wondering what they expected of him.

A third wolf appeared and while his scent wasn't recognizable, it was vaguely familiar—which sometimes happened when you got siblings. The hair on the back of Bram's neck rose.

The she-wolf noticed his change in demeanor, turned towards the newest wolf and barked, telling him to back off. Which was even more baffling.

Another scent came to him on the wind. This he recognized absolutely, of course he recognized it, but he rejected the fact that he smelled Ethan. Impossible. Ethan was long gone and safe and not near wolves tracking Bram.

My cousin Trey is a cat killer. Doug's voice, explaining how he knew about Ethan. Bram rose to his full height, snarling, ready to take on the new wolf who smelled alarmingly like Gabriel—these wolves were all related and to Bram's mind that boded ill for Ethan.

Bram didn't care that there were three, no four, against one. If he could take out one or two, Ethan would have better odds of escaping. It would be hard for two, even three wolves, to bring Ethan down.

Bram focused on the one who had to be Trey, Gabriel's brother, and was preparing himself to go at him when the she-wolf stepped between them. She whined in greeting and Bram snapped at her, not willing to hurt her unless it became absolutely necessary.

The white wolf immediately stepped in front of the she-wolf, and Bram expected to be attacked. Except that Trey was backing off, quickly, even as the white wolf shouldered the she-wolf away. She was annoyed, seemingly determined to make friends.

Bram couldn't imagine what the hell any of them were thinking.

To Bram's dismay, Ethan's scent grew stronger. When he appeared, heading right into the middle of the wolf pack and putting himself at grave risk, Bram barked once in warning. Ethan ignored him and came straight at him, knocking Bram to the ground with a shoulder block. Before Bram could regain his feet and try to better communicate the danger, the cat draped his entire body over Bram and used his extra weight to prevent Bram from rising.

Jesus, he needed to speak, and could not. Bram tried, growling and snapping, to convey the urgency of the situation but to no avail because Ethan simply held him down. It wasn't even aggression. The cat's actions were all affection, purring, rubbing his large head against Bram, overwhelming him with the rumble of his full-body vibration.

After months of loneliness, Bram felt a sensory overload, what with the danger and the anger, and this body tackle. Ethan licked Bram's face, his eyes, his ears, over and over, stunning Bram until he was whining, pleading with Ethan to listen.

As if finally realizing something might be wrong, Ethan moved off and Bram stood, stunned and confused by the fact that the wolves hadn't yet attacked and Ethan was *here*. He braced himself for a fight and found...the wolves were gone.

What the fuck? He swerved his gaze towards Ethan, trying to take it in. Had he been imagining things? Was he going crazy? Had the wolves vaporized? Bram moved forward and found their scents, proof of their existence. The wolves had been there, all four of them, and they'd fled upon Ethan's arrival.

Bram started shaking, feeling like he was in some kind of shock, and this time Ethan approached him more slowly, chirping once, that weird cat greeting of his. Again he rubbed his head against Bram and while Bram wasn't exactly conversant in cat speak, it became evident that Ethan was glad to see him. The how and why of it—and the wolves—left Bram feeling utterly dumbfounded. Ethan pressed Bram down to the ground once more, grooming him affectionately, and Bram allowed himself to whine, both a greeting and a question, allowed himself to bask in the heat of the cat's body and the rumble of Ethan's purr.

Eventually Bram's heart rate returned to normal, though God knows it took a while. It had been a scare and a shock. Only then did Ethan stop with his attentions. He moved off, just a little, and Bram watched those hazel eyes blink at him as if Ethan had a purpose.

Then Ethan lay down and began to shift.

Bram, too, wanted to shift, to join Ethan as human and *talk*—it had been months without speaking. But Bram resisted. In fact, if he'd realized sooner—his brain was not working all that quickly, overcome by all these events after three months of close to nothing happening—he would have tried to dissuade Ethan from changing into his more vulnerable form. But it was too late. Ethan's body was already in limbo. During the cat's shift, Bram could only stand guard in case the wolves returned.

Ethan woke. No, not waking exactly, for he hadn't slept, he'd shifted—in a field, which was a poor choice. One shifted in safe, sheltered places, not open areas where you could be easily attacked. What had his cat been thinking?

As his vision swam into focus, he saw a dark wolf watching over him, which made the scenario even odder. To top it off, a wolf should have alarmed the shit out of him, but this one was familiar and...

Bram. It was Bram.

Relief flushed through Ethan like a drug. After months of

worry and guilt, they'd found the wolf whole, in one piece, not a mauled, disjointed, rotting carcass. Lila had deserved a better fate.

But it wasn't Bram's fate. Ethan shook his head, trying to reorder his most recent memories, and the pieces fell into place—Trey and company out searching, Bram being found, Ethan running towards the wolves to find Bram was alive and not even crazy-feral, though admittedly a little on edge and surprisingly aggressive given what Ethan knew about him. Ethan had tackled him before he could attempt a misguided attack on Trey or Liam.

Even now, Bram was alert to danger, watching over Ethan and guarding him while he'd shifted, guarding him while he was human.

Ethan rolled from his side onto his stomach and pushed up on his knees. "Bram?"

The response was an impatient bark. Ethan knew something about wolf communication, having been with Lila for those years, and he recognized that Bram was displeased. By what specifically, he could only guess.

"Shift. We can talk."

Bram glared, then blew out air through his nostrils as if Ethan was a fool.

"It's safe—"

Here, Bram emphatically shook his head, a very non-wolf-like gesture.

Ethan smiled. "You must think I'm a complete fool to shift when it's unsafe. I wouldn't do that."

Bram watched him warily, so Ethan rose and walked the few steps over to his friend. He ran fingers through the fur on Bram's head and neck, and Bram trembled.

"Shift," Ethan coaxed. "You know you want to. The moon is setting."

Bram barked in negation and pulled away.

"Okay," said Ethan, shifting gears. "Wait and shift when you're comfortable doing so, that works too. Talking is a luxury anyway. That said, I need to get home. Can you come with me?"

After a pause, Bram gave what sounded like an affirmative bark, so Ethan started walking. When he glanced back Bram was following him, admittedly at a distance, ears facing forward, all senses on alert.

No doubt about it, Bram intended to guard Ethan.

It was about a half-an-hour walk to the parking lot in the conservation area. A little chilled, Ethan retrieved his clothes and pulled them on.

The wolves and their car were already gone, but by Bram's growling and snarling, he'd evidently picked up that they'd been here. He looked at Ethan as if trying to communicate telepathically: *danger.*

"Bram." Ethan waited until those dark eyes looked directly into his. "That was Trey, Veronica, Seth and Liam. They're all related, though not really a pack as such. We've been working together to find you."

That Bram looked unimpressed with this news was an understatement. His lips curled, revealing sharp canine teeth.

"Okay, why are you so suspicious?"

The response was growling, nothing Ethan could really understand. "Look, I've known them for three months. I was also suspicious at first. But they haven't hurt me, they've helped me. They're sincerely concerned about you. Trey—"

Bram snarled.

Ethan eyed him. "Not Trey's biggest fan then? I'll admit he

takes a while to warm up to, but he's been helpful." The wolf remained utterly unconvinced, and Ethan wished Bram were human and could tell him about his concerns.

"I promise you. You're going to have to give me some credit for knowing who is not my enemy. You aren't. They aren't." Ethan decided now was not the time to tell Bram the wolves might be back at Ethan's house. He needed Bram to get in that car. "Come home with me? I'm renting a house." Now was also not the time to say that the place belonged to Trey.

He walked to the car and unlocked it, opened the passenger door and swept his hand towards the interior. "Please?"

Bram circled the car twice before he deigned to get in. As Ethan shut the door, he let out a long breath and jogged around to the driver's side and jumped in. He started the engine and drove out of there as fast as possible, because he didn't want Bram changing his mind and leaping out of the car.

Trey had warned Ethan that feral wolves could deteriorate quickly. Even if both Veronica and Liam had protested, claiming they had been feral for *years*, Trey with his signature slashing-hand motion had silenced them.

"Bram," Trey had said, "is coming out of a bad situation."

Veronica had snorted. "Whereas it was just peachy-keen for Liam and me."

Ignoring her, Trey continued, "The pack dynamics were terrible, still are. Not only that, from his perspective he betrayed them. Now three months out, I've got a lot of hope, but we have to be careful. I don't want assumptions made about this guy and how safe he is to approach." His expression turned grim. "I have seen vicious-feral wolves, and it's not pretty."

Veronica still hadn't been convinced. "'This guy' obviously has a moral compass if he set you free." She nodded at Ethan. "He'll be okay."

Trey had simply raised his eyebrows whereupon Veronica had expounded, "Stronger morals, stronger mind."

It was then Trey had slung his gaze back at Ethan. "Or he was bonding with a cougar."

Chapter Thirteen

The truth was Bram didn't have a clue if he could trust Ethan's judgment. Given his history, the cat should perceive wolves as enemies, not friends. But perhaps, too, Ethan wasn't aware of how devious wolves could be. Or perhaps Ethan had had very little choice.

Except Ethan wasn't stupid and he didn't seem to be under any kind of coercion. Bram could smell Ethan and that wasn't stress but happiness. And while it might be that Ethan was happy to see him again, it was going to be some time before Bram allowed himself to shift. He needed to understand what was going on.

It was bizarre sitting in the passenger seat as wolf. Dawn was lightening the sky, and the forest skimmed by, disorienting Bram whose wolf had never traveled like this. It made him want to whine. As a point of pride, he held the sound in.

Sensing his tension, Ethan glanced over. "Should only be about twenty minutes more."

God knows how long it had been. It was hard to gauge hours or minutes when he was wolf. He didn't think like that. He only thought about sunrise and sunset.

"You can lie down in the back if you're tired."

Bram lifted his head away to look out the window. He sure as hell wasn't going to sleep. Ambush was a possibility. It had happened before.

"Or not." After a long silence, Ethan observed, "You haven't been eating properly."

Bram swung his head back towards Ethan and closely observed him. The cat had filled out, post-captivity. The sharp planes of his face had softened, the hollows of his cheeks had lessened. A good sign. It would suggest he'd been able to look after himself properly, maybe with these new wolves' help.

Careful, he warned himself. *Don't get your hopes up.* Because he wanted to hope, was a sucker for hope.

The sun had broken past the horizon by the time Ethan turned into a long driveway. He apparently lived down this road. A small house, Ethan had explained, not all that well kept up, but unremarkable and a little isolated, which was what he needed. Humans weren't around, a relief to Bram since he wasn't fit to be anywhere near them. Never had been. If he was going to stay here, he'd have to eventually explain his lack of control to Ethan.

The scent of wolves came in through the vents of the car first, jolting Bram to alertness. The female's smell was most distinctive, but the others could also be discerned.

They'd probably arrived here not that long ago. Bram rose on all fours, not the easiest thing given that he was in the passenger seat of a compact car. His fur bristled, he snarled.

"Calm down, Bram. It'll be okay. I promise." Ethan turned off the ignition and went to open his door. Without thinking, Bram threw himself across Ethan's lap and clamped down on his wrist, careful not to break the skin. He whined in apology and wished he could communicate his desire for Ethan to back the car out of the driveway. *Now.*

Ethan sighed. While it was good that Bram's hold didn't unduly upset the cat, that Ethan trusted Bram not to hurt him,

arm in his mouth, it would have helped if Ethan
[?] to be alarmed by the presence of wolves at his
very

"Bram. Come on. Trust me here. They're the good guys."
With his free hand he stroked along Bram's spine. The contact
caused him to shiver. "Too skinny," Ethan murmured. "I know,
so was I. That's why we shouldn't run around in our animal
skins for months or years on end, hmmm? That's why we've
been trying to find you. They've been very helpful in this search,
Bram."

He kept stroking Bram's back and didn't try to disengage
his wrist from Bram's mouth. Eventually Bram released the arm
and licked Ethan's palm in apology.

"It's okay. Why don't we sit here until you get comfortable
with the idea of getting out?" Ethan placed his face against the
back of Bram's neck and hugged him. "Your heart is racing."

Sure his heart was racing. He was waiting for a four-wolf
attack, but they didn't hurry at all. After a time, the wolves
wandered out of the house, dressed and human, weaponless.
Not really attack-mode, Bram had to admit, despite his distrust.

"Listen, I'll put down the window a smidge, so we can talk,
okay?"

Bram couldn't come up with a coherent argument why not,
and even if he could have, he was unable to communicate it.

It was the she-wolf who approached, alone, though Bram
seriously doubted she was their leader, not given the postures
of the men. One lounged against a van, but the blond and the
large man stood nearby, arms akimbo, prepared to help the
woman if she showed any sign of distress.

She bent forward, looked into Bram's eyes, her gaze still
golden and kind, or faux-kind. Bram was in no position to tell.
Though he was beginning to feel a little foolish. A natural

138

reaction when a wolf refused to shift and everyone around him did.

"Hi, Bram. I'm Veronica." She listed off the men's names—Seth, Liam, Trey—though Bram didn't quite line them up with the men. He just knew that Trey was the cat killer.

According to Doug who was never your most reliable source of information.

She continued, "We've been looking for you for a while and we're glad we found you. But I understand it's an odd situation from your point of view, and you have no reason to trust us. So listen, we're all going to take off, we have to get back to our families or, in Trey's case, his job. One of us will visit in the future. I assure you we're not a threat to either you or Ethan. Ethan can fill you in on more and he has our phone numbers if you want to talk to any of us. Feel free to call me if you have any questions, okay?"

Her expression was sincere, friendly, honest. Bram could smell her earnestness. But he didn't react.

She switched her gaze to Ethan. "Take care. Phone me if you want."

"Sure." Ethan ran his hand once again down Bram's back in reassurance. "But we'll be fine."

She smiled, straightened up and angled her head towards the empty minivan in the drive. "Let's get to the airport, guys."

They obeyed her, piling in. The blond turned on the engine and drove off. Bram could hardly believe it had been that easy.

Ethan waited until they were out of sight before he said, "Bram?"

As Bram rose off him, Ethan opened the car door, and Bram leaped out and shook himself, feeling suddenly exhausted. He hadn't eaten last night and now, even if he'd wanted to shift, he felt like he barely had the resources to do so. Still, he gazed down that driveway.

"They're not coming back anytime soon," Ethan assured him. "Their flights leave in a few hours. So, come on, let's get something to eat."

Two days had passed, and still Bram remained wolf. Not that Ethan didn't enjoy his company. It felt much less lonely in the house to have a companion. But the one-sided conversation wasn't satisfying, and Ethan's anticipation at meeting the human Bram was growing stronger each day.

However, Bram remained on guard against some kind of attack. It was evident by the way Bram did regular checks inside and outside the house, and refused to sleep through the night.

Well, if nothing else, Ethan could feed the guy, who was always hungry. Fortunately he had stocked up for the week of the full moon—given his regular visitors—and had plenty of supplies, so feeding Bram till he was stuffed was not a problem.

The problem was that he couldn't place a hand on Bram anymore. The wolf shied away from it, and not only because he was skittish. Ethan understood that Bram didn't want to be tempted to turn because of the human contact.

Ethan tried not to pressure Bram, wanting him to be comfortable with the idea of shifting, of returning to the human world. But the presence of wolf-Bram was starting to weigh on Ethan. He toyed with the idea of changing to cougar himself and that was a bad, bad idea. The last three months hadn't always been easy. There'd been temptation to go back to the feral life. The quartet of wolves had even taken turns visiting with him. At first Ethan had resented the surveillance, mostly because he didn't initially trust them. But it hadn't taken long for him to appreciate their presence and their offer of friendship.

"Trouble is," Ethan said abruptly to Bram the third night, after the wolf had circled around the throw rug and lain down. "I'd love someone to talk to. I continue to struggle a little with being human. Eight years has taken a toll. I need the company. The conversation at work is extremely limited."

Slowly Bram raised his head and gazed at Ethan.

"Sometimes, one of those four wolves stays and visits with me for a while. After the moon run."

Bram cocked his head.

"They come and go, each of them, because they all have busy lives at home. Seth is pretty quiet, earnest. Veronica is the friendliest and most at ease with me, not sure why exactly. And then there's Liam, who flirts with me." Bram's gaze seemed to intensify. "Without meaning anything behind it," Ethan added. "And Trey is pretty damn quiet, more of a presence or an acquaintance than a friend."

Ethan threw himself back on the chair and scrubbed his face. He heard Bram rise and walk towards him as he spoke into his hands. "I don't want to force you, but I'd be, well, grateful, if you would shift to human. I'm not entirely comfortable in this skin, especially when you're hanging around me in wolf form. You make me want to shift back to cat."

Bram stood within reach and Ethan lifted his hand, pressed it upon Bram's head, ran fingers through that coarse fur. "Come back to me, Bram, okay? Besides, we really need to talk about a few things."

Bram turned his head and licked Ethan's hand, then

141

walked out of the living room into the guest bedroom.

He gave Bram time. Shifting itself is a silent process, so Ethan was polite and waited for Bram to signal that he was done. After ten minutes, anticipation began to build. Shifting time was highly variable. Rarely below fifteen minutes, but it was possible with some wolves. Others could take longer.

A half an hour later and after some amount of pacing, Ethan became anxious. Bram should have finished surely. Fearing something had gone wrong, he walked towards the room Bram had entered. The door had been left ajar. He knocked and the door swung open a little.

"Bram? Can I come in?"

No answer, and Ethan felt alarm.

"Bram. I'm opening the door, okay?" Ethan pushed and the hinges creaked as the door swung inward.

Bram lay on the bed, still wolf. Silent, unmoving, eyes closed, though Ethan could see him breathing.

He cocked his head at the sight of an unchanged, motionless Bram and walked towards the bed. "Hey, what's going on?"

For the first time, Bram whined. He looked miserable. Ethan suddenly had the terrible thought that maybe Bram was having trouble shifting. Was that possible? Could three months of being feral be causing Bram problems? Ethan wasn't exactly expert on this and for the first time he wished that one of the wolves had stayed behind even if he wanted Bram to himself.

Slowly, Ethan settled himself on the bed near the wolf, then edged closer, so his leg came in contact with Bram's side. Ethan leaned over to hug Bram and the wolf shuddered.

"Come on, buddy, I'm waiting for you."

He whined again, as if in distress, and Ethan wasn't

entirely sure what to do. That wolf's heart was speeding again. "Shhh, it's okay, it really is. Just come say hello to me." He rubbed his face into the back of Bram's neck.

It took Ethan a moment to realize the shudder this time was the beginning of a shift. The strange sensation of rippling flesh and fur had him jolting back, getting out of the way, as Bram's body made its journey from wolf to human.

Chapter Fourteen

Shifting was private, so Ethan turned his back on Bram, rose from the bed and walked a few steps away. He could have left the room, but being polite and staying away hadn't worked so well for the first half hour. Besides, he wanted to be there when Bram came back to himself as waking from a shift could be very disorienting.

Not so much when you were going from human to cat, because the human was prepared. The cat always less so.

The sound of shifting was silence. It was hard not to look around, so Ethan sat in the chair facing the desk and made himself turn on the computer Trey had left him. Much to Ethan's embarrassment. The instrument unfortunately baffled Ethan, which made him look stupid. He'd missed too much education and his years as cat hadn't done anything to catch him up.

A familiar feeling of panic caught at Ethan's chest. He was twenty-nine and essentially useless in the human world. Trey had got him work moving boxes and the physical labor earned him some cash, but Ethan needed a longer-term plan.

It might help if he could read properly. In self-disgust, he switched the computer off. What was he playing at, pretending he could do something with the computer? Sometimes he feared this was to be a brief sojourn into the human world before he permanently returned to the life of a cougar.

He'd been so lonely. It would be hard to go back. But it might be harder to stay. Well, not in the short-term, not when he wanted to talk to Bram, find out what had happened that weird night he'd escaped, and make sure Bram was in a safe place, not with that asshole Doug.

The expression on Trey's face, when Ethan had told him Bram and Doug were lovers, had alarmed Ethan. Trey rarely displayed much emotion, but disgust had been there and it sure as hell hadn't been about anyone being gay. Trey was gay. It had been about Doug abusing his power.

It might take a while to ask Bram about that.

Ethan frowned, thinking Bram was overdue with his shift, and yet still so silent. After wrestling with his decision for a few more minutes, Ethan pushed himself to standing and made himself turn.

To watch a shift was rare and rather wondrous. Bram still shimmered, his body stretched between wolf and human. A dark shadow, a light aura. A thing neither nor. Ethan was scared, scared that Bram could somehow stay in limbo though that didn't happen. He'd never heard of it.

"Bram?" he whispered. What was going on? He racked his brain trying to remember if this was within the range of normal, ten minutes into a shift and still no final form. The bulk of the time with shifting was spent in recovery, not changing form. Because, yes, often a shifter remained unconscious as his body healed from the dramatic change. But this seemed wrong.

Ethan walked slowly to the bed, crouched down beside it and rested his elbows on the mattress. He was scared to touch Bram and cause him physical damage when his body was so vulnerable.

"Come on, Bram. I need to talk to you." It might have been

his imagination, or maybe hope, but the shimmer seemed to recede, and Bram appeared more human. Ethan forced himself to say more though he thought he'd exhausted the one-sided conversational possibilities a day ago. "I, uh, I've been having conversations with you in my head for the past three months. A little embarrassing and I don't know that I'd tell you if I really thought you could hear. Sometimes I think I'm like one of those ducklings who imprint on the first creature they see and follow them around, not interested in anyone else in the world."

Ethan bit his lip. It wasn't his imagination. Bram's skin, his long limbs and his dark head were becoming more substantial, less shadowy. "Why am I talking about imprinting, you ask? Well, I think I've imprinted on you after my years in the wild. I think about you all the time, and I've missed you. I mean I've talked more to Trey, but despite how helpful he's been, he's a pretty cold guy. The others are nice, but they're with me out of duty. They have families they're eager to get back to.

"Maybe you're here out of duty too, but in my head, you're not. You're here because..." Ethan faltered. Not only because telling Bram he hoped the wolf liked him back was a bit embarrassing, but also because Bram was fully human now.

He'd turned onto his side, facing Ethan, legs up against his chest as if protecting himself. He had long, dark limbs. Beautifully muscled of course—what shifter wasn't?—but the way Bram pulled in on himself tugged at Ethan's emotions.

He wanted to reach over and caress Bram's shoulder but he didn't have permission for that act of affection. If they'd been lovers, Ethan would have done it. They weren't, even if Bram had been there one time when Ethan jerked off.

His face heated remembering that and wondering what Bram had made of it.

Bram frowned, eyes still closed, but he was stirring, getting close to waking. His shifting time had been unusually long, but his recovery time fast. His breathing changed, less deep, then he took in a sudden breath.

His eyes opened, dazed.

"Hey, Bram." Ethan tried to sound casual, laid-back, though he felt neither of those things.

Bram blinked twice, gaze not quite focused.

"You're just in one of the bedrooms. The one with a computer I don't know how to use..." He was babbling. So what. "Do you know anything about computers?"

Something in Bram's expression sharpened, as he became more aware. He pulled in a long, loud breath and pushed up, almost losing his balance. Fear played across his face.

"Bram." Ethan wanted to reach for him, but the wolf had backed away. "It's fine. Everything's fine."

Bram's expression turned haunted. His dark eyes seemed bruised. A shudder ran through him. "Where...?"

"My temporary home."

"I'm sorry, I'm sorry."

Ethan shook his head sharply. "There is nothing to be sorry for."

"I...I." Confusion now, though the anxiety was not dispelled. "You're not a wolf? You shouldn't be here with me."

"Do you not remember me, Bram?"

Bram's gaze slid away. He looked down at his hands and, making a decision, pushed off the bed. "I have to go. *Now.*"

"It's Ethan, Bram. Ethan." He rose from his crouch and walked around the bed to Bram. As he approached, Bram retreated, so Ethan stopped. What the fuck was going on?

"Stay back. I might hurt you," Bram warned.

"What?" Ethan took another step. It seemed imperative that he reach Bram. Yes, sometimes shifting scrambled the brain and the memories, making it difficult to process for the first few minutes. But Ethan hadn't known of this kind of panic before. "You're not going to hurt me. You saved me, remember, Bram?"

Bram breathed in. "You're not human." This reassured him. "But..." his expression turned incredulous, "...*cat shifter?*"

Ethan nodded and Bram's face cleared. He took another step forward and Bram appeared to wonder what was going on, as if it were bizarre for Ethan to approach him. But he couldn't help himself. He walked right up to Bram, who was now plastering himself against the wall.

Ethan reached for him, slowly, letting Bram register what Ethan was going to do. He picked up a strong hand, darker and slightly larger than his own. More significantly, the hand was shaking. Ethan hadn't meant to say anything of the sort but as he took the hand and placed it between his two protectively, the words came out. "I missed you."

Somewhere between the touch and the words, recognition lit in Bram's eyes.

"Ethan?" Bram asked, his eyes shimmering with emotion, and Ethan smiled.

This had to be the worst shift he'd ever experienced, and Bram didn't know why. He didn't even know where he was, only that Ethan was here, a rather strained, concerned expression on his face. Ethan's warm hands held one of Bram's and the touch was a welcome respite.

Then memories exploded and Bram stiffened right up. Christ. "Doug. He's going to..." But he didn't want to alarm Ethan any more than he already was. "You've got to get away from me, Ethan."

"Doug's not here," Ethan said quickly.

"He will be. He'll find me." Bram pulled in a breath, trying to figure out if there were others in this place, but he could only find his and Ethan's scent.

"No, he won't," insisted Ethan. "This is a safe place."

Safe? No such thing. However, Bram got distracted by the way Ethan tugged his arm, pulled him over to the bed and pushed down on his shoulders so Bram sat. "Doug is going to kill me."

Ethan ran a hand through Bram's hair and he shuddered in reaction, an awkward mix of emotions running through him: yearning, embarrassment, lust. When Ethan proceeded to run the flat of his hand up and down Bram's back, his chest grew tight, the sudden tenderness of that caress almost painful.

"You've just shifted. You might have been a wolf for three months. That's probably why you're so confused. But listen, Doug is not here, okay?"

"*Three* months?" It felt like just yesterday when Bram had betrayed his alpha and freed Ethan.

"Yes." Again that hand slid down Bram's back. And up. The sensation overwhelmed him and he didn't know if he could continue to sit so close to Ethan. Yet he couldn't bring himself to move away.

His dick felt overwhelmed too and he didn't want Ethan to know, so he pulled his legs up onto the bed and hunched over them. It almost didn't matter if Ethan wasn't fooled, as long as they could pretend. A wolf would smell Bram's arousal, as well as all his other emotions. A cougar's sense of smell was not as strongly developed. Bram hoped.

He put his face on his knees and closed his eyes. Let the

hand, Ethan's hand, rub his back. He pushed out a breath, pulled it in again.

"Doug doesn't know where we are, Bram. I promise." Ethan paused. "You believe he wants to kill you?"

Bram nodded against his knees.

"Because you let me go?"

Bram turned his face sideways, cheek on knee, and really looked at Ethan this time. He was clean-shaven, his face still beautiful but not so sharp. No longer giving the impression he was possibly starving. "I attacked Doug."

Regret filled Ethan's eyes. "I'm so sorry, Bram."

"Not your fault." Bram wanted to look away, but something in Ethan's face wouldn't let him. "I'm not sorry. I just think it's safer if you stay away from me. Doug can be tenacious. He'll find me eventually."

Now Ethan was tracing a pattern on Bram's back. Bram wasn't sure if he was getting used to the sensation of this kind of caress or if somehow a finger was less overwhelming than the entire palm.

Offering him the slightest smile, Ethan murmured, "I can be tenacious too. After all, we've been looking for you for months."

Bram frowned. "We?"

"Do you not remember the past few days?"

"Not right now. I will," Bram added hurriedly, in case Ethan thought him mentally impaired. Yes, his shifting had always caused him problems, but he did recover, given time and a little peace.

"Sure you will," Ethan agreed. "You must be hungry."

Bram felt like he'd always been hungry, but he nodded.

The finger continued to trace that pattern on Bram's back,

across muscle, down the bumpy line of his spine, across another muscle. Ethan didn't say anything for a few moments, seemingly intent on stroking Bram's back. Finally he rested his palm on Bram's shoulder, squeezed once.

"Why don't you come to the kitchen?"

"Can I have some clothes?" Bram's face felt hot. It was obvious why he needed clothes, and it was an effort not to turn his head and bury his face in his knees, but he didn't want to act like an infant. Besides, Ethan wasn't a wolf demanding Bram show submission by lowering his gaze.

"Sure." Ethan slid off the bed and disappeared. He promptly came back. "These are a bit big on me, I hope they're okay."

"That's great." Bram waited while Ethan put the clothes down beside him. He didn't move.

Jabbing a thumb backwards, Ethan said, "I'll be out in the kitchen, pulling some stuff out of the fridge."

"Okay."

"The bathroom's down the hall."

Bram nodded and, strangely, Ethan hesitated before he reached for Bram, hugged him and planted a kiss on his cheek. "I'm glad you're here."

Unable to even manage a thank-you, Bram just stared into the tawny gaze and felt like he was drowning.

Then Ethan was gone from the room, and Bram got up and hurried to the bathroom, found a towel and showered. It wasn't difficult, taking care of his erection in the shower. Shifting made him horny and shifting after three months made it even worse. He understood that it was probably the same for Ethan, but the idea of talking about it was beyond him. He leaned against the shower stall as he came. It didn't release any tension though, he simply felt more tired and found it harder to focus. He wished he could remember how he'd got here. At least he'd recognized Ethan. Those first few moments, of staring into the face of a beautiful stranger, had thrown him off.

While toweling off, Bram reminded himself that Ethan, despite everything, was glad to see Bram. Ethan had sounded sincere on that subject. He'd sounded sincere about everything. Bram was uneasy about Doug, and should probably not stay long, but company for one evening, after a very long bad patch, was impossible to reject.

Besides, he was starving and exhausted.

Chapter Fifteen

Bram hovered at the kitchen door as if Ethan might kick him out. It almost made Ethan laugh, given the months he'd spent looking for the wolf, except Bram's uncertainty was painful to see. Obviously it was going to take some time for him to feel comfortable which was not surprising for any number of reasons.

Ethan smiled. "Come in. Sit down. I'm not the world's greatest cook, but I'm a good shopper. The bread and cold cuts are quite good."

"Oh, I like everything," Bram assured him a little too earnestly.

Ethan beckoned him, since the wolf wasn't moving, and Bram walked into the kitchen. The T-shirt he wore was tight across the shoulders and a little short. The narrow line of skin between the top of his sweats and the bottom of his shirt was something Ethan found appealing.

"You don't have to like everything, as long as you like something. I know you must be starving." Ethan gestured to the table. "Pull up a chair."

Movements a little jerky, Bram did. He very carefully took some cold cuts and bread from the communal platters, and his actions looked almost practiced because it had been months. Once Bram started eating there was no time for conversation as he vacuumed in desperately needed food. The downside of shifting was the enormous caloric requirements involved.

Ethan waited until Bram eased up on eating before he came to stand beside him. Bram glanced up, wary. Slowly, Ethan brought a hand to Bram's shoulder, watched him jump slightly as Ethan traced the shoulder blade.

"Too thin." Ethan observed Bram's eyes. The dark pupils went even darker. He felt he knew what the wolf was thinking. Shifters often wanted sex after shifting back to human. It was as if everything in them had been rejuvenated, as if after being an animal they needed to connect to their human, or someone else's human. An excess of longing—Lila had described it as such once. Back then Ethan had snorted, embarrassed by the topic of sex education that Lila had felt obliged to give, but somehow that description seemed apt now.

However Bram was too skittish for Ethan to make any kind of move. Earlier Bram had attempted to hide his erection.

Well, they had time. Yes, years ago Ethan had enjoyed the game of seduction, but that had been with older, experienced men, humans. Now he was dealing with an inexperienced, nervous werewolf, younger than himself. Not only that, despite his desire, Ethan felt way out of practice.

He dragged a chair over, so he could sit next to Bram. Their legs brushed together and Bram didn't jump this time, instead his breath hitched.

Ethan nudged Bram's shoulder with his own. "Are your recent memories coming back?" Memory confusion was common after a shift, but it didn't necessarily take long for the brain to sort itself out.

Bram nodded, staring down at his hands on the table. Those hands flexed once. "I remember I was protecting you from four wolves."

154

"They're our friends."

Bram picked up a knife, put it down again. "One is named Trey."

"That's right."

He lined the knife up with the fork, a slight tremor in his hand. "Doug calls Trey the cat killer."

Not exactly what Ethan had expected to hear. "*Cat killer?*"

Bram nodded, darting an apologetic glance at Ethan. "Sorry."

Ethan waved off the apology and chose his words carefully. "I don't think that's right. Trey hasn't killed this cat." Ethan placed a hand against his own chest. "And believe me, he's had plenty of opportunity."

Bram's dark gaze looked doubtful.

"I can't believe Trey wants to hurt me."

Looking away, Bram moved the knife and fork again, lined them up. "Trey is Doug's cousin."

That information gave Ethan pause. In three months, Trey had never mentioned that Doug was family, only that Doug was an asshole. "So, you're saying they're close?"

"No, actually. But Doug researched cat shifters before he decided to find you and bring you in. Trey was a big source of information. Very helpful, said Doug."

"Cousins, huh?" Ethan didn't like it.

"For whatever it's worth, you may have noticed they share the same eye color."

Ethan had noticed that, had thought it was likely a common werewolf color. "Oh."

He felt a bit of a fool, like maybe Trey had been sneaking something past him. Pack dynamics were not easy for him to read. Cougar dynamics, which consisted of just being alone, were much easier.

He heard Bram breathing, even the faint thump of heart. Ethan could imagine the heat of Bram's body if they touched, and he couldn't help himself, he leaned against Bram, half-expecting the wolf to push him away or rise.

Instead Bram stayed there, not inhaling for a moment, his lungs seizing in surprise. What Ethan really wanted was for Bram to put his arm around him, but he didn't think it was likely.

The idea that Trey was untrustworthy, after Ethan had spent three months trusting him... Well, it made Ethan feel a little unsteady. And Bram here was Doug's sometime lover.

He forced himself to push away from Bram.

"Don't be scared." Bram spoke in a low voice.

"Huh?"

"I can smell your fear," Bram said apologetically.

Ethan decided to ignore that detail, that Bram could smell all his emotions. He might as well wear his heart on his sleeve.

"I'm not handling this very well. I'm sorry."

Ethan slashed a hand through the air. "Don't apologize." He found Bram's constant apologies unnerving.

"Doug and Trey weren't close, but I don't trust him." Bram paused. "Trey is also Gabriel's brother."

"Jesus Christ." Ethan stood up. This wasn't exactly how he'd hoped the evening would go, with unsettling revelations from Bram about Trey.

The anxiety was back in Bram's eyes, but it all focused on Ethan. "I think you should get away from here."

Ethan rounded on him. "And go where? I have nowhere to go unless I want to return to being cougar. Which I do *not*. I probably cannot describe how much I don't want that."

Bram's face went blank.

"What? That surprises you?" Bram opened his mouth to say something but Ethan overrode him. "Yes, I was furious that you and Doug drugged and imprisoned me when I didn't ask to be. I would have been okay staying cougar if you'd left me alone. But after three months as human, with some..." he'd have called them friends until this conversation, "...acquaintances, I can't give up my humanity. I can't give up this side of me. I lost close to a decade, Bram. I'm almost thirty."

They stared at each other and Ethan felt like his voice was echoing in the silence. He hadn't meant to yell, so he added softly, "I want to be human."

Bram looked down and Ethan couldn't stop talking. "Okay, *I* am sorry now. I think you deserved a quiet evening, not my outburst."

Bram rose, pushing away from the table. "I told you Trey was a cat killer. Of course you're mad at me."

Ethan frowned. "I'm not angry at you. You're giving me information you think I should have, and I'm a little rattled."

"But you trust this Trey?"

Ethan hesitated, taking a moment to think it through. "I think so. It doesn't make sense that he'd want to harm me. He, well, he wants to help and protect all shapeshifters, you included."

Bram didn't look terribly convinced.

"You don't think Trey would help you? I mean he's been searching for you."

Bram lifted a hand in a "who knows?" gesture. "Most alphas claim they want to help and protect me." His voice sounded a little dead. "I find it hard to attach much meaning to it."

Ethan thought there was a lot to unpack in those two sentences, but he couldn't do it now. Instead he nodded. "Okay, I can understand that. Listen, the thing with Trey is, I can't read him, barely at all. Very little emotion shows on his face. He has no interest in trying to convince you he's a good guy with words or meaningless gestures. But, Bram, he's worked his butt off for me. Finding me in the city. Bringing me here. Getting me ID. Getting me a paying job. Bringing in the other wolves to look for you. *He* wouldn't say he's trying to help and protect shapeshifters. He just does it."

Bram nodded back, though Ethan felt like it was to be polite.

"Look, why don't we sit in the living room? Want a beer?"

"No, thanks."

Ethan opened the fridge and pulled out a bottle of beer, as well as a bottle of water that he threw at Bram, who caught it. "I'm sure you're thirsty," said Ethan.

Again that polite nod. Ethan made a follow-me gesture and headed for the couch. Bram waited till Ethan sat, then lowered himself into the chair opposite to sit on its edge. Ethan wanted to tell him to relax. But saying something like that would make the tension worse. He cast about for something else to say. His conversational skills were not at their peak, and presumably Bram's weren't either.

Bram rolled the bottle between his palms and blurted out, "Has Trey ever talked about Doug?"

"Only to say that Doug's no longer the alpha."

Bram blinked. "What?"

"Trey challenged him, won the challenge and took over." At

Bram's stunned expression, Ethan added, "Trey isn't terribly talkative, so I don't have the details. My impression is that Trey disapproved of how Doug was running the pack so...he took charge. He doesn't particularly relish being alpha which, to my mind, is different from both Gabriel and Doug."

Nevertheless, Bram had gone pale, gripping the water bottle between his hands.

Ethan frowned. While Doug and Bram had obviously had some sort of relationship, Ethan had assumed they'd parted on bad terms. "You're upset by this news?"

"Where's Doug now?"

"I don't know. I think he's still there."

"If Doug lost his position because of me..." Bram didn't finish the sentence. But he put down the bottle and spread his hands, as if the situation was hopeless.

"Doesn't it point to Trey and Doug not being in cahoots?" Ethan suggested.

"Maybe." Bram's head fell forward. "I'm tired. I don't think I can figure out anything else tonight."

All that eating, after the shifting, would have made Bram extremely tired.

"Go sleep. We can talk more in the morning."

"If we're still safe in the morning." There was a slight slur to Bram's words, from his exhaustion.

"I've been safe for three months here, Bram. Let's try for another day. I will say that Trey says Doug's name with dislike and, oh, he doesn't like the term omega. Says it's bullshit."

"Huh?"

"Never mind." Ethan decided that playing it cool and hands-off when Bram was about to fall out of his chair wasn't going to work. He walked over, took his hand and pulled Bram

159

to his feet to lead him down the hall to the bedroom.

Though weariness dragged at Bram's features, his eyes were darkening again. Okay, so Ethan couldn't smell attraction, but he could observe it. He still hadn't released Bram's hand and Bram hadn't released his. In fact his grip remained strong.

Ethan pushed Bram to sit on the edge of the bed. "Lie down."

Watching him, Bram obeyed.

Finally Ethan released Bram's hand and ran fingers through Bram's tousled hair. The wolf stared up as if mesmerized and Ethan smiled.

Without warning, Ethan dropped a swift kiss on Bram's mouth. His lips parted in surprise as Ethan straightened.

"Sweet dreams, Bram."

Chapter Sixteen

Bram slept deeply, and he couldn't stop running as wolf. Running, running. Mostly from Doug, but sometimes other wolves. Sometimes he was being run out, sometimes he was being hunted.

They closed in, this round. It was no longer a game, but life and death, and Bram knew the wolf was going to catch him, punish him. He stopped, turned to fight though he wasn't a fighter, and suddenly found himself human, sitting on the ground helpless as the wolf's canines descended.

Bram screamed...

The scream was silent. Long ago, he'd taught himself not to make noise during his nightmares. He sat up, sweating, his lungs working double-time as he gasped as quietly as he could. Trying to catch his breath.

In someone's bedroom. Where the fuck was he?

Quiet, stay quiet.

"Sweet dreams, Bram." Words echoed from earlier, a friendly voice, even familiar. *Ethan.* Bram's memories swam to the forefront of his panicked, stupid brain, and he slumped forward.

He forced himself to breathe through his nose. Cat hearing was excellent and he didn't want Ethan to find him like this, waking from night terrors. Carefully Bram listened to the house, smelled it. No one here but himself and Ethan.

For now it was safe.

Bram slid his legs out from under the covers and placed feet on the floor. He walked with deliberate slowness to the bathroom down the hall, wishing he didn't have to pass by Ethan's room to do so.

Staring into the dark mirror, he was barely able to make out the shape of his face. It seemed oddly appropriate. He didn't know what to make of himself at the moment and he didn't trust himself. But Ethan was a shapeshifter too and could fend off Bram if he shifted and somehow got confused about who was friend and who was foe.

He pushed away from the sink, slowly and quietly turned the knob and opened the door to slip out. Ethan stood in the darkness right across the hall from him.

Bram sucked in a breath and Ethan said, "Hey, it's me." He tilted his head. "You remember, right? I know about memories after a recent shift." His tone was wry, sympathetic, and Bram managed a nod.

"You okay?"

He could have nodded again, but it would look stupid. He cleared his throat. It felt clogged by the nightmare and his discomfort. "I'm fine."

Ethan walked forward and Bram had to make an effort not to back up. The cat raised his palm and placed it on Bram's chest.

"You're all wet." He didn't remove that hand and it was warm against Bram's cooling skin, even through the damp cotton. "I'll get you a change of clothes, okay?"

Ethan spoke as if it were normal to need a change of

clothes when Bram quite definitely didn't have a fever. "I'd like to take a quick shower."

"Sure." Ethan nodded and Bram stepped back into the bathroom. "I'll hit the lights for you."

After the dimness of night, the fluorescent lighting was harsh and they squinted at each other. Bram turned away. He was trying to figure out if Ethan would want him to shut the door or not, and he couldn't. But it didn't matter because Ethan wasn't a wolf who thought he should call the shots.

Bram stripped and stepped into the cold water, let it shock him out of his stumbling, fumbling brain, let it wake him up. He made himself stay under the water until he was shivering and freezing before he shut off the tap. As he pulled back the shower curtain, he saw a set of clean clothes lying on the counter. He quickly dried himself and dressed with stiff, uncooperative fingers.

When he returned to his bedroom, Ethan was there and had brought water and a sandwich.

"Thank you," said Bram.

"Would you like something else?"

"I like this," Bram assured him through chattering teeth. It was stupid to have taken such a long shower. He hadn't thought it through, had just needed the distraction of feeling cold.

"How about coffee?" Ethan was frowning at him. The lamp was on, not as bright as the bathroom lighting, yet certainly enough to see each other.

"No. This is great. I'll warm up in a sec. I always do. I like cold showers, but I think I overdid it."

He wanted to apologize for his lack of judgment, but sensed that wouldn't be received well, with Ethan looking so concerned. Bram couldn't even trust himself to pick up the sandwich yet, and hoped his host wouldn't take offense at that. Instead he took the lid off the bottle and drank up the water. Once that was done, he felt suddenly famished and polished off the sandwich.

Ethan, who'd been perched on the edge of a short dresser, abruptly put down his drink and walked over. Bram felt helpless, he couldn't move or control himself or his thoughts. He remembered how Ethan had kissed him last night and run fingers through his hair.

"You're freezing." Ethan was all concern, not sentiment. "Get under the covers." The cat's hand wrapped around Bram's biceps, making him jump even as he was dragged backwards. "What are you punishing yourself for? It isn't necessary."

"N-not punishment." Between his body temperature and Ethan's proximity as he lay down beside him, Bram couldn't even speak properly. "S-sorry." He could feel Ethan staring at him.

"Shit." Ethan's warm bare foot touched Bram's. "Bram, what are you sorry for?"

Bram closed his eyes and gave up on thinking and speaking as Ethan ran a palm down his sternum.

"Is it better I go?" Ethan asked. Bram shook his head.

"I'm tired," he said, as if that explained anything at all or could explain how he felt strung out and worn out, tight when he wanted to be loose. Where had all this unease come from?

"I'm going to warm you up, okay?" Ethan settled closer to Bram, under the covers. He turned Bram on his side and spooned him so Bram could feel him chest to back, legs intertwined.

Ethan kissed his ear and whispered, "Go back to sleep."

Right. But Bram made a valiant effort by trying to take his mind someplace where he could relax, trying to think of anything but Ethan's heat, Ethan's body around him. And in that striving, Bram fell into half-sleep and warmth, and slid further away until he slept again.

Some omegas overdevelop their desire to please others so they can't even tell themselves what they want. This isn't some natural personality type thing, it's part of the exigencies of being at the bottom of the pack. Trey's expression had been grim, as it usually got when discussing pack dynamics. The man didn't like packs, Ethan realized early on. He was one of those rare lone wolves, now alpha. Veronica had found it rather funny, and the other two men hadn't. Ethan had mostly tried to forget about wolf packs because he hated them.

Still, as he stared down at the sleeping Bram, he thought that he didn't hate wolves when they came as singletons. In fact, he'd developed a crush on this one. The crush hadn't bloomed until after Ethan had fled the compound. Three months of trying to find Bram had worked in tandem with a few fantasies.

Also Ethan seemed to imagine that he and Bram had a lot in common. Perhaps it wasn't really true.

The phone rang, dispersing Ethan's thoughts, and he quietly slipped out of the room and ran for the phone, hoping the ringing wouldn't wake an exhausted, undernourished werewolf.

"Hello?"

"How is he?" It was, as Ethan had guessed, Trey.

"Um..." Ethan didn't know quite what to say. "Skittish?"

"I'd imagine," Trey said dryly. "I told you he had a hard time here. Omega wolves are generally treated like shit and then they buy into the idea that they should be treated like shit. Go easy on him."

Ethan was offended. "He saved my life. What do you think I'm going to do, kick him in the balls?"

"That's not remotely what I think you'll do, and that's not what I mean."

"Well, good."

"You'll figure it out."

"Figure what out?" Why couldn't Trey speak clearly sometimes?

"Just assure Bram that Doug is still here and will remain here, under my orders." Not exactly an answer, but still an important topic.

"Bram says Doug will want to kill him."

"Well, yeah. Bram brought him down."

"I was hoping Bram was exaggerating."

"No."

"Speaking of Doug, Bram also says you and he are cousins."

"Yes."

"You never mentioned that."

"No." Oh, good, Trey had retreated into his monosyllabic responses. Ethan waited, and Trey sighed. "I don't like Doug, to put it mildly. I think you know that. It doesn't matter that he's my cousin. Seth's my nephew, focus on that relationship instead."

Seth was a nice guy, but not someone Ethan needed to discuss with Trey right now. "Bram says Doug says you're a cat killer."

The pause was tense. "I've killed vicious cats, Ethan, yes."

"You didn't mention that either."

"At the beginning I didn't want you to run from me and afterwards it didn't come up."

"Didn't come up," Ethan repeated.

"Look, I think you'd better talk to Veronica, she's better at this than I am."

"She's killed cats too?"

"*No.* She's better at explaining...stuff. Look, I have to go. I'll check in again soon."

"Bram doesn't trust you," Ethan said quickly.

"Well, get him to trust you. We'll work from there. Bye." The phone went dead.

We'll work from there? Who was this *we*?

Still, the odd, truncated conversation with Trey, pretty typical actually, had made Ethan feel better.

A noise alerted Ethan that Bram was up. He decided to wait it out and let Bram come to him. It took about twenty minutes, but finally Bram appeared in the hallway, just outside the kitchen, as if waiting for permission to enter.

Ethan waved him in. "Hungry?" he asked while trying not to stare because Bram had evidently borrowed Ethan's shaver. He was clean shaven and his hair buzzed short.

The shy look Bram cast him made Ethan's heart turn over.

"Okay, silly question. Of course you're hungry. Sit down. I've got cereal to tide you over while I make bacon and eggs."

"Cereal's fine," protested Bram, not sitting, but at least he was hovering by the table instead of outside the kitchen.

So Ethan pointed to the cereal boxes on the shelves for Bram to grab, then retrieved juice, milk, eggs and bacon from the fridge.

After cracking the eggs and getting them cooking, he turned to see that while Bram had poured himself cereal, he was waiting. Ethan hoped it was extraordinary good manners and not some kind of weird pack dynamic about eating order. Lila had mentioned that once.

He walked over and raised his hand slowly, making sure his next move was obvious before he skimmed a palm over Bram's short dark hair.

"You gave yourself a haircut." Ethan bussed Bram's newly smooth cheek. "Eat. You're starving and I know it. Don't make me a bad host."

Bram frowned as if Ethan had suggested he were an elephant or something. "Of course not."

"Come on." Ethan rubbed Bram's bare nape and to his relief, the wolf, despite the slight tremor in his body, moved into that touch. "You know I'm glad you're here. You know you need to eat."

He went back to the eggs to turn them over and Bram dug in.

Ethan suddenly realized what Trey had meant when he said go easy on Bram. Trey hadn't expected Ethan to be harsh or cruel. He'd been referring to something else—desire. Ethan needed to not rush the wolf. Ethan wanted Bram, but before he could do anything about it Bram had to want Ethan back.

Chapter Seventeen

Bram didn't know what to do with himself. It was odd, the on-the-surface normality of it all. Ethan had gone food shopping while Bram napped. And now he waited after wandering the house. At the compound there'd always been work to do, since Bram had basically been Doug's gopher.

He turned on the computer that Ethan had offhandedly mentioned he was welcome to use. Reading up on the news offered some distraction, though Bram couldn't help listening for Ethan's return.

When the engine rumbled into the driveway, Bram was up and at the front door. He stopped for a moment, embarrassed by his eagerness and tension. If he didn't figure out a way to relax in front of Ethan soon, the cat was going to think he was hopeless.

Taking a deep breath, he opened the door to call out, "Can I help bring in the bags?"

Ethan hefted four of them from the trunk and walked towards him in a thin T-shirt and worn jeans. The ethereal look was gone, replaced by a sturdy frame and a strong face.

"Sure." He tilted his head towards the car. "I'll put the groceries away if you bring the rest in."

Bram got out of his way as Ethan entered the house, then fetched the rest of the bags. They ate and, after lunch, the rest of the day was all mundane stuff. But the mundane—cooking dinner, doing laundry, cutting the grass—reassured Bram who thought he wasn't quite as stressed as he had been. At least Ethan's brow wasn't constantly creasing in concern whenever he looked Bram's way.

How had Ethan described him to Trey that morning on the phone: *skittish.* Yeah. Well.

Eventually Ethan brought up that conversation, explaining that Trey had called that morning. "You probably heard."

Bram nodded.

"He doesn't want you to worry about Doug. He's apparently keeping a close watch on your former alpha."

Bram met Ethan's hazel gaze. His eyes were wide spaced and beautiful, the lashes a light brown, matching the color of his irises.

"He doesn't know about us—" Face heating, Bram broke off, embarrassed to have made them sound like a couple. "I mean, where we are. He doesn't know where we are, right? That's the most important thing. Because I doubt Trey can stop Doug if he decides to run. Well, unless Doug is imprisoned in some way, but that's unlikely."

Ethan's mouth twisted. "Only cats get imprisoned?"

"That's correct."

"Not you?"

Bram found he couldn't look away, though he wanted to. He could scent Ethan's attraction and he longed for it, even if he didn't deserve it. "It was never necessary to imprison me." It came out more bitter than Bram had expected.

Ethan stepped into Bram's space, carefully, watchfully, and Bram went still. He wasn't sure what to do next. Ethan's arms came around Bram's shoulders and he kissed Bram's neck. "I'm glad you set me free," Ethan murmured. "I wish it hadn't cost you so much."

He knew he was awkward, but Bram put his arms around Ethan too.

"Hey," said Ethan, nuzzling.

"Ethan."

"Mm-hmm?"

"I'm glad I got you free. So glad." Their loose embrace became closer as Ethan just kind of melted into him. It was the nicest feeling, this. "It was wrong of me to help catch you."

"Well, sure, but you were hardly the only one. There were at least six of you in the hunt. Besides, I think this Doug guy is manipulative and controlling."

"Doug."

The thought of his alpha caused Bram to stiffen and Ethan said, "Shhh. He's not here." Then he ran a hand over Bram's hair, kissed his cheek and stepped back. Much to Bram's befuddlement. He'd felt Ethan's erection, smelled his arousal. Ethan wanted to fuck.

Instead Ethan simply took his hand, led him down the hall. In the doorway of his bedroom, Ethan gave him a soft good-night kiss on the mouth, and told him to sleep well.

It continued like that over the next few days. Bram began to realize that while Ethan was very affectionate, he was not going to make a move. He didn't know how he felt about that. There was some relief, actually, that this relationship was utterly different from anything Bram had been in before. However, there was a yearning he couldn't ignore and it was growing.

He managed to stop jumping at Ethan's touch though. One

time Bram even grabbed his hand as Ethan was walking by, stopped him and pulled him into Bram's lap. Ethan laughed, which kind of filled Bram with light, before they stared at each other with a tension that left Bram feeling like he desperately wanted to do something if he could only make himself move.

Ethan's laugh went quiet, and he slipped off Bram's lap while sighing regretfully. "I have to go to work." And he disappeared for the night, because he worked shifts.

Sometimes Bram still slept for half the day. At other times he read a book or went on the computer. Said computer was set up, but it could use more security, even if Bram was careful about what he did on the internet. When Ethan returned, he asked about setting up additional passwords.

"Sure." Ethan shrugged.

"Any preferences?"

"For what?"

"Passwords."

"No," he said rather terse. "You choose. I don't even use the computer."

"No? I like it for the news. Though today I found this ridiculous site about werewolves. Let me show you." He pulled it up. "I actually find it a bit worrying, because they believe in them, which is not totally unusual, but they also believe we can convert by biting and I hate that bullshit." When he looked up, Ethan was staring at him stonily, an expression Bram hadn't seen before, and he couldn't figure out why.

His heart rate sped up. "I just found it a bit worrying," he said and realized he was repeating himself. "Doesn't mean it's something you want to read, of course. And don't worry, I'm set for private browsing and it's just one of many sites I've visited. I don't think this will set off anyone's alarm bells so..." Bram's voice trailed off because he was babbling and his explanations weren't making it better.

Ethan placed his hands on his hips and stared down.

"Ethan?"

"I can't read."

Bram stared as Ethan's reaction snapped into place. His stiff body, his embarrassment that Bram had mistaken for anger, though if he'd been using his nose at all he'd have known that.

He cocked his head and Ethan gave a crooked smile. "I'm quite useless, really. But I'm glad you're making use of the computer. Someone might as well do so. Trey thought I would and I haven't managed to tell him I'm too ignorant to do any such thing."

Bram blinked as he realized Ethan meant that, the "useless" and "ignorant" part. It had been a flat statement, self-deprecating and very real to Ethan. Bram reached out and took one of Ethan's hands. "You're not useless to me."

Ethan gave a small laugh. "Well, thank you."

"I can teach you."

His face reddened and Bram read shame in Ethan's expression. "I'm quite stupid about it, I'm afraid. Can't really learn anything. Never could."

Bram pulled Ethan to him, placed his cheek against Ethan's belly. "You're not stupid about anything. Let me teach you."

The smell of Ethan filled him and Bram realized what he wanted to do. He lifted Ethan's T-shirt and nuzzled his belly, licked his bellybutton. Grinned as Ethan sucked in a breath.

"Let me do this too." The anticipation filled him, even if he was the one who had to make the move.

Ethan remained motionless. "Bram." It was a warning, but

against what? Bram could smell Ethan's attraction to him. Those first days in the compound, Bram had assumed it was a kind of forced attraction because there was no one else. But Ethan wanted him here and now too.

"What?" murmured Bram as he undid the button on Ethan's jeans, pulled down the zipper. He smiled as Ethan's cock rose to greet him. No briefs. Bram didn't hesitate. He took Ethan to the back of his throat.

"Christ." Ethan gripped Bram's shoulders but didn't move.

Slowly Bram pulled back, then paid attention to the glans, swirling his tongue, licking the slit, listening to Ethan's labored breathing. Again he took Ethan to the back of his throat, this time cupping his balls. Doug had never allowed Bram to touch him like this, or to set his own rhythm. But Ethan was unwilling or unable to move, and Bram enjoyed this small amount of control.

He had to be careful not to linger too long on this part of the act though, and he wanted to make sure Ethan continued to harden, that Ethan's balls tightened. It had to be about Ethan, like a gift Bram had always longed to give. Bram wanted to make this feel right, from beginning to end, and his focus became all about making Ethan come.

It didn't take long. Under Bram's hands and mouth, Ethan went stiff, shuddering as he spurted. Bram concentrated to the very end, swallowing, the taste sweeter than any he was used to, which he managed to find appropriate even as he cleaned up Ethan with his tongue, catching the last drops from his slit.

"Bram?"

Bram realized Ethan's knees were buckling. With some anxiety, Bram looked up, remembering that this was generally where things went wrong. Instead of searching Ethan's face though, Bram caught Ethan as he collapsed, and gathered him up. Ethan's shoulders shook, which took a moment for Bram to process—Ethan was laughing quietly against his neck, happy about what had just happened. Bram loved holding him in his arms like this right after... Well, right after.

"Now why'd you go and do that?"

It wasn't a question Bram knew how to answer. *I wanted to* didn't seem to be what Ethan was looking for. But Ethan didn't wait for an answer as his kissed his way up Bram's neck and jawline before capturing Bram's mouth.

Their tongues met. Ethan would be tasting himself and Bram, and he appeared to like it. There was a laxness to Ethan's body that was extremely attractive to Bram. As was the thorough and lengthy and deep kiss. It made Bram feel shaky with relief, that sex had gone *right* between them.

Ethan pulled back, rested his forehead against Bram's. "This chair isn't quite the place, is it?"

"Huh?"

"You're spending all your energy keeping us from falling off, that's no good."

"I don't mind."

Ethan clambered off. "I do." He shucked his jeans that had been down around his knees and, hand warm in his, dragged Bram up and led him to the bed. There he made short work of undressing Bram, who tried not to stiffen at being suddenly naked. Then Ethan began the kissing again and Bram found himself relaxing into the embrace. They sat facing each other, Ethan's legs draped over Bram's thighs.

Sweeping a hand up and down Bram's back, Ethan felt some of the tension leave the wolf's body. He tamped down the kiss and pulled back to look at Bram, whose gaze was dark and unfocused but not, at this moment, wary.

"Tell me what you want," Ethan urged, but as soon as the words were out he saw he'd made a mistake. The tension crept back into Bram's spine and his gaze turned troubled.

"I want you."

"You have me. I'm not going anywhere." Those words seemed to help. "You're so beautiful," Ethan murmured.

The confusion that played across Bram's face at that statement made Ethan smile. "You need a little more weight, but I know what that's like, to be too skinny." He skimmed fingers across Bram's prominent clavicle. Traced a finger down to circle one brown nipple before going lower and criss-crossing back and forth over ribs. "Can I hold you?"

After a moment, Bram's brow cleared. "Oh. Uh..."

Ethan brushed Bram's lower belly with his fingers while watching the wolf's face. Then he slowly brought his hand to wrap around Bram's cock. It was hard, almost like steel, its head glistening, and Ethan didn't think it would take long. Ethan also thought it was exactly what Bram needed even if not very long ago he'd had a hands-off policy when it came to his houseguest.

"I sometimes take a while," Bram said apologetically.

"Yeah?" Ethan asked as he traced his thumb over the glans and was gratified to hear Bram suck in a breath. That was tension, but the right kind of tension. "We have time. Do you want to chat?"

"Chat?" Bram echoed, sounding a little strangled.

"About how beautiful you are."

"Don't. Joke."

"No joke, babe." Ethan palmed Bram's face, forcing him to look at him. "Your dark eyes do me in." He paused in his strokes, because Bram was very close to coming, despite his earlier concern. Ethan again traced the glans, spreading pre-come, making Bram shiver against him.

Fisting and pumping Bram's cock, Ethan asked, "Takes a while, huh?"

"I don't know." Bram's face fell into the crook of Ethan's neck and he wrapped an arm around the wolf's shoulder as he groaned. "I don't know anything right now."

Ethan felt Bram's mouth latch onto his neck, as if it was a way for the wolf to hang on. "You can let go anytime. I've got you, Bram." On his name, Bram began pulsing. Ethan smiled as he received a hickey and Bram continued to spurt in his hand.

He didn't stop pumping while Bram's body shuddered against his, didn't stop until Bram stopped making those sexy, deep, needy noises. The wolf just breathed against Ethan for the moment, like he couldn't move, and Ethan didn't urge him to. Holding was enough. At some point, though, Ethan sensed a rising tension and he murmured, "Hey."

"I'll clean up," Bram said quickly, trying to push off.

"Clean up what?" Ethan locked the wolf in his arms so he couldn't pull farther away, and Bram looked down. "What's sex without a wet spot?"

Still, Bram didn't look up, until slowly Ethan forced his gaze to rise to his. Bram's eyes were glistening.

"Okay?" asked Ethan, now tracing a pattern over Bram's back.

Bram gave a short, sudden nod.

"But?"

"No. No buts." He sounded emphatic about that.

"Good." Still Ethan waited, sensing Bram wanted to say more but he couldn't guess what that would be. Besides there was something too beguiling about staring into those dark liquid eyes. Ethan could have stayed there all day.

"Can we sleep together?" Bram blurted.

Ethan grinned and before Bram could regret the question, he swung them around so Bram lay on top of him.

"I'll squish you," Bram protested.

"Later, maybe. Today, you're too skinny."

"Oh." Bram dropped his head onto Ethan's shoulder. "I'm so tired."

"I missed you, Bram. I know it sounds odd, given how little we knew each other, given *the way* we knew each other. But I did. I missed you. I thought about you."

He melted into Ethan. "I missed you too," he whispered.

Ethan smiled into Bram's hair. "We're a matched set, then."

Chapter Eighteen

The next few days passed in a haze of kissing and hand jobs. Ethan found it excruciating, but in the best way possible. He wasn't going to make the next step until Bram was comfortable. The wolf had become increasingly so, his body turning looser and looser in Ethan's embrace. Bram had offered more than once to blow him again, but Ethan was waiting until it seemed less like Bram's gift and more like a mutual exchange.

They hadn't talked again about Ethan's reading, or lack thereof, and Ethan felt guilty that he'd reacted strongly enough to make Bram cringe, strongly enough to make Bram placate him by sucking his dick. That realization had only come in retrospect, which was perhaps a good thing. Whatever the initial cause, the sex had opened a dam between them, and now they couldn't get enough of the kissing and coming in each other's hands.

There was a lightness to Bram's expression after they were sated that always undid Ethan.

He hated going off to work, but the money was necessary, and there was Bram to welcome him home.

When Ethan walked in the door that evening though, Bram had tightened up all over again. Ethan just looked at Bram who didn't walk over, but stood in the hallway, shoulders hunched.

"Someone named Liam is coming to visit tomorrow."

Stifling his smile, because Bram made it sound like they were doomed by Liam's imminent visit, Ethan stepped out of his work boots. "Liam's okay."

"He *announced* the visit. I told him you weren't in and should talk to you, and he said he'd talk to you tomorrow in person and hung up."

Scratching his head, Ethan eyed Bram. "Haven't I mentioned someone usually comes to visit here?"

Something flashed in Bram's eyes, almost like betrayal.

"Hey, come on." Ethan reached for Bram's decidedly stiff arm. "Liam's a good guy." Though Ethan mentally made a note to tone down the entirely not-serious flirting they had going on. Instigated by Ethan, because he'd once been good at it, and Liam was married in Canada. "Really." Ethan wrapped his arms around Bram, who after a moment unbent enough to hug him back.

"Sorry," said Bram which made Ethan wince. He hated Bram's too-frequent apologies.

"Don't be sorry." Ethan captured Bram's face between his palms and smiled. "You shaved."

Bram's gaze darkened and while Ethan sometimes waited for Bram to kiss him, because it was sweet to let Bram take the lead, this time it wasn't going to happen. Ethan brought his mouth to Bram's, felt warm lips, mobile beneath his, and he smiled again, pulling back.

"Such a pretty mouth."

Bram, as usual, managed to look completely dumbfounded by the compliment, but before Bram had time to think about it more, Ethan leaned into him, opening his mouth, meeting Bram's shy tongue and tasting wolf and coffee and Bram.

He was in no hurry to end this leisurely kiss, exploring, teasing, tamping down, before going deep again. Bram's shyness evaporated and by the time the kiss ended they were both flushed and breathing hard.

Bram did something unusual. He reached up with his large hands and cradled Ethan's head, then he said fiercely, "I want you."

Ethan gazed back, trying to decipher what this meant in Bram-speak, because he was pretty sure that it didn't mean the same as what it had years ago when Ethan fucked older men.

"Okay...you can have me, beautiful."

There was that faint spasm of confusion that came after an endearment. Ethan had to watch that Bram didn't think he was being teased, even if it was clear that Bram thought Ethan's praise for his beauty was some attempt at kindness on Ethan's part.

Bram knelt and undid Ethan's belt. Ethan stilled his hands and Bram looked up. "God, Ethan, don't stop me again."

The corner of Ethan's mouth kicked up. Yeah, he'd stopped Bram more than once, not entirely sure of this one-way offering. "Can we go to bed? I'd like to lie down while you...have me."

Bram didn't answer right away. He silently undid Ethan's jeans and skimmed strong hands over Ethan's ass and legs as he pulled down the pants. Over the past few days, Bram had easily figured out that Ethan loved his hands on him. Bram nuzzled Ethan's thigh and Ethan rethought the idea of moving to the bed.

Bram sucked one ball into his mouth, gently, and Ethan's brain shut down. All he could think about was Bram and his mouth and his hands, lightly stroking the sensitive skin behind Ethan's knees.

Bram took the other ball in turn, and Ethan had to lean on

181

his shoulders.

"Bram," he murmured.

"Hmmm?" Bram released Ethan's sac and ran his tongue up the length of Ethan's dick and over the sensitive head, causing a shudder to flow up and down Ethan's body. Ethan's body sang *yes*.

When Bram opened his mouth to take all of Ethan in, Ethan fucked his mouth, the warmth impossible to resist. There was an ease in Bram's movements that reassured Ethan this was right.

Last time Bram had taken him in his mouth, Ethan had been so overcome by sex after an eight-year drought that he hadn't been able to process much beyond his own desire, but there was skill and experience in Bram's movements, no doubt about it.

He skimmed a palm over Bram's short-cropped hair and Bram stopped, looked up, eyes hazy with lust and wanting. "Can I work on myself at the same time?" he asked.

Ethan blinked, trying to understand Bram's question.

"Doesn't matter," Bram said quickly, not quite masking disappointment and even if Ethan was too lust-dumb to comprehend what specifically Bram was asking, Ethan wanted him to have it. He hauled Bram up.

"Hey," protested Bram. "I was doing something."

Ethan lifted Bram into his arms, not easy, but not difficult, given that Bram was skin and bones these days. He kicked off the jeans that had pooled at his feet and started walking to the bedroom, making Bram cling to him, arms around his shoulders, long legs wrapping around Ethan's waist. His face fell into the crook of Ethan's neck.

"I wanted that," he said, a bare whisper.

"Good," said Ethan dropping Bram on the bed and landing on top of him, framing his face with both his hands. "'Can I work on myself?' What does that mean?"

Bram stiffened, as if he were being ridiculed, but as he searched Ethan's face he relaxed a little. Ethan sat back, tugged off Bram's shirt and pulled down Bram's sweats to find that thick, beautiful cock hard and glistening.

"Does it mean...?" Ethan scooted back and, before Bram had time to protest, licked pre-come off Bram's slit.

"Hey!" Bram sat up on his elbows.

Ethan looked up while stroking Bram's lower belly with his fingertips. "Yes?"

"No."

"No, what?"

Bram licked his lips.

"Again?" Ethan asked.

"No."

Ethan was careful with noes; he listened to them. Though what he read on his lover's face was wanting and longing, not resistance. He moved back farther to settle between Bram's thighs. He was tempted to lift Bram's legs up, but perhaps not quite yet.

So he palmed Bram's inner thighs and asked, "No, what?"

Bram stared as if in a trance. "I don't know."

"Say no again, and I'll stop. Promise." Slowly Ethan leaned down and took Bram in his mouth, although what he really wanted to do was fuck Bram. Ethan's dick was aching and he couldn't remember the last time, if ever, that he'd stopped someone whose mouth was on him. But soon Ethan got distracted by what he was doing and the smell of Bram's musk rising in his nostrils. He liked Bram's body under his mouth and hands, reacting, responding, but oh-so-silent. A terrible, wonderful struggle. As Bram's cock became even harder, Ethan pulled back to lick the head almost apologetically and looked up.

"You stopped." It was a protest and Ethan grinned.

"I wasn't sure you liked it."

"Like hell you weren't."

Ethan rose over Bram and kissed him full on the mouth, lingering before he trailed kisses down his neck and stopped to attend to the tiny erect brown nipple.

"Ethan," Bram managed in a strangled voice, "you're making me even slower than usual."

Ethan backed down to Bram's straining cock. "You say the strangest things, Bram. Are we in a race?" And he took him into his mouth again while Bram surged up to greet him. Cupping Bram's balls, he returned to the deep, even rhythm Bram had responded to most strongly if the trembling was any indication and this time, Bram's breathing was harsher. This time, Ethan was not going to stop.

Bram's balls tightened, his back arched, Ethan kept going.

"God!" Bram bit off the word. Then he was coming in Ethan's mouth.

He swallowed while he kept up his strokes, making Bram react even as he was coming down from the orgasm, and Bram shouted, "God, Ethan. *Stop.*"

Slowly Ethan lifted his head, though he didn't let go of Bram's cock. "It's a bit late to stop, babe."

Bram shook his head and flung an arm over his face.

Crap. Ethan froze, as suddenly everything went off-kilter and he felt out of his depth. Had he misread Bram? Was he that stupid? He swallowed, feeling sick. "Bram?"

"Sorry."

Ethan winced. The last thing he wanted were Bram's sorrys.

"Give me a sec." Bram's chest heaved.

Ethan found it hard, but he removed his hand from Bram and sat there, staring down, his own erection wilting.

After a moment, Bram breathed in and declared, "No, no," before he was on Ethan, pushing him over, kissing him with a strange desperation, and sick worry fled as abruptly as it had arrived. While Ethan didn't understand Bram, he understood enough to know that Bram had not been pushed too far.

"You're so perfect."

"What I am is confused." Ethan clamped on to Bram and they held each other.

"Thank you."

"Babe, I don't understand what you're thanking me for but I need to know what's going on in that pretty head of yours. You scared me right now."

"I know, I'm sorry."

"Please don't be sorry. Just...talk."

Bram put his face against Ethan's neck. "I felt stupid."

Ethan stroked Bram's back. "Why? Because you came?"

"No."

"That was supposed to be a joke, Bram."

"Okay."

Ethan sighed, but he didn't let go of Bram. "Help me out here, okay?"

"I got..." Bram's voice choked up. "*Shit.*"

Ethan slowly forced Bram's head up so he could look into his eyes. His gaze sheered away as the eyes filled with tears.

"Shh, shh," said Ethan, wiping Bram's cheeks before pulling him back into a hug. "That's okay."

"I want to be with you." Bram clung closer.

"I want to be with you too. It's okay to be overwhelmed. Breathe in. Cry if you want." Ethan rocked him for a bit, and he couldn't help thinking rather wryly that it was going to be a while before they moved on to anal sex. First Bram needed to feel like oral sex was something he could handle okay.

Once Bram settled down, Ethan rolled until they were on their sides, looking at each other. He kept touching Bram's face, both because he liked the smooth-shaven feel and because he wanted Bram to look at him.

"So what did you think would happen when I realized you were crying?" Ethan kissed Bram.

"Some people don't like it."

From which Ethan could only infer that Doug had never allowed Bram to show much emotion. Ethan tucked away his anger for later. "You know what, Bram? I think you'd better just stick with me from now on. Okay?"

He spoke casually, lightly, as if he were suggesting a new diet or something. Bram didn't look away though. He stared into Ethan's eyes, searching for a moment, before he smiled shyly. "I'd like that."

"Good." As Ethan moved to rise, Bram placed a hand on his bare hip.

"Lie on your back, like you wanted to from the time you came home." Bram scooted down, nuzzled Ethan's belly. "I really did want you, you know."

"I'm all yours, Bram."

Chapter Nineteen

Bram spent the morning on the computer, trying to distract himself from the impending visit, Ethan figured. They'd already made love this morning, but Ethan stood behind Bram and leaned over him for a hug. Bram tilted his head back and they kissed. It started friendly and leisurely but moved to more intense.

Then Bram broke the kiss, his expression indicating he had something to say. Ethan stepped around to prop himself against the desk's edge, tilted his head.

"I've been doing some research."

Ethan nodded, trying not to feel defensive, because whatever Bram had researched was probably something he didn't know much about. He kept his expression neutral though.

"Researching about teaching adults how to read. There's a lot of information."

Ethan felt his face heat up, and he abruptly pushed away.

"Ethan."

He turned on him. "What?"

"It's just something to look into." Bram looked so earnest that some of Ethan's anger receded. He had to remember that he wasn't actually angry with Bram. He was angry at himself.

"I told you I'd teach you."

Ethan stared.

"What did I say wrong?" Bram lifted a hand in question. "It's not uncommon—"

"Stop. Okay." Ethan pulled in a breath because Bram was obviously struggling to understand Ethan's reaction. "Nothing you said was wrong." He attempted a smile and utterly failed.

Bram stood. "I don't think that's true."

Ethan smacked his chest. "I'm wrong. I can't read, remember?"

"And that's why I'll teach you." Bram eyed him as if he was making no sense.

"I couldn't learn when I was nine. I'm just as stupid now."

"You're not stupid."

"Oh yeah?" Ethan was getting seriously pissed. "How do you know that?"

"I know," he said in a low voice, as if it were something on which he would not give way.

"Point to one bright thing I've done, huh? Besides get caught by wolves. Twice. *That* was pretty stupid." Jesus, why did he have to get so upset, with Liam arriving and Bram too fragile for this kind of fight just because of Ethan's ego. Yet Ethan couldn't set his pride aside.

Bram's expression had turned mulish. "You're not stupid. Don't say that."

"You can't name me one thing clever I've done, Bram! One. Thing."

Bram set his hands on his hips and looked down.

"See," Ethan said, more bitterly.

"No." Bram was glaring. His face had heated up, like

Ethan's. They were a matched set, again. "You made me comfortable with you." It was spoken like an accusation which did funny things to Ethan's heart, despite his discomfort over discussing his being illiterate. "Nobody else can do that. It means a lot to me."

Ethan threw his arms out in frustration. "It means a lot to me too, Bram. But that's not smart."

"People-smart." Bram offered a half-smile. "Or werewolf-smart." They gazed at each other and this time it was Ethan who looked away.

"All right." Despite himself Ethan felt a bit better. Stupid, but he'd take what he could. "I'm a little Bram-smart, at least."

"I think you're perfect." With that Bram marched up to him and hugged him hard.

"Sorry," said Ethan. It was his turn to apologize, and Bram shook his head against Ethan's shoulder.

"I say things wrong."

Ethan gave Bram another squeeze and backed up. "No, Bram. You can't blame yourself because I'm unable to read and I find it limiting and upsetting and I don't want to talk about it. But maybe, well, maybe don't bring it up."

"Then how will I teach you?"

Ethan sighed. "Maybe not now, okay?"

Bram gave him a small shake. "Why not?"

"I need time to get used to the idea."

"We might not have enough time."

Ethan frowned. "What do you mean? Are you going somewhere or something?" He had to work at not getting angry again. *Dial it down, Ethan.*

"That's not what I meant. Just, the sooner the better."

Ethan felt like demanding to know if Bram was planning to leave. But he'd made a point not to demand things of Bram. Because he hated seeing his lover cringe.

"Come here." Then Bram did what Ethan was coming to love. He pulled him into his arms.

Bram kissed Ethan's neck, wishing he hadn't distressed him so. He'd known reading was a sensitive topic, but felt it was important enough to raise the issue again. He wanted to teach Ethan, who would be vulnerable if he remained illiterate.

Trouble was, Bram wasn't sure how much time they had, and he wasn't sure who would bother to teach Ethan after he was gone. It appeared the wolf friends were around occasionally, but nothing constant. And Ethan hadn't really met people at his work, though he had no problem working with them.

Bram knew he'd have to leave Ethan fairly soon. For Doug would never forgive Bram for what had happened, and Doug would never let Bram go unpunished. He refused to have Ethan caught up in that. If Doug set his sights on Ethan again, what had happened in the compound would simply be a warm-up before a second round of imprison the cat.

Bram wanted Ethan to have no part of his punishment. He deserved to stay free of Doug.

"I'm not upset anymore, Bram," Ethan said quietly.

"I know."

"You don't have to sound so smug about your sense of smell." Ethan ruffled Bram's hair, or would have if it were long enough to ruffle, and he wanted to sink into Ethan and never leave.

The doorbell ringing made him jump back. Ethan caught

him in the cage of his arms. "Don't worry. Liam's a nice guy. Honest."

"Let's make sure it's him." He escaped Ethan's embrace and headed to the front door, breathing in hard and long.

"Who else would it be?"

The scent came to him and it wasn't Doug's. Bram recognized the wolf's scent from that night last week when they'd briefly met.

Ethan came up behind him and kissed his cheek as he passed by. "Relax. Trust me."

Bram didn't say anything, simply watched as Ethan unlocked and opened the door. "Hey, Liam. Come on in."

Liam smiled at them both, but his gaze returned to Ethan. The wolf was blond, golden really, and beautiful. Gorgeous. Bram didn't think he'd seen a more beautiful wolf. He ignored a pang of jealousy, set it aside when there were so many things he was more concerned with.

Maybe Liam would look after Ethan once Bram was out of Ethan's life. The way Liam looked at Ethan indicated to Bram that he was pleased to see Ethan. But they didn't kiss, just said hello while Liam chucked Ethan on the shoulder.

"Bram?"

He blinked. Fuck, pay attention.

"This is Liam," Ethan was saying. "You actually met, though you were wolf at the time."

"Hi, Bram," Liam said easily, and they shook hands. "Pleased to meet you in person."

He nodded. "You too." He breathed in again, not caring if it was rude to track Liam's real feelings.

"Checking me out?" Liam asked bluntly. "That's all right," he added as Ethan frowned at the question. "Trey says your

191

pack's been a real shitty mess. Don't worry. I don't even have a pack. Only family."

Bram nodded again and Ethan jabbed his thumb backwards to the kitchen. "Well, how about some lunch?"

"Sure," said Liam.

The rest of the visit was fairly awkward, given that Bram spoke in monosyllables, if at all. The first night of Liam's visit, Bram had thought he and Ethan should sleep in separate beds, which left Ethan scratching his head.

"Uh, why? Liam's gay and married."

"Married?"

"Yeah, he lives in Canada. Besides, he can smell us on each other. He knows we're lovers."

At Bram's expression, a strange mix of disappointment and relief, Ethan shook his head. "I wish you would talk to me more. I'm an open book and you, well, you don't let me in. You know?"

Bram let some of his feelings out, at least, by muttering, "He's very pretty."

"Come on," said Ethan, pulling him into his lap. "You're prettier."

"I don't even know why you say these things."

"Because they're true."

Bram sniffed his neck. "You're not even lying." He sounded dumbfounded.

Ethan laughed and fell back, Bram falling with him. "I think you need some attention. I think you're jealous."

As Bram loomed over Ethan, his eyelashes fell. "Liam has a husband, eh?"

"*Exactement.*" That word courtesy of Ethan's one Quebecois

lover.

Bram held himself above Ethan, staring down the length of his body, and Ethan expected Bram to go with what he seemed most comfortable, focusing on Ethan's cock. Not that it wasn't heaven, Bram's mouth, but it had to make Ethan wonder what kind of sexual relationship he'd had with Doug.

Perhaps best not to wonder.

But Bram eased down beside Ethan and instead spent time exploring Ethan's chest in great detail, fingers tracing bone and muscle, mouth kissing such sensitive areas as his nipples, under his arm, his bellybutton.

Ethan palmed Bram's face as he rose back to kiss him. "We're taking the slow train."

Bram stopped moving. "Too slow?"

"*No.* I like it." When Bram didn't reply right away, Ethan asked, "Checking out whether or not I'm telling the truth?"

Bram just smiled to himself.

"But it's not a race. You often talk about yourself being too slow. What's that about?"

Bram fell into Ethan's neck, and under his arm, Ethan felt him shrug. Ethan stroked Bram's back, up and down.

"Doug got impatient," Bram finally murmured.

Jesus. Ethan turned to kiss Bram's temple. "I'm not Doug."

"I know *that.*" Bram licked Ethan's collarbone and he shivered a response. "I like being able to do all kinds of things with you."

Ethan was back to wondering again. Being in bed with Bram was absolutely wonderful, and there were all kinds of things they still had to do. "I like you doing things with me too. If you ever want to fuck me..."

Bram reared back to stare, blinking at Ethan as anger and

193

hurt pooled in those deep dark eyes of his. He retreated to sit away from Ethan.

"Okay, obviously not the right thing to say. I'm sorry. I wasn't even talking about now." Ethan could have kicked himself. So much for claims of being patient. But when he was with Bram in bed, he tended to share, or overshare, his feelings.

He reached for Bram who declared, "I don't want to hurt you. Why do you think I want to hurt you?"

"I do not," Ethan said slowly.

Bram rolled his eyes. "Oh, yeah, pretty it up."

"Come here." Ethan waited because when Bram tensed up, he reacted better to approaching Ethan than vice versa. "Bram. Come on. Do I seem keen on pain? I was not asking you to hurt me, believe me. Come here."

"I'll forget to be mad if I do."

"That's okay. Come here and explain what you mean by 'pretty it up'."

"Pleasure/pain and all that shit they talk about."

Ethan waited, then pulled off his pants.

"What are you doing?"

"*Not* preparing for you to fuck me. I like being naked in bed. You know that. I especially like being naked with you."

With jerky movements, Bram divested himself of his own clothing and crawled into Ethan's lap to wrap his arms around him. "Now I can't relax." It was almost a grumble.

"So Doug hurt you?"

"No." Bram snorted. "He didn't have sex with men."

"Uh-uh." Like hell. "Just you'd..."

"I took care of him."

"All right." Ethan paused, searching for what to say.

"That was the one good thing about Doug. He didn't hurt me. He didn't want to hurt me."

"Okay." Ethan waited, hoping Bram would offer more and not quite sure where to lead this conversation. "Did you ever go outside the pack for lovers?" Ethan couldn't help but think Bram might have benefited from less aggression.

"I couldn't." Bram let out a long sigh, loosening up as he sank into Ethan's embrace. In turn, Ethan relaxed a little. "I have to stay away from humans. You saw how bad my control is. Took me ages to shift to human. I shift to wolf too quickly. My weird tic. I need to stay away from nonshifters."

"Oh, Bram. I never knew this could even be an issue."

"It isn't usually," Bram whispered. "Just for me."

"Well that explains a few things."

"Does it." It wasn't really a question on Bram's part. The words were spoken with resignation, and Ethan realized he perceived Ethan's comment as a criticism.

"If you could have gotten away from your pack and met some humans, some nice ones, I think you might have a less...skewed idea about sex. Because, I repeat, it doesn't have to hurt."

Bram pulled back from Ethan's embrace, his face hot with embarrassment, anger, distress.

Ethan kissed him, coaxing at first then teasing, then full-on deep. He let Bram end it, and the embarrassment had ebbed, the hazy lust back in the wolf's eyes. It wasn't that the men Ethan had been with years ago hadn't been responsive, but Bram was extremely reactive and Ethan really liked it.

"There are a few things"—Bram became confused by the look on Ethan's face, which he imagined was part determination, part insinuation—"*I* intend to teach *you*."

"I'm a burden," Bram said in a low voice.

"No, babe." Ethan made that statement emphatic. Then he smiled and kissed him again. "I really like teaching. Believe me. Not so good at being taught, I have to admit. Also..."

"Also?"

"I didn't know it could be like this."

Bram blinked.

"I've never been so attached and so attracted to someone." Ethan laughed a little. "I didn't actually mean to tell you that any time soon."

"Why not?" Bram's face had lightened and Ethan had to ask himself, *yeah, why not?*

"Sometimes, the way you hold yourself back, I think you're planning on leaving me."

Bram froze like a deer caught in the headlights, which answered Ethan's question. Perhaps Bram looked into the future and asked himself how he could make a life with an illiterate worker who moved boxes around for a living. He was pretty sure Bram cared for him, and cared quite deeply. But it might be easy to recognize that there were limits to what Ethan could offer him. Bram was very smart and Ethan, well, Ethan was not.

"Yeah, well." Ethan wanted to turn away. Suddenly all of tonight's revelations felt overwhelming and he was tired.

"It's not like that." Bram slid a hand down Ethan's arm.

"What is it like?"

"It's because I'm a wolf with a pack. If they call me back, I don't know what will happen."

"Ignore them."

"Ethan. You don't know what they're like. They're not like Liam."

Ethan flopped down and Bram started investigating his body. It was the wolf's fascination that undid Ethan. Not that his body hadn't been appreciated by others, but Bram's interest was so intense, and lovely.

He allowed Bram to play him, take him in his mouth, and they came together, Bram's mouth on him, Bram's hand on himself.

"Oh, Ethan." Bram pulled him into his arms afterwards, offering him warmth, heat and affection. And Ethan took it while he could.

Chapter Twenty

The next day Ethan was off to work, and Bram didn't know how he felt about it. He'd hurt Ethan last night and even if Ethan had reached for him after they'd made love, and held him, it made Bram feel like shit.

Yeah, he planned on leaving Ethan, but not because he wanted to but because of Doug. The ex-alpha was under Trey's control now, but it wouldn't last forever. Better for Ethan if Doug found Bram when Bram was alone. There was no way to argue with that logic.

Eventually Bram dragged himself out of the bedroom and down to the kitchen though he knew that meant seeing Liam, talking to the wolf. Bram didn't much like wolves right now, including himself.

"Good morning," said the golden godlike creature. Even his voice was beautiful.

"Hi." Bram went to the coffeepot and saw it was half-full. He glanced at Liam and cleared his throat. "Would you like to finish the coffee?"

"God no. I've had my fill. Go ahead." Liam gestured encouragingly.

"Thanks." Bram really wanted to disappear back into the bedroom with his cup, but he was obedient and polite, so he sat at the table. And promptly couldn't think of a thing to say.

It didn't take him long to realize that Liam didn't know what to say either. Huh. So beautiful didn't mean knowing how to navigate gracefully past awkward social pauses. Bram decided to cut through the bullshit. "What do you want from me?"

Liam slowly took a seat opposite, as if the question was an invitation to sit. "Nothing."

Bram tried keeping quiet for a while, as that often shook loose those alphas who liked to play games. Silence bored them and they cut to the chase.

It worked as Liam added, "I just came to visit. We like to make sure Ethan's okay."

Bram deliberately lifted his gaze to Liam's, stared, and didn't look away.

Liam laughed, a little humorlessly. "You don't have to challenge me, Bram. I think I'd better bring my husband next time."

"Well, Liam, why don't you do that."

Liam frowned, like he was examining an interesting phenomenon.

"What?"

"Nothing." Though Liam clearly thought something.

"Sometimes a rogue would visit the pack. They were always curious about me. Know why?"

Liam actually dropped his gaze away. "You were omega."

"Got it in one."

"I don't always agree with Trey." Liam sipped his own coffee. "But he may be right about his claim that omega isn't a personality type, it's a pack position. At least, you don't seem very submissive to me. You're spoiling for a fight with me."

Bram had always been submissive, it was just that it made

199

him sick.

"What are you so angry about?"

There was no answer to such a question. Bram turned to anger to get him through most situations. This was no different. He shook his head.

"Ethan cares about you. I hope you appreciate that."

Bram felt his eyes burning, with anger, with guilt. "Ethan is perfect," he declared, then stiffened at the sound of his fervent words. He hadn't meant to say it out loud to Liam. It sounded stupid, here in the kitchen, with a stranger. It only sounded right when he said it to Ethan, who always softened at the words. Because Bram meant them. He loved Ethan, but he wasn't ever saying *that* aloud.

"Have you told him?" Liam asked quietly, and Bram could see that Liam might be alpha but had no interest in going alpha on him. It was a question, not a direction. He seemed to actually be concerned.

"Told him what?" Bram took a large gulp of coffee. He needed to wake up properly and stop blurting out stupid things.

"That you see him as your mate. Ethan knows about wolves and mates."

It wasn't in Bram to deny it. He couldn't deny Ethan to Liam. He stared at his empty coffee cup as he spoke. "It's too early. We barely know each other, and our first week together was wrong. Forced. He was my prisoner."

"It might not be too early." But Liam didn't push it. Instead he asked Bram if he wanted to go for a walk, and Bram seized on the idea because anything was better than this golden wolf who saw too much and asked too many questions.

✧

Ethan got home late and tired, and he and Bram simply slept that second night Liam was visiting. Then Ethan drove Liam to the airport and talked about God knows what. Probably what a mess Bram was. He cleaned up the house as best he could, even baked something, because Ethan deserved many things big and small.

When Ethan returned, he came right into the kitchen and grabbed Bram in a hard hug.

"What was that for?" Bram demanded, even if he welcomed it.

"I'm glad you're here."

"What did Liam say?" He tried not to sound suspicious.

"Well," Ethan said portentously. "Liam proposed, but I turned him down."

"All right," said Bram. "I wasn't *that* jealous, was I?"

"You were the right amount of jealous."

Despite himself, Bram laughed. "But, really, what did Liam say?"

"About you? What would he say about you?"

Bram swallowed. He wasn't ready to talk about mates, not in a world where Doug existed.

"Aw, Bram, he just said you're still scared." Ethan rocked him a little. "But I knew that."

"Sometimes I think I'm not scared so much as angry."

"Yeah?" Ethan moved his mouth to Bram's ear. "You still angry at me?"

"No." *For what?*

But Bram didn't have a chance to ask since Ethan was pulling down Bram's shorts. "Step out."

Bram blinked, but obeyed.

Next Ethan yanked off Bram's shirt. "I like you naked best."

"Well, not when you're dressed," Bram pointed out.

Ethan gripped the back of Bram's head. "All in due time." He stroked Bram's throat, a firm hold that made Bram feel vulnerable and yet safe. "Trust me?"

Bram stared as Ethan held him, one hand on his neck, the other on his throat. If a wolf had held him like that, he would have been fighting for his life, but Ethan was gentle. It was a strange kind of coaxing, and Bram wondered if Ethan was asking if he trusted Ethan to fuck him.

He did, so he said, "Yes."

"Kiss me."

Ethan placed his mouth on Bram's but didn't move. So strange. Bram pressed against those lips and they responded. He licked them, opened them, forced his tongue inside to be met by Ethan's, warm and tasty and eager.

Releasing his neck hold, Ethan skimmed hands over Bram's shoulders as they kissed, ran his thumbs down, stopping at both of Bram's nipples. Bram lifted his chest towards this touch. His dick rose, hardened, pressing against Ethan's jeans.

All the while they kissed, Ethan in control, owning Bram's mouth so Bram could barely breathe beyond Ethan's air, those thumbs pressing on his nipples, his dick pressing against Ethan.

He expected Ethan to move on, but all that changed was Ethan rolling Bram's nipples, catching them between his thumbs and fingers, and Bram yearned for his dick to be touched by Ethan.

As soon as his trembling started, Ethan lowered his hands,

cupping his ass cheeks, spreading those cheeks and before Bram could wonder, Ethan lifted Bram up, forcing Bram to throw arms around Ethan's neck, and wrap legs around Ethan's waist.

Bram found Ethan's carotid, sucking there as Ethan carried him out of the kitchen and into their bedroom.

When Ethan dropped Bram down on the bed, he had to release Ethan's neck.

"You'll have a hickey," Bram managed to say, though talking was difficult when he felt like this, so dazed with desire for Ethan's touch. He liked the idea of leaving a mark on Ethan.

Ethan smiled as he skimmed hands down Bram's chest and stomach, but as Bram started to sit up, not wanting Ethan to feel he was doing all the work, Ethan pushed him down again.

"Can you lie there?"

"Well, sure—"

"Good." Again those palms skimmed down Bram but instead of taking Bram in hand, as he yearned—his cock was practically straining towards his lover—Ethan's hands continued down along Bram's thighs. On top of them and under them. He lifted Bram's legs.

Bram closed his eyes. He'd taken it before, he could take it again. And he trusted Ethan to give him pleasure too, and to hold him afterwards. That's what mattered most. Being discarded had hurt worse than the pain.

He felt his legs draped on Ethan's shoulders, but Ethan didn't go for his hole. Instead he licked his way up Bram's cock and took Bram in his mouth.

Bram gasped and, in reassurance, Ethan stroked Bram's legs. Bram expected to be released, for Ethan to focus elsewhere, but instead Ethan set a rhythm, moving up and down Bram's cock, until all Bram could think about was how hard he was. He became dimly aware that Ethan's hands had shifted. They were on Bram's ass, even as Ethan kept making love to Bram's cock with his mouth. He caressed Bram's ass and spread his cheeks, as the head of Bram's cock hit the back of his mouth.

He never quite touched Bram's hole, though his thumbs skimmed near it.

Bram's balls tightened, he was going to come.

Ethan stopped, almost apologetically licking Bram's glans before withdrawing, letting Bram's feet fall to the bed, though he kept his knees bent. "Just a sec."

"I..." began Bram.

"You?"

Bram turned his head, saw Ethan digging something out of his drawer. "What?"

"You'll see."

Oil. Needed for Ethan's cock. Of course. Bram exhaled and just concentrated on breathing, remembering that feeling of Ethan's mouth on him. Ethan had given him that.

Oddly, Ethan returned to Bram's cock, though this time he didn't set a rhythm, he just licked the slit, the glans, ran his tongue up and down Bram's length, sucked in a ball, and Bram was trembling again.

He was never going to come this way, but he might die of pleasure.

Ethan's oiled hands touched Bram's cheeks. "Let your knees fall."

Bram couldn't quite register the words but, with his arms, Ethan pushed Bram's knees outward so he was more exposed.

Ethan slid a finger along Bram's crease, right over his hole without stopping.

"Jesus," said Bram. Back down the finger came again, never stopping. Back and forth across the hole. And Bram's body was jittering, but whether from nerves or desire, he wasn't sure. He wanted that finger to...

Ethan stopped at his hole. *Yes.* Bram moaned.

"Oh, babe, that is a nice sound." Ethan ran a finger around the muscle.

"Oh my God."

"Like that."

A new and foreign warmth, a kind of laxness, traveled up Bram's body.

"I'd suck you too, but I think you'd come. And I want this to go slow."

Round and round the muscle that finger went, and Bram's chest went loose, his arms began to sink into the bed.

The finger slid in and Bram shot up to half-sitting.

Ethan kept his finger there, even as he leaned over and kissed Bram. After a while the twin invasion of the finger up his ass doing crazy things and Ethan's tongue inside Bram's mouth made him collapse back on the bed, his mouth falling away from Ethan's.

Immediately a second finger went in, but instead of shock, it felt right. Bram thought his eyes might roll back inside his head.

"Ethan?"

"I'm here. You're here." Ethan moved the fingers, in and out, a scissoring motion and the stretching felt incredibly good. Bram wasn't only melting, he was liquefying.

Ethan placed a palm on Bram's belly, in reassurance

perhaps. The hand anchored him as a third finger entered his hole. It burned, but in a good way. The stretching continued and all Bram knew was that Ethan was taking care of him and he'd never felt so softened in all his life.

The fingers disappeared and Bram made a noise of protest.

"Shhh. Don't worry, I'm coming back." Then Ethan's cock was there, at Bram's hole, pushing, not hard, but insistent nevertheless, filling the empty space the fingers had left. The ring of muscle gave ever so slowly. Wider and wider, and Ethan's head was in.

He didn't move.

Bram opened his eyes to see Ethan above him, his face wet with sweat, with effort, with restraint, and Bram smiled. "Come in. I want it."

Ethan slid the rest of the way, making Bram writhe. It wasn't bad, it wasn't even painful, but he wasn't used to it either. Overwhelming.

Before Bram could process it all, Ethan was leaning over, kissing him, touching his oversensitive nipples.

Bram broke the kiss. "I. Can't. Breathe." It was too much. He was...

He was going to come, he realized.

"*Ethan.*"

Ethan held him as he arched, shouting as he spurted.

The orgasm rocked through him, stronger than anything he'd ever felt, and as it rocked him, Ethan pulled out and pushed his way back in, pushing Bram's body higher into sensation, something like flight. Out went Ethan, scraping Bram's nerves and the orgasm didn't let go. It flowed over and over again, making Bram temporarily blind and mindless.

Gasping, he came down, but Ethan was still with him, still

holding him, still making love. Bram never wanted Ethan to leave. He lifted his boneless arms and hugged Ethan.

Though the orgasm had drained Bram, the pleasure hadn't stopped and his body welcomed Ethan in a way that amazed Bram.

Again and again, Ethan entered him until that one last time when Ethan stroked in and held on, groaning as he stiffened. Bram caressed Ethan's face above him while Ethan held himself up, emptying himself into Bram, and Bram said, "Come to me, because I love you and you're mine right now."

Ethan fell onto Bram, face pressed against Bram's shoulder as Bram wrapped a hand around Ethan's head.

It took a while for them both to catch their breaths. Ethan shifted and Bram clamped down on him. "Don't move."

Ethan lifted his head, a sated expression on his face. The tenderness there was going to bring tears to Bram's eyes if he wasn't careful. "You like me like this, inside you?"

"Yes. I didn't think I would."

Ethan kissed Bram's cheek. "Trust me, okay?"

Bram knew Ethan was talking about more than anal sex, but he just smiled at Ethan, because words were getting beyond him.

"Did I hurt you?"

"No."

"Do you believe I wasn't asking you to hurt me last night?"

"Yes."

Ethan flopped back against him and sleep threatened to claim Bram.

"Bram?"

"Hmmm?"

"I need to clean us up."

Before Bram could protest, Ethan slipped out of him and away. The water was running, as sleep started to make its way through him again. Then Ethan was back with a damp cloth, cleaning Bram everywhere.

Slowly Bram blinked, thinking about how he'd always been the one to clean up, and how he simply couldn't summon the energy.

Ethan returned and stroked fingertips across Bram's brow. "So solemn."

"I can barely stay awake."

"You might be sore later, but it'll be okay."

Bram opened his arms. "Sleep with me?"

Ethan slid down beside him, and they wrapped themselves around each other as Bram slipped under.

Chapter Twenty-One

Bram woke in an empty bed and jerked up to sitting, worried about where Ethan might be. Then he heard him in the kitchen, prowling softly but insistently, and smelled something cooking.

He was surprised how long he'd been out. Five hours, and he didn't usually sleep like that during the day. Sex with Ethan was apparently a soporific.

Pulling his legs up to his chin, he sat there for a little while, trying to gather his thoughts and feelings together. He felt tender, and not only physically. He wanted to go directly to the kitchen because Ethan, even if he hadn't been half so affected by the lovemaking, would still welcome him with open arms.

But Bram had intended to keep a part of himself away from Ethan, so that when he left it wouldn't hurt so much. For both of them. This reasoning was unraveling completely.

He couldn't last much longer here. Yet he wasn't going to leave at this moment. There were a number of days left still, until the week of the full moon, when Bram would have to turn wolf anyway. He'd leave then, deal with Doug and, if he wasn't dead or ruined, come back to Ethan afterwards. Perhaps Ethan would forgive him.

His heart hurt. Liam had been right. To Bram, Ethan was his mate and the idea of leaving him was wrenching. But Liam hadn't, Bram didn't think, told Ethan anything about mates.

Eventually Bram rolled off the bed, took a shower, dried himself, and decided to walk into the kitchen naked.

Ethan was stirring something in a pot, and he glanced over.

"Well, well," Ethan mused. He turned off the stove. He himself had only a pair of shorts on. "What have we here? If I fuck you, then I get to have you around naked afterwards?"

Bram gazed at him. He couldn't say *I love you*, or *You have me*, or *I wish I didn't have to go so I want to give and give and give*. And none of that made much sense given that on top of all that, he felt shy.

Ethan leaned his butt against the edge of the table and spread his legs and arms. "Come here."

Bram walked over and Ethan caught him, rubbing hands up and down his ribs, and turned him sideways between Ethan's legs. He palmed Bram's ass. "I think it's too early for round two. Are you sore?"

Bram moved in against Ethan, still sideways, but twisting to hug Ethan. "Tender but in a good way." He mouthed Ethan's neck.

Ethan held him there, hand on Bram's stomach, rubbing the soft area. Shifters always felt the most vulnerable there, at the belly, where all the critical organs were unprotected by bone or muscle, but it was relaxing to have Ethan's palm on him stroking up and down, around and around.

The action continued and Bram sighed against Ethan's collarbone. Odd how just one warm hand's caress had Bram's cock filling with blood.

Ethan's hand slipped south. "What have we here?" He stroked Bram's inner thigh, the crease between thigh and groin, then cupped Bram's sac. "You are so relaxed, Bram. I love it."

"This is..." Bram couldn't find the words. In a leisurely fashion, Ethan wrapped his hand around Bram's cock and slowly pumped up and down. His other arm encircled Bram's waist and a hand returned to Bram's belly, stroking that skin as Ethan alternated between cupping Bram's balls and pumping Bram's cock.

Bram hadn't recovered from the body-melting fuck of earlier and he felt like he might slump to the floor. When he'd been younger, he'd had dreams of being held, but he'd never imagined it would be like this.

There was endless patience in Ethan's touch as he continued his sensual assault on Bram, never stopping, never intensifying either. Bram kept expecting Ethan to explore his hole again, despite what had been said earlier, or for Ethan to kiss him mindless. But Ethan remained fascinated by these relatively simple touches.

Bram leaned into Ethan even more. He was gradually getting harder. "If you keep this up, it will end exactly like this."

"Yeah?" The hand on Bram's belly rose up to find Bram's nipple and tweak it, which sent a ripple of tension, good tension, through him. "Would you like to come, Bram?"

"What...kind of question is that?"

"A silly one."

Bram was losing his breath. That hand cupped his balls one last time before it slid up and pumped him, strong, even strokes from base to head, and even though Bram had thought he was too relaxed to come again, his back arched, the pleasure-tension running up his spine as he spurted into Ethan's hand. Ethan didn't stop pumping though and Bram began to shake in Ethan's embrace because of his oversensitive cock.

"Too much."

"Yeah?" But Ethan stopped, wiped his hand on his shorts and placed it on Bram's hip, turning him so he could pull him close and hold him tight.

Bram was about to protest that he hadn't cleaned up when he just shut his mouth and enjoyed the afterglow and Ethan's body around him. Ethan was clearly aware that Bram had come.

"I want to tell you something." Ethan's words sounded a little tentative, and Bram struggled to come back to alertness. He kissed Ethan's neck and pulled away enough that they could look at each other.

"I, um..." Ethan glanced away and laughed, self-deprecation there. "Somehow this is easier to say in theory."

Bram was fully alert. "You can tell me anything."

"Well. It hasn't been like this for me before."

If Bram could have been more sure of what Ethan meant, he could have responded in an effective way. As it was, he blinked.

"Of course it's been eight years, it's normal I would have changed, even if I haven't been human." Ethan frowned. "I tended to go after older men and there were certain expectations that went with that."

Bram felt out of his league, trying to figure out what Ethan was telling him. "Were they not good to you?"

"No," Ethan replied immediately. "It wasn't that. I was careful about who I chose to be with. I went after the nice ones. I made sure I sincerely liked them too." Ethan rolled his eyes, not at Bram but at himself. "I didn't make much money or anything, Bram." He paused before he blurted, "They'd support me. I'm uneducated, as you know, and was not rolling in money at twenty."

Bram snuggled closer.

"I'm telling you this for two reasons. Liam—" Ethan stopped as Bram no doubt stiffened in his arms. "You don't like Liam?"

"He seemed fine," said Bram in a neutral tone.

Ethan eyed Bram, unsure. "Well. Liam said you might think this was somehow one-sided because..."

Bram gestured for Ethan to continue.

"Because you were the pack's omega."

Heat rose in Bram's face, and Ethan stroked his cheeks and kissed them, as if to take away the shame. "Do they choose the prettiest wolf to be omega, or what? I doubt you were the smallest or the biggest or the whateverest."

"I was nothing special," Bram assured him. Ethan waited and Bram sighed, before he gave more of an explanation. Not his favorite topic in the world but Ethan had asked and Ethan deserved to know the truth. "I had no protectors. I didn't know my father, and my mother left a long time ago, left me with my uncle. He didn't care if I was omega or not. My control issues were frowned upon. All these things added up, I guess." Bram shrugged. He could talk as if it wasn't personal, but it never felt that way.

"I don't want you ever to go back to that pack, Bram. Even if you leave me."

"God. I'm not going to leave you for the *pack*." Bram almost spit out the word.

"Good." Ethan was tracing patterns on Bram's back again. "The other reason I wanted to tell you about me and my previous relationships was, well... I think you should understand how little I have to offer, outside myself."

"You've given me everything!"

Ethan laughed. "It feels like that right now, doesn't it?

213

You're a sweetheart, Bram. But, if you leave, I'll understand. You've got a lot going for you—"

Bram pushed back from Ethan, angry. "Stop that. Stop talking like that."

Ethan's gaze saw right through him. "Why? I get the feeling you plan on leaving. Am I wrong?"

Bram pulled in a long breath, trying to buy time, trying to figure out what to say without lying. "I need to clean up," he said abruptly and bolted for the bathroom.

God, yes, he needed to leave. But not because of Ethan's supposed shortcomings. The idea of leaving Ethan tore at him. Bram stepped back into the shower, put it on cold, cleaned himself up and then stared at the door. He didn't know how to face Ethan. What to say. If he told Ethan he wanted to save him from Doug's wrath, well, Ethan would want to help Bram. He simply couldn't endanger Ethan again. Not after he'd helped capture him. What if Doug had his contact with him? Bram might have a chance against Doug, but Ethan would have none against someone associated with the paramilitary, some powerful group of people out to contain a cat shifter for God knows what reason.

Too dangerous. Bram was shaking. He had to get out of here. He'd stayed too long as it was. He'd wanted to wait until the next full moon. But he couldn't even manage that. If Ethan hadn't been a shifter, Bram would have climbed out the bathroom window, turned wolf and ran. But Ethan would hear him and chase him. So Bram rather grimly went to the bedroom and put on clothes.

Ethan had messed that up and bad. Bram was utterly spooked, even as he gulped down the canned chili Ethan had heated up. Liam had stressed that Bram would still feel ties to

214

his pack, it was impossible for a wolf not to. So Ethan had thought he should make it clear that he had feelings for Bram. Offer Bram another kind of tie.

It had made sense at the time. And Liam being wolf, Ethan had thought he'd have better insight into an omega's situation than a cat who'd spent the past eight years essentially by himself.

Of course, if Ethan had left it at declaring his deepening feelings, Bram might not have freaked. But no, he had to mention that Bram seemed to be planning on leaving. Something he couldn't bring himself to deny.

"I'm sorry I upset you."

Bram lifted his gaze from his chili, his eyes burning. "*You* haven't upset me."

Okay. "If you do feel you need to go, I would always welcome you back."

"I have to do something."

Realization dawned and Ethan couldn't help but think he really was stupid not to understand what was going on in Bram's mind. "Does this something have to do with Doug?"

Bram's gaze slid away. "I don't want to talk about it."

For the first time since he'd settled in this house, Ethan felt frightened, and it wasn't for himself. "Does Doug have some kind of hold on you?"

"No." The word came out strangled.

"Do you feel you owe Doug something?"

"*No.*" Bram put down his spoon and clenched his fist. "I was never any fucking good at lying or dissembling or any such thing."

"The last time we discussed Doug, you said he wanted to kill you. So I didn't think you were bonded to him."

"I am not bonded to *Doug*." Bram almost spat out his alpha's name as he shoved away from the table. "He will kill me, or die trying. I don't want you anywhere near me when that happens. Don't you understand that! I'm a danger to you."

"Oh, Bram." Ethan ached as he watched Bram tremble.

"You don't know what he's like. You think it's safe because he's with Trey, but Doug will bide his time when he has to. God knows, he did it for years with Gabriel." His chest heaved. "You're not safe with me and you *never will be*."

"I'm not questioning your assessment of Doug here, okay, Bram? But can you explain to me why Doug would be so focused on you?"

"I attacked him. I set you free. I cost him his leadership. But it's not only that, I belonged to him. In return for protecting me, I couldn't do anything without his permission. And I rejected that in the worst way possible."

"Okay." Ethan rose slowly, walked around the table as if approaching a wary animal.

Suddenly Bram hung his head. "Don't touch me."

Ethan stopped. "Why not?"

Bram released a shuddery sigh. "You make me weak."

"I don't think that's true," Ethan said softly as he pulled Bram into his arms. "You *belonged* to him?"

"If I did everything as he asked, no one could touch me, no one could hurt me."

"Except Doug."

"Except Doug," Bram agreed.

Chapter Twenty-Two

"He's convinced Doug will come after him." Ethan waited for Trey's response. Silence, he'd come to realize, meant Trey was thinking. Repeating himself never did much to hurry along Trey's reply.

"I won't just execute a shapeshifter, Ethan. I don't do that. Even when that person has dubbed me a *cat killer*." The last two words were said with scorn. "Doug knows the rules. He can't go out of the compound, for fear of imprisonment or death. I am the law here. He knows I mean what I say."

"None of this will convince Bram."

"Look, I've been very careful. Doug does not know where you are. Only Liam, Veronica, Seth and myself know this. You're not in the same state. I don't believe Bram or you are in danger. If I did, I would do something about it."

"But Bram…" Ethan found it hard to describe the fear that rode Bram when they discussed Doug.

"Bram has been Doug's omega for four years. It will take more than a month to deprogram him. Patience."

"This is not about patience," Ethan snapped. "I have no problem being patient when it comes to this. It's about the fact that Bram judges Doug to be a real threat, even under the current conditions. Doug has told Bram, on more than one occasion, that if Bram ever betrayed him, he was dead. I wish you would kill the motherfucker."

"I'll consider it."

"Are you serious?"

"Sure, I'm serious about considering it."

Which meant more wait and see. "Bram wants to save me from all this danger by taking off. Which...infuriates me." Here Ethan glared at Bram who started wiping down the counter. "We're in this together. I mean if I hadn't existed, none of this would have happened to him."

"And he'd still be with Doug. Is that what you'd want for him?"

"Of course not."

"So stop feeling guilty for existing. Doug is here. Doug is contained. Doug does not know where you are. Both of you sit tight, okay? I'm prepared to have another chat with Doug. I'll talk to you again in a couple of days."

"Okay."

"Ethan? How's the job?"

He tried not to sound too irritated. Who cared about the fucking job? It paid the bills. "It's fine. It's a job."

"Good. Talk to you later." Trey clicked off.

Ethan sighed. It did not feel "good".

Bram observed him from the other side of the counter. "So nothing's changed."

"Doug has no way to find you, Bram."

He shrugged, as if that was a technicality. But Doug couldn't find them if he didn't know where they were. It wasn't possible. Ethan held on to that.

"You're not going to suddenly take off, are you?"

Bram shook his head a little wearily.

"Is that a promise?" Ethan pushed.

"I'll make a deal with you."

Ethan raised his brows, since making a deal didn't sound very Bram-like.

"You let me teach you how to read and I won't take off."

Groaning, Ethan leaned on the counter, bowing his head for a moment.

"It won't be so bad," Bram said softly. "I like teaching too."

Which was hardly the point. Trying to read swung Ethan back two decades to when he was nine years old, in a classroom with kids who knew what was going on, and he didn't. He felt *stupid*. And he strongly disliked feeling nine years old *and* stupid.

Bram's hand slid around Ethan's neck, blunt fingers coaxing him into an embrace, Bram kissing his neck and jawline, then plundering Ethan's mouth. Also un-Bram-like, but Ethan liked it.

He should tamp it down, he had to go to work, but Ethan couldn't bring himself to pull back.

When Bram broke away they were both flushed and a little startled. "Work." Bram pointed out the door. "Better go."

"Like this?" Ethan was hard and wanting.

Bram actually smirked. "I'll be here when you come home."

Ethan didn't exactly remember agreeing to their bargain, but by the time he was driving away from the house, he figured he was stuck with it.

Well, if that was the way he convinced Bram to stay around, he'd take it.

✧

When Ethan got home that night—this week he was working days—Bram had not only made supper, chicken-something-or-other, he had a stack of worksheets on the kitchen table.

Good that Bram was here and keeping himself busy, bad that he was busily determined to teach Ethan.

Bram took one look at Ethan, burst out laughing, and walked up to kiss him on the cheek. "Sit. Eat."

"What are you laughing about?" Ethan grumbled.

"The look on your face. As if you're doomed."

Though he could have worked up to indignation, Ethan didn't have the energy, especially with the food taking up his attention. He'd forgotten to bring lunch today, given the way he'd left the house late.

Bram sat opposite and began shoveling down as well. Ethan was pleased to see that he wasn't quite so bony looking. Also the distraction of teaching Ethan had gotten rid of the worst of Bram's edginess. Or maybe that was all the sex.

Hmmm. There might be inventive ways to avoid these dreaded worksheets, at least for one more night.

Bram let Ethan use sex to distract him the first night. It was simply too much fun. But the second night they started this new kind of tug-of-war where Bram refused to play if Ethan didn't work. Bram managed to get through one worksheet before he gave up and let Ethan seduce him.

But even that one worksheet was enough to ease up Ethan's resistance to the whole endeavor. Not that Ethan enjoyed working on his word recognition the third night, but the stress reaction was gone and mostly he found it tiresome and carried an air about him that suggested he was doing Bram a huge favor.

By the fourth night, Bram had the sense there was some interest on Ethan's part, though he seemed loath to admit it. He also noted that Ethan's problem might be partly dyslexia-based, but decided this topic could wait a while, given how touchy Ethan was about his reading ability.

Their pattern continued, even through Ethan's different work hours. The following week Bram ran under the full moon at nights, sometimes with Ethan, sometimes without depending on his work schedule. Always Bram tried not to think about Doug. Trey claimed all was under his control, Ethan believed him and who was Bram to know differently? But sometimes he woke up shivering with foreboding, and even if Ethan could soothe away the immediacy of the fear, the threat of Doug's retribution remained.

Chapter Twenty-Three

Ethan cranked up the radio. He didn't particularly like the song. It made him feel old, like he'd missed the past decade of his life, which he had. But he wanted to drive to a beat, and by the third time the chorus came around, he joined in, singing "going for you" three times in a row off-key.

As the song wound down, a car pulled over to pass him and Ethan eased up on the gas to allow it. But instead of speeding on, the gray car with tinted windows slowed down, forcing Ethan to follow suit.

A second car pulled up behind him.

Ethan's heart picked up like a jackhammer, the danger so sudden and unexpected it took a moment to process what was happening to him. He was sandwiched between two cars. He'd only ever been trapped by people who wanted to do him harm and he refused to be trapped again. Once this year had been hell enough.

Yeah, the tinted-window cars didn't much resemble werewolves, but someone was sure as hell targeting him.

He decelerated, as if he were cooperating with these assholes. At the curve he slammed down on the gas and jumped around the car ahead. He listened to his own vehicle trying to pick up speed. Trey had lent him a nice-enough Ford, but it wasn't exactly going to outrace anything.

The gray car rolled up behind him again, this time bumping his back end slightly before it pulled alongside, and all Ethan could think was there was going to be a fucking accident on this two-lane highway and he had to get off the road, out of this car and out of this human skin. He unhitched his seat belt and hit the button on the side of his door so his window descended.

The car pulled in front to slow him down a second time and, just before the guardrail started, Ethan swerved right. As the car began to hurtle down the slope, he threw himself out the open window.

His Ford whipped past him, too close for comfort. Ethan rolled, hitting his shoulder harder than he liked, somersaulting three times through the brush, but eventually, and a little shakily, landing on his feet.

He ran.

Bram printed out another bunch of worksheets, not that Ethan would be thrilled—though he could actually read to some extent. It was a frustrating, slow experience, however, and his reading vocabulary had stalled with that of a nine-year-old. Bram's heart constricted a little, thinking of Ethan losing his mother and having to fend for himself. It kind of amazed Bram that Ethan was so strong.

His mother had loved him those nine years, that much was obvious. Ethan didn't speak much about her, except that he couldn't remember what she looked like and that bothered him. Bram wondered if Trey, with his many resources, would be able to track down a picture of Ethan's mother. She had stressed to Ethan that his shapeshifting ability was a gift not a curse. That ended up counting for a lot, Bram thought, her refusing to allow Ethan to consider himself a freak. She apparently hadn't held a high opinion of education when it came to her son, but maybe for good reason. It was hard for a werewolf to adapt to regular school, and it might have been worse for a lone werecat with dyslexia.

The phone rang, startling Bram out of his reverie. He stared for a moment, wondering if he should leave it for the answering machine. He didn't particularly enjoy talking to Trey or Liam or Veronica or whatshisname. As it rang a fourth time, he gave a labored sigh and lifted the handset.

"Hello."

"Hi, Bram." Trey's voice was grim and he didn't wait for Bram to return the greeting. "You should know that Doug is gone and his guard is dead."

He reached for the counter to steady himself and clutched the phone tighter. He choked out the word "How?"

"This happened at most two hours ago so there is no way he is in your neighborhood right now. In fact, I see no way that he can even know *where* you are. However, to be safe, I think you and Ethan need to move out as soon as possible.

"We're setting off to find him, but there's a chance he got in a vehicle which—"

"Will make him impossible to track."

"That is correct." Trey paused. "I won't simply execute people. I had to give him a chance to adapt to his new role. That's over."

Over? Doug was on the run.

"Bram, is Ethan there?"

"He's at work."

"I want to talk to him when he gets home."

"Okay."

"Bram, I'm sending Liam over to stay with you guys until this gets resolved. He'll be flying in tonight."

If this gets resolved. Doug could go into hiding for a while and choose his moment. Liam couldn't exactly stay with them forever. He had a business and a husband and a brother to look after.

"Okay."

Trey sighed. "Look, obviously you don't think it's okay."

Bram bristled but stopped short of responding.

"Get Ethan to call me."

"I will."

They hung up, and Bram immediately called Ethan at work to find out, as he expected since Ethan's shift was over, that he'd already left. He got a time of departure—twenty minutes ago. Ethan should have been home, unless he stopped for groceries.

Bram paced the house, weighing possibilities, waiting for the gravel to crunch under the sound of Ethan's tires.

Twenty minutes later he was convinced something was wrong and not only because the stress was driving him nuts. His skin itched and he didn't want to be human any longer. It wasn't safe. He'd wait here for Ethan, but not as human. Bram stripped off his clothes, slipped out the back door and jogged to the woods. There, he shifted.

Ethan wasn't quite sure how Doug could have managed to arrange for two cars with tinted windows to run him off the road. It didn't add up. Doug liked to be in charge, do things himself, according to Bram. Doug was also under Trey's thumb in the Winter compound. Or at least he had been.

Didn't matter right this moment. What Ethan had to do was get to Bram and warn him.

Ethan had run farther into the woods before shifting. He

was a fast shifter, and while he was disoriented upon waking from the change, it hadn't taken him long to recover and remember that cars had run him off the road. He heard their occupants. The men were on foot, chasing him, but he was cougar and they had no chance. Ethan raced towards the house and Bram, who would be vulnerable and human and waiting for him to come home from work.

He ran for half an hour maybe, aiming straight for the house, racing through brush, past trees, over hills. As he got close, he didn't slow down, desperate to see Bram safe. He almost missed Bram in his headlong run for that back door. The wolf cut off his approach and Ethan screeched to a halt to stare.

Being wolf could only mean that Bram had had some warning too, hopefully not as dangerous a warning as Ethan's had been.

Didn't matter how Bram knew of the danger, they needed to flee. Bram evidently thought the same thing, given that he lifted his head in a gesture that said, *Let's go.*

Ethan knew what to do. He'd explored this area carefully the first month he'd lived here when he couldn't bring himself to trust Trey. There was a cave where they could shelter, the same cave he'd set up as an escape route if the friendly wolves suddenly turned vicious on him. It was about a four-hour run from here. They needed that distance, they needed to get far away from here, then shift, talk and reassess the situation.

Bram allowed Ethan to take the lead.

While Ethan could run faster, Bram had more stamina, despite his skinniness. They had to stop a few times for Ethan's sake and it was close to four hours later when Ethan led Bram directly into the cave.

They turned and faced each other. It was awkward being

animals, even if they were comfortable as lovers. So Ethan stalked over and purred, rubbing his head against Bram's face and neck, and was licked in response.

After that mutual reassurance, Ethan retreated to shift to human. Because, God, they really had to talk. Shifting twice in a short period of time took its toll and he braced himself for the forcible rearrangement of muscle and bone. He fell into grayness, then black.

When he woke, he didn't know where he was and why the fuck he wasn't panicked that nearby a werewolf lay on his side, panting heavily.

He just knew this was a friend. Ethan crawled over and memory descended. Bram. Lover. Wolf. On the run.

Bram, Ethan managed to recall—two shifts in one day was disorienting—had trouble shifting to human. So Ethan sat beside him, stroking his warm, dark fur until it finally began to recede. At that point Ethan sang the song he'd heard on the radio on the way home, before switching over to some Beatles songs his mother had sung to him as a boy. Anything to lure Bram's body over to the human side.

It worked. The wolf receded and Bram came to the forefront, first unconscious but then quickly waking, even more confused by the shift back and forth than Ethan had been. Bram blinked, fear entering his eyes but leaving with a gratifyingly rapid speed. "Hello?"

"Hi, Bram, it's Ethan."

Bram's gaze circled around the cave as if that could give him more context.

Ethan smiled and said the words he'd, rightly or wrongly, been withholding, waiting for the perfect time. "I love you."

Bram looked behind him, as if Ethan might be talking to someone else. Okay, Ethan had not made such a declaration before and Bram didn't quite yet remember who he was or what they were doing. But still Ethan was scared enough by the events of today to speak it. In case he wasn't able to in the future.

"Yeah, *you*, Bram." He touched Bram's face lightly with a knuckle, wanting to make contact without overwhelming him. "But never mind. We've been living together for, well, not too long. We're in trouble right now."

At that, recognition and memory took hold, and Bram jerked to sitting, gasping, hand on his heart. Ethan slid a palm over Bram's shoulders and he trembled at the touch, rather like those first few days, but then he leaned into Ethan, wrapping his arms around him, and spoke against Ethan's neck. "Doug's disappeared. Trey probably can't even track him."

"Shit."

They sat there for a moment, taking the news in, Ethan for the first time, and Bram for the second time. Eventually, Bram asked, "How did you know?"

"I didn't," Ethan said quietly. "Someone ran me off the road."

Bram jolted back and looked at Ethan full on. "Are you okay?"

"Better than the car," Ethan said wryly. "I jumped out the window. Only some scrapes and bruises which are mostly healed from the shifts."

Bram kissed him, hands sinking into Ethan's hair as he took possession of Ethan's mouth, tasting, searching, reassuring. Ethan returned the kiss, wishing that this was somehow a way to protect Bram, but it wasn't. He tamped down the kiss. Normally he was wired after a shift, but it had been two shifts and four hours of running and a lot of fear and adrenaline. They needed to eat and drink from Ethan's

228

supplies, and Ethan needed to listen.

Because something didn't make sense about this afternoon. He scrambled to the back of the cave and picked up energy drinks and nutrition bars.

He shoved them both into Bram's hands, and then they were guzzling and vacuuming up food. Bram was even worse off than Ethan because he had fewer resources and still needed to fatten up after being too skinny for too long.

By the time they were done eating, Bram was fading and fast. He reached for Ethan. "No sex?"

"I think not right at this moment."

"I thought that was a big benefit of being, uh, together after a shift." He was slurring his words.

Ethan pulled him into his arms and held him. "Usually. Today's a bit of an exception."

At that Bram opened his eyes and stared at Ethan, worry there, and fear. He reached up a hand and brushed hair off of Ethan's forehead.

Ethan smiled and he tried to make it reassuring. "Sleep. We need it. In the morning, we'll figure things out."

Bram acquiesced, his eyelids fluttered shut, and he was out in less than a minute. Ethan lasted long enough to pull a blanket over both of them, but the events of the day overwhelmed him, and he too fell asleep.

The motor entered his dreams slowly, as if from far, far away. Ethan the cat wondered why a car had driven off the highway, down that hill and still chased him. Hadn't he escaped? Hadn't he jumped out of that window and run and run and run? They couldn't catch the cougar.

But he was human.

Abruptly Ethan was fully awake, staring into the pitch black of the cave. He lay there, curled around Bram who continued to sleep. The forest was quiet except for insect and small-animal noises. And the sound of a motor in the far distance. Not a car, exactly, but something.

Ethan slipped away from Bram and went to the edge of the cave to listen carefully. After ten minutes he was sure the motor was getting closer. To him. To Bram.

How the fuck could they be found at night in the wilderness in a cave? In that moment, Ethan became convinced this was not Doug out there chasing down Bram.

Someone else was chasing down Ethan. Somehow. He shivered as a memory of Trey in Robert's kitchen surfaced. *There are very sophisticated tracking devices.* But he'd avoided that fate, hadn't he? Doug hadn't managed to pass him over to the people who could have tagged him.

He glanced back at the wolf, *his* wolf, who slept on, who had thought to leave him in order to save Ethan from Doug's wrath. Doug may have wanted to hunt Bram down, but Bram wasn't being hunted now. Ethan knew what a hunt felt like and this was it.

There was one way to find out who was the real target. Ethan crept away from the cave. There he shifted, one last time, he told himself, for if he was right, he wasn't going to be human for a while, perhaps a very long while.

Then he ran, putting distance between himself and Bram. When he stopped he again listened carefully to the motor and where it was now headed. He'd positioned himself so that they formed a triangle: he, Bram and the vehicle. It no longer aimed for Bram. It had changed direction so that it headed towards Ethan and away from the cave.

Ethan turned and ran farther. The most important thing

was that Bram didn't get caught in whatever net was closing in on Ethan.

It wasn't the longest run of his life, but it was the grimmest, because Ethan knew how it would end. It took them seven hours and three ATVs, but the tranq gun eventually hit its mark and Ethan, exhausted, went down.

He didn't want to wake, so he didn't fight going under.

Chapter Twenty-Four

Bram woke cold, hungry and alone.

He'd overslept and Ethan had gone to work.

No. Bram jack-knifed to sitting. He was in a strange cave, one he and Ethan had fled to yesterday, and Ethan was long gone.

Bram shoved his panic down. No time for that. He had to figure out what the hell had happened. Ethan wouldn't have just left him. Had they somehow abducted Ethan from the cave without Bram waking?

Impossible. Besides, the only scents here were of Ethan and himself.

Bram chugged down as much energy drink and nutrition bars as he could, and as quickly as he could. The calories would carry him for some time, even after a shift.

Then he lay down and his world faded out as he turned to wolf.

He shook off the shift immediately. With his heightened wolf senses, it didn't take him long to determine that Ethan had left the cave under his own steam, first as human, then shifting to cat, then running.

Why Ethan would do this Bram couldn't fathom, but he would follow that trail. Bram had always thought he was a source of danger to Ethan, bringing Doug's vengeance down on them both. But despite Trey's phone call, it had not been Bram driven off the road on his way home from work.

Someone had gone after Ethan. But why?

It took hours, but at some point Bram came upon the scene that made his blood run cold. It was only an hour or two old. Here, Ethan had stopped, his trail ended. At that same spot were the scents of eight different men. None of them shifters.

The scenario didn't make sense. Ethan should never have had a problem evading humans. Cougars knew how to be elusive. Something had gone seriously wrong and there was only one person Bram could turn to in order to understand what had become of Ethan.

After one last sweep of the scene, making sure his nose hadn't missed any clues, Bram began his long trek back to the house he and Ethan shared. It took him all night and it felt like the longest night of his life, running under the cloudy sky and through drizzle. He couldn't stop fearing the worst, that Ethan had been captured by those who wanted to do him harm, who wanted to kill him.

When Bram finally arrived home, the house was not empty. He'd held on to the futile hope that Ethan was somehow safely home. But no cat shifter was here. Only two wolves, and Trey's and Liam's presence did not bode well.

Trey opened the back door to Bram's bark and without preamble said, "Shift so we can talk. Ethan's in serious trouble and we need your help."

Exhausted, Bram nevertheless dragged himself into their room and crawled into Ethan's bed, surrounding himself with his lover's smell. His body resisted the shift but his mind forced it. For Ethan's sake, he had to push through this change as quickly as possible. Bram worked so that his entire focus went into his shift. Though it took forever, he pushed his bones and muscle towards human, and refused to give in to his despair. Finally he moved through the painful change and faded out.

"Bram. Bram." When he woke, his limbs felt heavy, as if he couldn't move, and it took him a while to realize someone was repeating his name, had been for some time. "*Bram.*" His name came again.

"Is he all right?" A second voice, recognizable, but from where?

"I think so." That was Trey's voice and Trey knew something about Ethan. Bram forced his eyes open.

"How many times have you shifted in the last day or two?" Trey was frowning. At a guess, this was the alpha's way of showing concern.

"Four," Bram croaked.

"You need to drink, eat and sleep, in that order."

"I think he probably knows that, Trey," Liam said wryly as he took Bram's arm to help him sit. He was shivering but he wasn't cold. "Rustle up some food for him." Liam jerked his head towards the kitchen and, to Bram's surprise, Trey left.

Doug would never have accepted being given a directive like that. Trey was no kind of alpha Bram understood, which was something of a relief.

It was a little embarrassing that he almost fell over twice while getting dressed. But all Liam said was, "We're really not made to shift this often, are we?"

Bram grunted. He made his way to the kitchen and shoveled in as much food and drink as possible. He barely noticed what it was.

Trey took a seat opposite him, eyeing him carefully. "You need to sleep, but first, tell me what happened. I want to know everything you know."

Bram made himself go over the events as thoroughly as he could, while Trey questioned him on the details. By the time he was asking if Bram was sure that he'd smelled eight men at the last scene, Bram was listing to the right and almost fell off his chair.

Abruptly, Trey stopped with the questions. "Okay, that's enough. Bed. But we'll definitely talk again."

"Ethan." Bram shook his head to keep himself awake. "We need to find Ethan."

"We need to find Ethan," Trey repeated grimly while Liam led him out of the kitchen. Bram didn't remember hitting the mattress.

This time Bram knew where he was when he woke, because he'd been sleeping, not shifting. He even knew that Ethan was gone, and that knowledge felt like a ragged hole in his chest.

It was hard to know how long he'd slept, but he dragged himself into the shower to wake up and get his brain working. When he walked into the kitchen, he expected more grim looks but instead Trey was, well, not smiling, but there was a look of satisfaction on his face.

"They called," he said.

"*They*? Doug?"

Trey shook his head. "This isn't Doug, though he may well have precipitated the week's events. This is my old job. One of my ex-colleagues called because they need my help." His voice went deadpan. "They have a cat shifter they can't handle, and they think I can help." His mouth quirked. "It's known that I have a way with shifters."

Bram lurched from the table and Trey immediately rapped out, "Sit. Eat."

Bram's first instinct was to obey but he didn't want to so he stood there, glaring, and Trey's face softened. "I'll fill you in while you eat, but we don't have much time, and you have to come with me."

"Is Ethan okay?" Bram sat down.

"He's alive, so we'll work with that. They have him in a room. He won't shift, he won't eat. He goes nuts if anyone tries to talk to him. They actually don't want a psycho-cat." Trey paused. "And I've planted the idea that they may not have a shifter at all, only a cougar."

Bram choked. "They'll buy that?"

"Depends on how long Ethan can hold out. Unlike his time with you, they have no one who dares go in that room and coax him to turn human. But we have to hurry."

"Don't they know anything about shifters?"

"Most of them don't." Trey slammed a drink down beside Bram's plate of bacon and eggs. "I'm the expert and a fount of disinformation, when necessary. You're going to be my assistant."

Bram frowned. "Will they know we're wolves?"

"Not you, there's no reason."

"But they'll assume?"

"No, because only one knows of my true nature, and he likes keeping that secret to himself." Trey didn't look entirely pleased by this, more resigned. Having been with his pack his entire life, Bram didn't know what it was like for a human to know about a shifter. Trey sighed before he elaborated. "One of the benefits of these slightly shady organizations that are sort-of-government-approved-but-not-really is that different parts of the organization don't always play well together. The players like to have secrets and to call in favors. I'm calling one in now and Kingley will pay it."

Kingley. Bram would remember that name. He shoveled in more food. "Liam coming?"

"No. He's going to hold the fort here while we drive eight hours. Not much faster to fly and I hate flying."

"Okay." When Bram was finished eating he voiced the question that had been plaguing him since Ethan was run off the road. "How the hell did they find him? Was it through me?"

Trey's gaze was measured. "There are very clever tracking devices these days. It seems Doug gave Ethan one in a drink and it's been swimming around in his stomach ever since. He just had to alert these people at a time of his choosing."

Bram thought he might throw up. "I helped make Ethan finish those drinks."

"You didn't know." Trey shrugged as if it were of no consequence. "Bram, look at me." This time Bram obeyed. "We don't have time for self-recrimination, okay? You don't, and I don't. I'm the one who offered Doug information on cats in the first place, remember? I thought I could trust him to use the information wisely. I thought he was doing okay as alpha of the Winter pack. I was wrong."

Bram nodded. Somehow the fact that Trey also felt like shit made the burden a little easier to bear. He tried to unclench his fist. "But...I don't understand. Why didn't Doug notify these people months ago, right after Ethan and I escaped?"

"That's easy for me to answer." Trey's smile was twisted. "We alphas understand each other too well. Doug would have wanted to keep control of the situation as long as possible. He hoped to find Ethan the old-fashioned way, without their help, and haul him back into the pack compound. Better than having to admit he'd been outsmarted by his omega. Face is important, especially in dealing with these guys who despise shapeshifters."

Great, they were going to visit people who despised shifters and held Ethan captive in their prison.

Trey continued, "Doug was trying to increase his currency, not decrease it. And then, once I arrived, he had no chance to contact anyone. Till now."

"Till now," Bram echoed, and he swallowed the lump in his throat.

"Bram," Trey said softly. "We need to go."

He nodded and rose.

Fifteen minutes later they were out the door, in the car and driving towards Ethan.

The rage rolled through him, and Ethan, for the first time in his life, knew he could become a killer. Somewhere between the drugs and the walls, Ethan could barely see straight he was so angry.

He prowled the small room, snarling, and he didn't eat their fucking food or drink their fucking drinks and a godawful voice came into the room and he didn't even register the words.

They put him out with some regularity. Maybe they hoped he'd shift under the influence, but that wasn't going to happen. Not with this fury engulfing him, his cat wild and locked on to him like never before.

Time passed and Ethan couldn't measure anything, not even the number of times he circled the room. The voice came on again, and he roared and hissed until it shut up.

He didn't care if he died here, but he wanted to warn Bram.

These men weren't werewolves, but they had talked about Doug. Doug had connections Trey hadn't realized and Bram needed to know he was in danger.

Bram hadn't expected much conversation from Trey, but given the fact that Bram slept for most of the journey there wasn't much opportunity either.

"Ready?" asked Trey near the end of their trip. Bram nodded and not long after, they drove up to a large but plain building that sat in the middle of nowhere. They had to pass through three sets of guards and two fences, one looking decidedly high tech, and Bram could only hope that Trey's plan worked, because the odds of escaping without help were low.

People recognized Trey and were happy to see him, so Bram thought that was a good omen. Trey even seemed pleased to see them too, and it wasn't a fake reaction. One of the few things he'd said on the way over that wasn't directly related to their plan was that most of the people at the facility were "good", whatever that meant.

Trey had also cracked his first joke by telling Bram he'd be presented to them as the cat whisperer. It would have been funnier if it hadn't meant that Ethan was perceived as being out of control.

Ethan must be going through hell.

They were ushered into the building and someone was striding across the foyer. "Trey." The voice almost boomed. "Am I glad to see you."

"I'm surprised you *could* see me." Trey shook hands firmly.

"I have some discretion, and this is what I consider an emergency." The man paused, with a glance at Bram, but spoke only to Trey. "You'll be going in yourself?"

"No." Trey made the introductions. "Abraham Carson. Shaun Kingley."

Abraham Carson wasn't even his name, but he didn't have to give ID so Bram shook hands.

"Your specialty then?" Kingley asked.

"Yes." Bram worked on sounding dispassionate, not desperate. "Where is he?"

"We'll show you soon. He's sleeping now."

"Drugged?" asked Trey.

"Yes." It quickly became apparent that Kingley wanted to speak to Trey in private, as Trey had anticipated. It was part of the deal. So while Bram was chomping at the bit, he allowed himself to be led by a guard to an area for refreshments.

Although his stomach was not exactly welcoming, Bram forced himself to eat and drink. He might need it. It wasn't much distraction though, with Bram anxious to see Ethan, to rescue Ethan.

In the middle of his second serving of food, another guard entered the room to call the first away. Bram thought little of it and continued to eat. He sure hoped he didn't have to shift for a while, as he found the process exhausting and the necessity of eating so much a burden. Halfway through his second meal, the hair on the back of his neck rose, he breathed in deeply, and froze.

He identified Doug just before his alpha entered the room and closed the door, leaving just the two of them present.

"Hello, Bram." His smile was predatory, and Bram choked. "What? You aren't happy to see me? Why not? Given that you've betrayed me, don't you want to gloat? Though perhaps it's a little too soon for gloating on your part. The stronger one always wins out, Bram, I think I've told you that."

Bram pushed away from the table.

Doug stepped forward. "Yes, you should be frightened. But I'll admit it. I enjoy the smell of fear. And I have time. Trey is happy to let me discipline you."

He was lying, and something in Bram's face must have said so, because Doug insisted on the lie. "It is true. Trey doesn't care about you. All Trey cares about is his career here. He's making a power move behind closed doors. He's out to prove that only he can control shifters, cat or wolf. He wants this job back, and Kingley wants to give it to him. I've been told they work well together."

Maybe Doug believed this. Bram didn't detect deception so much as fury, tightly leashed, and a desire to hurt. But Bram refused to be hurt by Doug again, let alone be killed. If that happened, he wouldn't be able to save Ethan, and Bram would not leave his lover here, caged and drugged. His gaze darted around the room, looking for a weapon.

Doug smiled again—ugly when he smiled like that. "There's no escaping this time. I've made sure of it."

Bram's plate had been hard plastic and he'd drunk out of bottles, both useless. The only thing Bram could focus on was the window and its glass pane. He backed up.

"Come here, Bram."

He recoiled. Ethan had uttered the same words, but with such a different meaning. He retreated farther.

"It will be easier if you come to me. You know that."

Bram slammed a fist backwards against the windowpane. Glass shattered, skin slit open on a ragged edge, but he managed to clasp a shard in his hand. Not as big as he'd like, but he couldn't afford to be choosy.

"Really, Bram, you are the oddest wolf I have ever met.

What do you propose to do? Prick me with that? *Scratch* me?"
Doug strode over and Bram clutched the shard harder, making
his hand bleed. It was going to slip soon, if he kept this up.

"Jesus, you're useless. Breaking a window for what? To
make your hand bleed." Doug crowded him and Bram was
gripped by the panic of knowing his alpha was in control and he
had to listen no matter what he was told to do.

"I don't know why I even bothered with you these last few
years," Doug said in quiet contempt. "Pity, I guess. Misplaced as
it's proven to be." He brought both hands to Bram's neck.
Squeezed. "I could kill you now and you'd deserve it."

He couldn't breathe.

"Drop the piece of glass, Bram, and I might let you live." He
squeezed more. "If you don't, I'll break your neck because you
attacked me."

Bram's world began to go gray.

"You've attacked me a second time. The first time was to
release a feral cougar. It won't look good for you here, Bram.
They're trying to study these feral creatures in order to prevent
future human bloodbaths, to prevent feral shifters from
becoming murderers. They are very concerned about humans.
Ethan is a danger to us all and I will let them know it."

Ethan. Bram grabbed hold of that name. Tried to speak but
couldn't because of Doug's grip.

"You'd like to say something?"

Bram managed a nod before Doug squeezed even harder.

"Fuck that, Bram. You're going to die and Ethan is going to
be their experiment. That's how it is."

Bram raised his right arm and slashed Doug's wrist where
it counted.

The pressure dropped away, Doug cursing, and Bram

moved again, aiming that small shard for Doug's carotid, jamming it in before Doug could block with his uninjured arm.

Wide-eyed, Doug stared at him then jerked the piece of glass out of his throat. A mistake, because blood gushed a red fountain and Doug paled rapidly. For a few seconds he tried to remain standing before he collapsed.

His alpha had always had a problem with overconfidence, Bram thought rather abstractedly, staring at the growing pool of blood.

"More than a scratch," he murmured and edged around Doug's body to walk to the sink and wash his hands. After which he licked his hand wounds repeatedly. He needed the healing agents in his saliva to stop the bleeding. Once he wasn't dripping blood—it took a good ten minutes—he left Doug trying to shift behind him. His alpha had never had trouble shifting before, but this time he was badly wounded.

Bram couldn't think about that anymore.

He walked out and saw his first guard, had his question prepared. "Can you take me to Trey, please?"

The guard conferred and hemmed and hawed, implying that Trey and Kingley had important things to discuss. Kingley apparently valued Trey's presence. Bram was asked if he had eaten enough. Like he ever wanted to go back into that kitchen again. He should have been worried about people finding Doug but, and maybe it was shock, he could only think that he needed to get Ethan out of here. *Now.* It took far too long before he was led to Trey, who went on alert immediately, probably from the smell of Doug on Bram's body.

"I'd like Bram to see the cat now," demanded Trey of Kingley.

They waited forever, or more like five minutes, before Shaun Kingley returned to inform them, "Okay, the cat is waking up, but still groggy. I'm not sure how safe it will be."

"That's fine," said Bram while at the same time Trey declared, "We're good to go."

Bram paid attention to the three halls they traipsed down, in case that information came in useful later. The plan was to calmly walk out of here, but Bram wanted to be aware of where he was.

They had to step through two doors, rather like the set-up back in the Winter pack compound. Kingley looked pretty solemn, as if he had some misgivings.

"The cat won't attack Abraham," Trey assured him.

"If you say so." Kingley looked directly at Bram, allowing him to voice any doubts.

"I'm ready." His fear had little to do with Ethan and everything to do with this facility. Bram pushed open the door and slid inside the room, scared he might see Ethan's broken body, scared he'd arrived too late. The moment he realized Ethan was alive, if not precisely well, Bram's chest squeezed, full of emotion.

"Ethan?" he whispered.

The cougar, so familiar, lifted his head, his gaze muddy and unfocused. After a moment he lurched to his feet and Bram walked over, not wanting to startle Ethan but wanting to reach for him. He crouched down and Ethan half-jumped, half-fell on him, knocking him to the ground.

The purr started up and Bram couldn't help but laugh, even as Ethan's very rough tongue began sandpapering his face.

"Okay, listen."

Ethan hissed.

"Yes, I know. I know." Their conversation would be

watched, listened to. Ethan nosed around Bram's injured hand, growling, probably tasting something of Doug on Bram. "Don't worry about that. It's under control. I need you to show that you'll listen to me. Okay?" He added, subvocally, "You're going to pretend to be my cougar pet. Got that?"

Ethan flopped down on him, rubbing his head against Bram, and relief flooded through Bram at having this contact with his mate, even under the least desirable conditions. He hoped Ethan had registered his words.

"Uh, Ethan, can't really breathe here."

Upon hearing that, Ethan crouched over him and Bram realized he was being guarded. He crawled out from under Ethan, gave him a hug and subvocalized again. "Do everything I say, no hesitation, no questions, okay? Whatever you do, do *not* shift to human."

Then he stood and waved at the camera.

Fifteen seconds later, Trey walked in with a bag, as planned, and Bram gestured to Ethan with one hand. "Sit."

Ethan shot a look of disbelief at him. But he sat, even twitched his tail, and Bram had to stifle a laugh. "He's my cougar."

Trey approached and shook his head. He put his hands on his hips and glanced backwards. "Kingley. Honest to God. It's a real cougar. No wonder it wouldn't 'shift'. I told you Doug was not reliable. He's a glory seeker and a bit of a nutcase. Which is why I was keeping him under guard in the first place. He killed someone. You might want to be more careful with him in the future."

Kingley entered the room, and Ethan snarled but quieted obediently when Bram waved his arm.

Kingley surveyed the room from a safe distance. "Since when are male cougars affectionate? They kill, Trey. The

245

females won't even let them near their young."

"I raised this one," said Bram immediately.

Kingley eyed Trey. "Uh-huh. You owe me, Walters."

Trey inclined his head in agreement. "Here's your bag, Abraham, if you would."

"Lie down, Ethan." Bram pressed his palm downwards and Ethan with a bit of a put-out sigh settled on the floor. Bram started chattering like he would to a pet dog, which was pretty much how Ethan was acting, and put the collar on him. He winced a little at it and apologized.

"He doesn't really like this," Bram explained to no one in particular.

"Sure is tame with you," Kingley observed. "Amazingly so."

"Abraham works wonders," Trey said flatly. Bram turned to Trey expectantly. "Let's go."

Down the halls they went, Bram trying to remember to breathe, because the closer they got to freedom, the more tightly wound he felt. And while Ethan walked quietly beside him, there was a stiffness in his prowl which indicated nerves and perhaps sickness. He hadn't eaten for too long, or drank.

"Hey!"

Bram stiffened.

"There's a fucking dead wolf in the kitchen." The guard turned his suspicious gaze on Bram. "What the hell did you do in there?"

Bram couldn't think of how to respond so he just looked puzzled, as if he knew nothing about it. Impatiently, the guard turned to Kingley, "And Doug Jensen is missing."

Kingley gazed back. "No one can leave the premises without me knowing. Find him. He may be dangerous."

"What are you guys doing with all these animals?" Trey

demanded. "Since when did you specialize in wildlife?"

Trey and Kingley stared at each other, Kingley's expression giving nothing away but Bram smelled...relief.

Kingley *knew*. At least about Doug being a werewolf. "We'll look after the dead wolf in a moment," he told his subordinate. "Let me say goodbye to these men first, please."

"Yes, sir."

Bram was so light-headed he felt like he wasn't quite in his body during the last five minutes it took to get back to the van. He and Ethan clambered into the back while Trey took his leave of Kingley.

"Call me if you have any other problems," Trey said, tone totally neutral.

"Oh, you bet," came back the bland reply.

Trey climbed into the driver's seat, took some kind of instrument from Kingley and pointed it at Ethan's chest for about ten seconds. After which he checked something on it. "Dead," he said with a glance at Kingley. "That's it?"

"Yep." Kingley took back the instrument and turned on his heel, leaving them be.

As Trey backed up, Ethan hissed, his front paw scratching at the collar.

"Yeah, I know, but not yet. Just wait." Bram rubbed his face against the top of Ethan's head. "So sorry. Look, you've got to drink." He pulled out a water bottle that Ethan guzzled with Bram's help.

After they passed through the two sets of fences and the guards, and were outside the facility, Ethan hissed again and Bram took the collar right off.

A shudder rippled through Ethan.

"I think it's over," said Trey as Ethan climbed on top of

Bram, draping his body all over him.

"Don't shift yet," Bram said holding him tight for a moment. "You need some energy first."

As Ethan ate hungrily, Bram asked Trey, "What the hell were you doing at the end there? What was that thing of Kingley's?"

"I was killing the transponder."

"Huh?"

"That 'thing' was a transmitter. I gave Ethan's stomach a burst of radio-wave frequency to kill dead the RFID so it'd stop swimming around in his acidic stomach and pass on through him. Is that helpful?"

"I guess," said Bram dubiously. He felt too tired to make sense of Trey's explanation.

"I disabled the tracking device. The last thing I want is for them to be able to follow us."

"Well, *no*." Bram would look this all up later. He needed to understand it better. "Where are we going?"

"Not back there, I can assure you. Kingley was useful, but he's not to be trusted."

"So why did he help you?"

"Because I pay back favors. I'm reliable that way." There was a slight edge to those words, and for the first time, Bram felt a little worried for Trey. He went silent, wondering just what kind of burden Trey had taken on.

"I'm driving to Liam's, by the way. I think you guys'll do better there."

"Liam's?" Bram said in dismay while Ethan made a chirp. "You mean, Canada?"

"Yup. Ethan likes Liam. Or is that the problem?" Trey actually grinned into the mirror, to Bram's amazement.

"No," said Bram, feeling about ten years old because he was blushing even if there was something rather reassuring about being teased by Trey. It made him sound like he thought the ordeal was over. But Canada? He wanted Ethan to himself, no matter how grateful he felt.

Ethan purred against him in reassurance, before pulling away to curl up in the corner.

He was fast compared to Bram, shifting to human in less than fifteen minutes, and when he woke he looked absolutely wiped out by the past few days, wan and thin. Haggard. But it was the sweetest moment ever when Bram took Ethan back into his arms to rest against him.

"Christ, Bram," he muttered against Bram's neck. "You killed Doug. Are you okay?"

Bram kept forgetting he'd killed Doug. It might take more than an hour or two for it to properly sink in. He ran fingers through Ethan's hair and focused on his lover instead. "If you're okay, I'm okay."

Ethan laughed. Or Bram thought it was a laugh at first, until he realized it was more of a sob. "No more of this pet business, okay?"

"Shhh. You did good."

Ethan shook his head against Bram. "Jesus. Too much."

"Yeah. But it's over."

Epilogue

The snow was falling thickly, like a curtain. And through it, Ethan glided, pushing himself up the hill. It was a long hill and the cross-country skis slipped back a few times because he wasn't used to them. When he reached the top he stopped to catch his breath. Cougars didn't have quite the stamina of wolves and sometimes it showed, even in human form.

"So?" asked Bram who came alongside, not nearly so breathless, and grinning. "What do you think?"

"Well, skiing is different than running through a blizzard, I'll grant you that."

Bram shot him a look of disdain. "This is no blizzard. It's barely more than flurries. Kind of beautiful when it's coming down this thick, don't you think?"

"Sure." At Bram's consternation—just because he couldn't contain his own enthusiasm, Bram thought Ethan would be equally enthused—Ethan laughed. "What? I saw a lot of snow in my twenties. But, okay, it is different to see it through human eyes. It's fun to brave the elements as human."

"Well, I *need* to get out of the house, now and then." Bram worked from home, contract work programming stuff, which was about as far as Ethan understood.

"Sure, and I wanted to come with you." Ethan tipped his head towards the path. "Let's go farther."

The next couple of hours passed by quickly, and enjoyably, Ethan had to admit. Getting home was easier, a long gradual glide downwards. By the time they reached their house, they were ravenous, and Bram pulled out the chili he had made earlier in the day.

They'd bought this house the year before, a real fixer-upper, but that was Ethan's job, plus some part-time work in Liam's woodworking business. Ethan might not be the greatest reader in the world, but he was good with his hands.

Ethan was washing up the dishes—that was usually how they split the meal chores—when Bram called him over to the computer. Squashing his defensive reflex, given that the computer made him feel stupid, Ethan walked over and tried not to look grudging.

"Sit down," Bram said quietly and something in his voice had Ethan obeying. Bram sank a hand into Ethan's hair and kissed him hard, then tender, and while Ethan appreciated any and all of Bram's caresses, this gave him pause. It was like Bram was preparing him for something.

"What?"

Bram picked up his hand and squeezed. "I asked Trey to look into this. To see if he could find a picture of your mother. It's taken him a while, obviously." He gestured towards the screen.

Ethan turned to see, although it took him a moment to register what was on the screen, and what Bram had said. He was dimly aware of Bram holding his hand. He'd thought he'd forgotten what his mother had looked like, and maybe he had, but the force with which he recognized her took his breath away.

A shiver traveled up through him, making him shake as memory surged to the fore. There she was. It was summertime and she was smiling into the camera, in a T-shirt and shorts. A little boy, Ethan, clutched her leg while she laid a protective hand on his shoulder.

Her short hair was dark brown, as were her eyes, but he recognized that smile as his—and hers from so long ago.

The screen went blurry and Ethan dragged in a shuddery breath, then let Bram pull him into a hug. He wanted to look at that picture again, just needed a minute to regroup.

The words spilled out. "I never got to say goodbye to her. They just took her away." Trey had let him know that the records showed his mother had gone into a diabetic coma before she died. She had hidden her sickness from the child he'd been.

"I know." Bram rocked him a little.

"I always wanted to see her one more time."

"Well, the picture isn't enough to say goodbye, I know that."

"But it's something. Thank you." Ethan scrubbed his eyes and made himself look again. She'd loved him, this woman. That love, he'd never doubted, and it had probably sheltered him more than he realized. Just like Bram sheltered him now.

"She was very beautiful," Bram said softly.

Ethan tilted his head, as if that would give him another view of her. Then he smiled. "I always thought so."

About the Author

Joely Skye is an introvert, a Spooks (MI5) fan, a wife and a mother. One of her favorite books ever is Ellen Kushner's *Swordspoint* and, while she doesn't watch much TV, she couldn't resist *Queer as Folk*.

She writes male/male romance. Don't ask her why. Men fascinate her, as does romance, so gay romance is the perfect fit.

To learn more about Joely Skye, please visit www.joelyskye.com. Send an email to Joely at Joely.Skye@gmail.com or join her Yahoo! group to join in the fun with other readers as well as Joely. http://groups.yahoo.com/group/joelyskye/

She also writes as Jorrie Spencer (www.jorriespencer.com).

In this world, trust is hard to find...
and the one thing they need to survive.

Poison
© 2008 Joely Skye

Tobias Smator lives down his late father's execution by avoiding the spotlight—and responsibility. He doesn't mind what people think of him as long as they leave him alone. Still, in this unremarkable half-life he's fashioned for himself on deceptively low-tech Rimania, he's not safe from political intrigue. Someone wants him dead.

Alliance operative Geln Marac's orders for his first assignment were simple: Stay uninvolved. Those orders go out the window, however, when he delivers an antidote to save Tobias from death by poisoning. His reward? Possible betrayal that lands him in the hands of police interrogators. To protect the Alliance, Geln resorts to a temporary mindwipe.

Tobias is fascinated by the amnesiac man who saved his life. But Geln has attracted the attention of the high-powered Lord Eberly, who would use him as a pawn. Rather than sacrifice Geln to the political wolves, Tobias chooses to embrace his heritage.

Geln's memory reawakens to a precarious situation with no source of protection—except Tobias. There's only one way forward for both of them.

Trust—or die.

Warning: this book contains hot nekkid otherplanetary manlove.

Available now in ebook and print from Samhain Publishing.

LaVergne, TN USA
18 March 2010
176476LV00006BA/4/P